# Out Of Reach

## The Day Hartford Hospital Burned

# Out Of Reach

## The Day Hartford Hospital Burned

A Novel By

F. Mark Granato



F. Mark Granato
fmgranato@aol.com
www.facebook.com at Author F. Mark Granato



Published in the United States of America 2014

# Out Of Reach

## The Day Hartford Hospital Burned

A Novel by

F. Mark Granato

## Also by F. Mark Granato

*Titanic: The Final Voyage*

*Beneath His Wings:*
*The Plot to Murder Lindbergh*

*Of Winds and Rage*

*Finding David*

*The Barn Find*

For my wife,
whose admiration of firemen
began as just a little girl
when she would lie awake at night and pray
for the safety of her cherished father,
a kind, loving man who was a volunteer fireman,
but more importantly, her hero.

*Capt. Richard "Spec" Hughes*

"They say in Football
that the game is measured in yards,
yet a good coach will tell you
it's really all about inches.
For a Fireman, life is not about minutes.
It's the seconds that count."

*Captain Timothy F. Kelliher, Sr.*
*Hartford Fire Department*

# Prologue

~~~ ~~~

Perhaps if the fiery-tipped stub of a cigarette hadn't been flicked into the center of the trash chute where tons of flammable refuse was piled high a half-dozen floors below, it might have slid down one of the smooth metal walls of the ductwork and miraculously fallen, harmlessly, into the bottom of a waiting garbage bin and simply burned itself out.

Or what if it had fallen deeply and unimpeded into the black hole and landed on a scrap of non-combustible rubbish? Might the bit of burning tobacco have gone cold from lack of fuel?

What if the strong gusts of air naturally funneling up the long trash chute had caught the tiny remnants of the cigarette with its few grams of weight and held it in mid air, causing it to dance on currents of wind until its deadly crimson ember had cooled?

Or if the maintenance workers in the basement below had caught the first scent or seen whiffs of smoke coming from the chute just a few minutes earlier – might they have used their long hooked poles to drag
~~~

the miniscule remains of burning tobacco from its lethal perch?

What if... what if... what if?

Then perchance those who had come to this refuge of care – the sick seeking to be healed, the healers determined to cure, loved ones hoping to provide comfort – might have lived.

The innocents would not have suffocated or burned to death in their hospital beds. A young doctor, his brilliant future ahead, might not have suffered a hideous death trying to save his patients. Nurses would not have been incinerated at their posts or immolated as they fled the inferno. Visitors would not have died gruesomely, clawing at doors and windows for air, for escape, for freedom.

And mercy from the fire monster.

# One

~~~ ৯ ~~~

*The Allen Executive Conference Room*
*Hartford Hospital*

Like a graveyard fog, a haze of tobacco smoke hung in the air, filling the ornate, mahogany paneled first floor conference room with a grey pallor and a noxious, crypt-like odor that permeated nearly everything – ceiling tiles, window drapes, carpeting, wall paper, upholstery – and tinted the entire chamber in the yellowish-brown stain of nicotine.

The 20 or so Hartford Hospital department heads and administrators seated around the long formal conference table took no notice. Each held a lighted cigarette, cigar or pipe throughout the meeting and sat in the comfort of a sumptuously padded, leather covered, high-backed armchair. The only modicum of protection each enormously expensive chair had from the scar of an aberrant hot spark was an oversized
~~~

polished brass ashtray that was placed on the table before each participant.

When one of the room's oversized doors was occasionally swung open by kitchen help arriving with fresh coffee or sandwiches for the working lunch, the act of stepping into the meeting chamber from the adjoining anteroom was like walking into a low hanging stratus cloud.

Such was the pervasiveness of tobacco use that even those few non-smokers present were oblivious to it. In fact, throughout the sprawling, high-rise Hartford Hospital complex, smoking was barely regulated and common in all but the surgical and nursery facilities. Patients, staff and visitors alike were all welcomed to light up. An entire staff on the hospital's payroll was charged with nothing other than emptying and cleaning ashtrays throughout the building, day and night.

Dr. T. Stewart Hamilton, president and chief executive officer of the second largest hospital in the State of Connecticut and biggest in the capital city of Hartford, took notice of the habitual practice ongoing during the regularly scheduled December meeting of the hospital's leadership only because he needed to briefly address a related safety issue that had been brought to his attention some weeks before. He took a long drag from his own filter-less Lucky Strike before snuffing the tiny butt remaining in his ashtray. In a minute or so, he would light another.

Unconsciously blocking out the annoyingly droning voice of a man addressing the hospital's senior staff from the podium at the end of the room, Hamilton thought back to the afternoon before.

In a few brief moments of solace while touring the 13th floor of the hospital, he had been drawn to stand at the oversized windows looking out over Retreat Avenue and the south end of Hartford. From there, he could see Barry Square and the tall steeple of St. Augustine's Church, Park Street and its Green, and the central thoroughfares of Wethersfield and Franklin Avenues and Broad Street.

The city was growing fast and the demographics of the once mostly Irish–Italian population were changing just as quickly. The north end of the small metropolis was evolving into a black community and the west end was experiencing a migration of immigrants from Puerto Rico, a short flight to Bradley Airfield in nearby Windsor Locks. He had pondered how Hartford Hospital was going to be able to handle the growing demand for its services and the ethnic shift that was coming with it. The thought was still heavy on his mind this afternoon.

But for the moment, the tall, thin, prematurely grey-haired chief administrator was preoccupied with a presenter (whose name he was embarrassed to admit he couldn't remember) that had been going on about the state of the artwork decorating the hospital halls and patient rooms for at least the last 30 minutes.

The 50-year old Hamilton, a Harvard Medical School graduate who already had 10 years of hospital administration experience under his belt, including four years running battlefield hospitals in Casablanca and Rome as a Lieutenant Colonel in the Army during the War, was a man of little patience or tolerance. He had sized up the gentleman at the podium as a hapless bureaucrat long ago, and within 60-seconds after the presenter opened his mouth, Hamilton's opinion was reaffirmed. He was seething at the waste of time the man represented with each additional word. Who in their right mind had hired this guy, he wondered. Hamilton had already made a mental note to speak with his assistant about the quality of meeting agendas in the future. Time was just too precious a commodity to waste on a subject that shouldn't have taken more than a two-paragraph memo to resolve. Finally, the presenter hesitated and the hospital president seized the opportunity.

"Yes, yes, why thank you, uh…" he said awkwardly, still unable to recall the man's name. With years of dancing around clumsy business etiquette situations in his holster of management experience, he was hardly to be stopped by such an inconvenience.

"Thank you for that enlightening information and my assistant, Mr. Markus, will be in touch with you." There was a collective sigh of relief from around the table as Hamilton essentially shut off the grating presentation. "Now, if you will excuse us, we have more pressing items to discuss in the short amount of time left to us this afternoon." He glanced at his watch. It was now just before 12:30 p.m.

The presenter's jaw dropped at the realization of what was happening.

"But Mr. Hamilton, sir, it is important to recognize that part of the hospital's reputation hinges on the value…"

The last shred of Hamilton's patience evaporated. "Mr… oh, hell, what is your name, man?" he interrupted again.

"Why… it's Anglan, James Anglan, Mr. Hamilton," he replied haltingly, mortified by the shocking show of disrespect aimed at him. Anglan shot a glance at Markus who had approved his slot on the agenda. The President's assistant lowered his eyes to avoid those of the Hospital's Vice President of Facilities Management.

"Why yes, of course James, how silly of me. I'm afraid my mind is too filled with more important matters," Hamilton responded, only pouring salt into the wound.

"I only need a few more minutes," the slight, bespectacled Anglan explained. He adjusted his bow tie and cleared his throat. "I was just about to discuss the appropriations request that I will be forwarding for your approval," he explained.

Hamilton nearly lost it.

"Appropriations request? For new artwork? Are you daft man? This is a hospital, not a museum, for heaven's sake!"

Heads around the table bowed in embarrassment for their colleague. Hamilton was not known for his patience, nor was his wrath something to be taken lightly. He had a vision and had no time for those who would cloud it.

"Tom, I'm not sure how this ended up on our agenda," Hamilton said pointedly, turning to Thomas Markus, "but this can't happen in the future, understand?" He jabbed at a sheet of paper in front of him on the table with his forefinger. "We have at least another 90-minutes of far more vital issues to discuss. Please, handle this with Mr. Anglan, off line." Markus shook his head and took a note, still refusing to look up at Anglan or to come to his rescue.

Hamilton addressed his subordinate directly. "James, forgive me, but we must move on. If I'm not mistaken, the next item on our agenda is a presentation on the unexpected increase in activity in the Emergency Room and what we're going to do about it," Hamilton said. "I'm afraid that supersedes the importance of discussions regarding artwork at this time."

"That's right, Dr. Hamilton, the ER presentation is up next," Markus finally spoke, glancing towards Anglan, flustered and angry, who was removing his papers from the podium. The assistant quickly turned back to saving his own skin.

Markus continued on, introducing the next topic as if nothing unusual had happened. "As you will note, gentlemen, to summarize we have seen a 30-percent rise in demand for Emergency Room..."

Anglan shut out the voice as he walked from the podium back to his seat at the table, thoroughly embarrassed and betrayed. As Vice President of Hospital Facilities Management, the appearance and upkeep of the building was his responsibility and he and Markus had spent several hours discussing the need for investment in redecorating sections of the Hospital, including replacing artwork and wall hangings that contributed to the overall ambience of the environment. Markus had enthusiastically embraced Anglan's recommendations in private conversations prior to the December management meeting but had failed to support him when pressed by Hamilton.

Anglan was seething as he took a seat. Immediately, he pulled a Camel cigarette from one of the three packs he smoked each day, lit it and swiveled his chair in the direction of the new presenter, more to turn his back on Hamilton and Markus than to engage in the new discussion item. Visions of wrapping his fingers around Markus' throat and choking the bastard danced before his eyes as he all but ignored the conversation that ate up the next 45-minutes and a subsequent and final presentation that followed. Later that day, he would have no recollection of the subject matter.

Precisely at 1:40 p.m. that afternoon, T. Stewart Hamilton ended the meeting with a final brief item.

"Gentlemen, it has come to my attention from the head of maintenance – as well as a telephone call directly from the Hartford Fire Chief's office," he said, pausing to shake his head in embarrassment, "that our staff has become increasingly indiscriminant about the disposal of cigarettes within the hospital. I have been informed by maintenance that it is not unusual for small fires to break out in either of the laundry and dry trash chutes that run the height of this building at least once if not several times each week."

Hamilton looked around the table to be sure he had everyone's attention. This was hardly the type of subject matter that should be on the agenda for discussion at a meeting at this management level, but it was extremely troubling to the CEO. He had learned long ago as a manager that it was the annoying, trivial problems that snuck up and bit you in the ass if left unattended.

"Chief Lee has informed me that he is becoming increasingly aggravated, but much more importantly worried by the situation and will take it up with the Mayor's Office if something isn't done. Embarrassingly, he 'suggested' – in the strongest possible language, I emphasize – that the hospital's behavior in this matter is not only reckless in consideration of the safety of the patients and staff of this institution, but also that every time his men have to respond to a false alarm here, he is putting them needlessly in harm's way."

He looked around the room. Each of the men, including James Anglan, were remarkably talented and educated, in some cases representing the best in their field of expertise, and it pained him to have to lecture them on such a seemingly inconsequential subject. Nonetheless, he'd learned as a hospital administrator that the devil was in the details. And fires in the laundry and trash chutes of the city's largest hospital were definitely the work of the devil.

"Gentlemen, quite frankly I could not debate the Chief's objection. You will recall I took the time to write a memo on this subject just several weeks ago that was addressed to each of you. It obviously needs to be discussed with each member of your staff, and must carry your personal note of urgency." He paused to let his urgency sink in.

"Am I understood? Please attend to this matter immediately." He looked around the room again, being sure that he had made his point.

"On that unfortunately troubling note, our meeting comes to a close. However, I'm sure I will see you this evening at my home for our holiday party, which should lighten things up," he said forcing a smile.

"But do allow me, as the year comes to a close, a moment to thank you for your continued dedicated service to Hartford Hospital. I am very grateful for your support and continual excellence in making this hospital a world class facility."

He glanced at his watch. 1:45 p.m. Time still for some other very important business before rushing home to join his wife Amy in meeting their guests for the annual staff holiday party at their west end home. She so enjoyed the merrymaking and he knew that every detail would be attended to.

"So with that, gentleman, enjoy a productive afternoon and Amy and I look forward to your company this evening."

The room emptied quickly with Hamilton leading the charge for the door. Oddly, James Anglan remained in his chair, his head down, leaning over the table as if he were studying some notes. He had done a remarkable job of hiding his anger, but inside he was still seething with rage. Tom Markus had completely betrayed him and caused him to be ridiculed before the entire senior staff. It was hard enough to be considered a peer of department heads responsible for surgery, radiology, the emergency room and other such critical functions. He knew that few of them took him seriously or had time for him unless they required special assistance. But this slight was more than he could bear.

For Hamilton to forget his name was cruelly unprofessional. He had little interaction with the Hospital's president but that hardly made up for the way he had been treated. He felt like a fool and his hands shook with anger even now, more than an hour later.

Anglan sat for perhaps another fifteen minutes after the conference room had cleared out, stewing in his rage. He had a mind to walk into Hamilton's office and resign, but he was smart enough not to cut off his own nose to spite his face. However, he'd made up his mind that Markus was going to get an earful from him this very afternoon that would leave the president's assistant reeling.

Finally, he stubbed out his cigarette in the overflowing ashtray at his seat and gathered his notes before quietly exiting the room located on the far south end of the first floor. His goal was to make his way back to his office without confronting anyone else who had been present at the meeting. He hadn't yet formulated how he would respond to those who would undoubtedly chide him this afternoon or later at Hamilton's festive party. What would he say to his wife?

Head down, he began the long walk to his office, but then had second thoughts. He needed to be alone, to think through his predicament. He continued on past his office and into the lobby, where he boarded an elevator and pressed the button for the 13th Floor. It would be somewhat quiet there. The 13th floor was used for storage but also housed the hospital pharmacy and was where the sterilization of equipment was performed.

Anglan walked to the same windows his boss had stared out of just the day before and pondered what had just happened to him. He was despondent and couldn't shake the enormous feeling of embarrassment and inadequacy that Hamilton's tirade had caused him. He stared out at the city for perhaps 30-minutes, chain-smoking, considering everything from resigning to boycotting Hamilton's holiday party. Finally, he lit a last cigarette and decided to spend the rest of the afternoon quietly hiding in his office, licking his wounds.

Just before reaching the bank of elevators to return to the lobby, he stepped through the open fire doors of the south wing. Out of the corner of his eye, he noticed the trash and laundry hatches that had been the subject of Hamilton's final consternation at the management meeting. The sight of the side-by-side, 18-inch round aluminum doors abruptly stopped him in his tracks.

He didn't know why but he stood and stared at them for several long minutes. The trash chute door bore the words, *"Dry trash only. For safety of incinerator attendant, burnable waste only. Do not force large boxes into the chute."*

He studied the words. Then slowly, a sneer came to his lips and his eyes drifted to the cigarette he was holding between his fingers. He studied it. The normally proper gentleman was struck by an unusually devilish thought that simmered out of his still steaming rage. He took a long drag on the Camel while considering an act so insane, so out of his character that he would have normally tossed it aside as adolescent tomfoolery.

But he had already made up his mind.

"Screw you, Hamilton," he said glancing up and down the hallway to make certain he was still unobserved. Then he stepped forward and pulled down on the latch, unlocking the trash chute cover and eased the door open on its double hinges. Behind it was nothing but sheet metal in the form of round ductwork and a black hole that he knew descended 150-feet to the basement. Anglan squeamishly leaned over the edge and looked down. Only darkness met his gaze. The emptiness made him queasy.

He took another drag on the cigarette and considered the consequences of his sudden intentions. If he proceeded, at the least Hamilton's afternoon would probably be shot, tied up with the Fire Department. It gave Anglan a bit of satisfaction to know that his boss might share a taste of the same rage and embarrassment that had brought him to this moment. There was a certain comedic twist to it.

Without another thought, he brought the burning end of the cigarette to his lips and held it there, staring at it. The crimson ember reflected in his eyes and cast an eerie hue across his face, a cruel look that his wife and two young children would not recognize, being so out of character.

He blew on its super-heated tip, burning at some 550 °F. The rush of oxygen turned the cigarette the color of glowing, molten lava. Insanely, it occurred to him that although the stub of cigarette was an inanimate object, in his hand it was now a living thing that could and would destroy upon his impulse. This tiny remnant of red-hot tobacco could satisfy his immediate need for vengeance. All he had to do was unleash it.

Mindlessly, he placed the butt between his thumb and forefinger and nonchalantly flicked it dead center into the trash chute. Then he smiled, amused that he had just repaid Hamilton's cruelty with such ease. But the look of amusement faded from his face quickly, as cognizance of what he had done suddenly came to him, dousing the satisfaction. Panicking, he stuck his head into the entrance of the chute, desperate to retrieve the cigarette. It was long gone, but nothing had changed. Only the blackness stared back at him.

"No..." he said, unexpectedly feeling very stupid. "What an idiotic thing to do."

Quickly, he slammed the door shut and dogged the latch, glancing up and down the length of the hall for anyone who might have observed his actions. He was still alone. Thank God, he thought. How would he explain the impulsive thing he had just done?

Anglan rushed to the elevator lobby and stepped into an empty car. He repeatedly stabbed the button for the first floor where his office was located. The doors closed. He was in the clear. The elevator car slowly picked up downward momentum, stopping only at the fourth floor for several passengers who were also headed for the main lobby. He turned away from them, trying to hide his face. But they were chatting, oblivious to his presence.

He grit his teeth, waiting to hear the shrill sound of the fire alarm abruptly reverberate in the stillness of the elevator. The administrator shut his eyes and held his breath. Nothing. Relax, he told himself. No one had seen him and the chance of anything more than a bit of smoke as the consequence of his action was remote.

The Otis elevator smoothly glided to a stop and the doors opened. Anglan brushed past several people in front of him to make his escape and hurried through the main lobby, past the receptionist and down the hall to his office. He ignored his secretary who held out a handful of notes and telephone messages as he entered his office and closed the door behind him. He sat at his desk, holding his breath again, still anticipating the fire alarm. Five minute passed. Nothing.

He thought quickly. An alibi. He needed an alibi. Anglan jumped up from his desk chair and swung open the door, hollering to his secretary.

"Marjorie," he said, forcing himself to maintain his composure," call Tom Markus and tell him he god damned well better be in his office when I get there." He rushed by her and out the door as abruptly as he had arrived. The secretary raised her eyes.

"Must have been some meeting," Marjorie thought as she picked up the phone. She had never seen her boss quite so flustered. He was usually such a gentle guy.

"Angela?" she said into the telephone. "Marjorie. Listen, my boss is headed to see Tom and you might want to warn him..."

# Two

~~~ ~~~

*A Mild December Day*

All over the city of Hartford, midday had come and gone as usual and the small metropolis went about its daily business without interruption. It was Friday. The weekend beckoned and in the small New England city and all across America, a tumultuous year that had endured some ominous rumblings was thankfully coming to a quiet, peaceful close.

There was a new President in the White House in 1961. Young John F. Kennedy had been inaugurated in January. It only took until April for the inexperienced President to find himself in hot water when he was embarrassed by the failed Bay of Pigs invasion of Cuba. Just months later, in June, a disastrous summit with Russian Premier Nikita Khrushchev had ended with the untested President taking a verbal beating from the pretentious and bullying Communist leader. Then, a tense standoff between American and German tanks in Berlin in October raised the stakes of the "Cold War."
~~~

School children across the nation practiced preparing for nuclear air raid attacks by hiding under their desks. Later in the year, despite the continuing stalemate of American involvement in the Korean Conflict, Kennedy announced that he would send 18,000 military "advisors" to the growing conflict in Vietnam. America was a bit nervous, but still had not lost the confidence and swagger earned from its great victory in WWII and its subsequent standing on the world stage as a global superpower.

But there was good news for the nation as well in 1961 and even a vibration of excitement here and there. Alan Shepard had become the first American in space and Kennedy announced a goal to put the first man on the Moon before the end of the decade. With sincere enthusiasm, he established the Peace Corps sending a message to the world that America had much to offer those less fortunate and was willing to share the knowledge and commitment of its best and brightest. The Civil Rights Movement, although fraught with confrontation and even violence, was growing, as was American support. Author Harper Lee's *To Kill A Mockingbird* won the 1961 Pulitzer Prize.

The musical film *West Side Story*, a contemporary interpretation of Shakespeare's *Romeo and Juliet*, won 10 out of 11 Academy Award nominations including Best Picture. To the elation of New York Yankees fans but the consternation of others, Roger Maris hit his 61$^{st}$ home run in the very last game of the season, finally breaking the 34-year-old record set by Babe Ruth. Wilt Chamberlain scored 78 points and snared 43 rebounds in a game against the Lakers, electrifying the sports world. Chubby Checker had teenagers all over America gyrating to the "Twist," his hit rock and roll single topping the charts and tapping into an emerging generation eager for a musical revolution.

This was the kind of news that was filling the newspapers in the last days of 1961, a relief for war-weary Americans who were anxious for peace and the promise of prolonged prosperity.

In Hartford, the weather had been unusually mild since Thanksgiving, with temperatures hovering in the low to mid 40's. It was a bit colder today, with the mercury fluctuating in the high 30's, but a strong westerly wind made it feel colder.

There was a growing holiday festivity in the air as Christmas, Hanukkah and the New Year approached, but without the season's first snowfall or a real cold snap, it hadn't quite taken hold yet. Nevertheless, Main Street saw a constant stream of traffic, as families from all over the city and the surrounding suburbs loaded up in their cars to cruise past the remarkable annual holiday display on the portico of G. Fox & Company, a department store that was the anchor of the city's business community. Throngs of shoppers also filled the Sage Allen's, E. J. Korvettes and Brown Thomson's department stores and hundreds of other retail businesses that thrived off the customers who came to see the G. Fox's display. The threat of a snowstorm later in the weekend lent some urgency to gift buyers who worried about the last minute holiday "rush."

Hartford was one of New England's best-kept secrets at the turn of the decade, and the slightly more than 160,000 people who lived there were in no hurry to share it. Just a shade over three centuries years old, it was the fourth largest city in New England but lingered largely unnoticed between the bustling urban giants of New York City and Boston.

For those who chose Hartford as home, it had its share of attractions and celebrated citizens, but most people liked the city for what it was: a safe, relatively slow paced gem of a community with tightly knit neighborhoods that boasted the nation's oldest continually published newspaper, the *Hartford Courant*, the country's oldest public art museum in the *Wadsworth*, and a bevy of well manicured, delightfully landscaped public parks. Mark Twain, who wrote some of his most important works in his mansion off Farmington Avenue, said before he died, "Of all the beautiful towns it has been my fortune to see, this is the chief."

The city's civil servants saw it pretty much the same way Twain did. In fact, the rank and file of Hartford's Fire Department took it on their own to commission a patch to wear on their uniforms which read: "All American City."

The small metropolis had come a long way over the last three centuries of development as a center of commerce along the banks of the Connecticut River, but was today surprisingly known as the Insurance Capital of the world. The city's business leadership may have come from the giant Hartford, Travelers and Aetna insurance companies, but its real strength lay in the pride of the Irish-Italian communities that were the bedrock of the city. And for them, the most coveted jobs were with the Fire and Police Departments.

It was a thing of pride to say you were a Hartford firefighter or cop, and there were a good number of families whose bloodlines were steeped with generations of one or the other.

For the Fire Department, much of that pride had been hard won – painfully emanating from an event that had shocked the nation and rocked Hartford's City Hall on July 6, 1944 – a day that had promised some respite from the news of GI's advancing quickly through France under heavy fire from the retreating Germans just a month after D-Day. The circus had come to town and the city welcomed the distraction from the war.

But by day's end, the Hartford Circus Fire, one of the worst disasters in the history of the United States, had claimed 169 lives in a vacant lot on Barbour Street in Hartford's north end.

The canvas big top of the Ringling Bros. and Barnum and Bailey Circus, which held upwards of 7,000 people that day, had been waterproofed with a mixture of 1,800 pounds of wax paraffin dissolved in some 6,000 gallons of gasoline. During the war years, with fireproof canvas in short supply, it was a common alternative method of waterproofing. When the fire started – by accident or arson, the cause was never determined – survivors reported that the burning wax paraffin had "rained down" upon them as they fled.

Who was to blame? Five circus officials were convicted of manslaughter in the disaster, but at City Hall, the question was which municipal department had signed off on the permit allowing the tent, waterproofed with such a lethal combination, to be erected in the first place. The Fire and Police Department brass pointed fingers at each other. Ultimately it was proven that a Police official had given the go ahead without consulting the Fire Department. The resulting scandal resulted in a major overhaul of policy and protocol for the two civil services and clear lines of authority. The modern Hartford Fire Department was the result of this painful experience, and there was an unspoken vow throughout City Hall and the Fire service: Never again.

In the Hartford Fire Department, you were either a "Trucky" assigned to the huge Ladder trucks or a "Pony" working the smaller pumpers or hose wagons. The tags were the source of great pride, even though their history only had to do with the size of the horses needed to pull the antique horse drawn fire equipment of a hundred years before. The heavier the apparatus, the bigger the horses needed to pull it. "Truck horses" were oversized beasts. Lighter apparatus needed lighter, faster "Ponies" to pull it.

Whether one was a Trucky or a Pony ultimately didn't contribute much to the significance of being a Hartford firefighter. What was more important was the "Brotherhood" that came with the job, a loyalty among men that drove them to a level of performance and dedication not seen or even possible in the halls of the city's prestigious insurance companies for which it was better known.

There may have been Blue Chip stock behind the greatness of the Travelers, Aetna and Hartford Insurance companies, but it was the bedrock of the Hartford Fire Department that made it the pride of the city.

What gave the Department such an unshakeable foundation were unpretentious, straightforward men like Lieutenant Fred Bartlett, a lieutenant for HFD's Engine Company 15 on New Britain Avenue.

Before becoming a firefighter, he was an Army medic that miraculously waded ashore on to the beaches of Normandy unharmed on June 6, 1944 despite murderous German machine gun and mortar fire that mowed down men by the thousands. There wasn't a day that passed when Bartlett didn't remember the red tinged breakers rolling on to blood soaked sands as he hopelessly administered what little aid he could to young GI's who were slaughtered before they took their first steps on European soil.

Being a Hartford firefighter was almost cathartic for Bartlett. Here he had a fighting chance and could actually save people. In his off hours, he built the Fire Department's Credit Union, living a life steeped in the rigid order and the regulation of an accountant. He found peace in maintaining strict orderliness and discipline within his family as well, raising three children with the same structured values that he brought to his work. His wife Doris, sons Fred Jr. and Bill and daughter Mary found their Army hero husband and father a loving taskmaster, devoted to them but also to his principles.

The Hartford Fire Department found more bedrock in men like Bob King, a Trucky. King was a life-long south-end boy with Hollywood good looks who became a lieutenant of Ladder 5 on South Whitney Street – after surviving the last hellacious year of the War in the Pacific aboard the Light Cruiser *USS Oklahoma City*.

King was one of the thousands of Navy men who supported the final island hopping strategy, facing the desperate last stands by the Japanese at Okinawa and Iwo Jima and countless Kamikaze attacks. He spent more hours at "Battle Stations" than in his bunk. It was another year, after a prolonged stay with the Allied Occupation Forces stationed near Hiroshima before he would see Hartford again. And when he came home, he carried with him the vision of the ultimate destruction, the smell of death and decay and the sight of those hideously burned survivors of the world's first nuclear attack.

There was John Larkin, another rock-solid, life-long south-end boy, an Irishman who had managed to live through the debacle of the first Allied invasion of Europe at Anzio in Italy in 1944 as a sergeant with the Fifth Army's 240$^{th}$ Howitzer Field Artillery unit. He spent four months pinned down in the bloody battle for Monte Cassino before the breakthrough that led to the liberation of Rome.

It was here, where Larkin stepped over the bodies of friends and comrades who had died for another foot of ground that he learned a brutal lesson that would serve him well as a firefighter.

"You gotta be at your best when things are at there worst," he would often share with his sons. For Lieutenant Larkin, sitting in the right hand seat of Engine 6 as a firefighter racing to a multi-alarm blaze was like a Sunday drive compared to the hell he had tasted.

There was Frank Droney, another Irish truck man assigned to Ladder 6 at Main and Pearl Streets on this day, who saw the front lines of the Allied push in North Korea up close. Too close. He froze in winter and baked in the summer over a year on the Korean peninsula fighting for every inch of every rocky hill that stood between the Allies and victory. He saw a lot of blood flow down those hills. To his comrades in the department, he was fearless. There was no better feeling than looking over your shoulder in a real bad working fire and seeing Frank Droney at your back.

There were countless such men in the Hartford Fire Department in 1961. Men who had left their city as innocent boys and returned as battle-hardened war veterans. Men who had gladly, joyfully come home to their birthplace and the peace it represented. Hartford was a place where they could push down the horrors of all they had seen and done. A place where they could build and live normal, satisfying lives. A place where they could help people, where they could harness their hardcore values and hardboiled nerves to save lives.

The Fire Department offered them an honest living if not wealth, but perhaps more importantly a continuation of the military-like daily regime and leadership that kept the now quick-witted and quick-fisted vets in line and out of trouble. It put them back in a uniform that made them proud, gave them buddies in whom they trusted their lives and a sense of camaraderie they would carry all their years. Yes, the work was dangerous. You could be killed, injured or crippled on the job. But after surviving Anzio, Normandy, Iwo Jima, Hiroshima and Pork Chop Hill – most of them laughed at the inherent job risks.

After their wartime experiences, after looking death in the eye every day for years, after surviving or witnessing every conceivable horror of war, the dangers a fireman faced were almost laughable by comparison. Most of them felt invincible. And for those younger men who hadn't seen war, the culture of invincibility built by the "bedrock" of the department was infectious.

And so it was on this early winter day in December 1961. Hartford was operating smoothly and efficiently, in good social and financial health, with the city fathers hardly wrestling with any pressing issues save the slow, but only slightly alarming exodus of its residents to the suburbs as men built financial security after returning from war. It was a safe place to live, with a well-respected Police Department and a small city Fire Department second to none. In Hartford, life was good and the holiday festivities were about to fill the streets with even more harmony.

For the Fire Department, the preceding night and early morning had been very busy, with 12 calls spread out over the city. But luckily for the men assigned to 21 fire companies, the fire monster had been unusually calm with none of the alarms adding up to much real action. In fact, the slow pace of activity gave some fire companies the opportunity to put up a Christmas tree or hang garland or a wreath outside their station house.

The men who were on that day remember it well as the calm before the storm.

Like an armistice shattered, the peace evaporated slightly after one o'clock when an alarm from Box 417, a four-story apartment building at the corner of Zion and Ward Streets, breeched the peacefulness of the quiet afternoon that Dispatchers Dan Kelley and Dick Walsh were enjoying. From their post on the third floor of the Fire Department's Headquarters at 275 Pearl Street, they sprang into the routine that would send men and apparatus speeding to the fire within minutes. No big deal, they thought. And as city fires go, ultimately it wasn't. But little could they know that the fire monster was just warming up.

He was saving his best for later in the day.

# Three

~~~ ❧ ~~~

*"Let's hope it's a quiet one, sweetheart."*

At 6 a.m. that morning, fourteen-year-old Tim Kelliher, Jr. lay awake in his bedroom on Evergreen Street, plotting how he might sneak the 1947 Cadillac his father had let him buy just days before out for a drive, despite the small obstacle of being too young to have a drivers license.

It was a Holy Day of Obligation for Roman Catholics, the Feast of the Immaculate Conception of the Blessed Virgin Mary. That meant no school for Kelliher, a freshman at Northwest Catholic High School, but mandatory appearance at Mass. He figured he'd work his way through one complication at a time. For now, some time at the wheel of the Caddy was a priority. He couldn't get his license until he was 16, but a friend of his dad's had offered to sell him the pristine car for a few hundred bucks. Even his old man couldn't let him pass up the deal. Young Tim listened as his father
~~~

moved around the kitchen of their flat, getting ready to go to work.

The Senior Kelliher was a captain in the Fire Department and already was dressed and geared up for another day, his mind racing with the responsibilities of leadership. He was a natural at leading men – even leading them into danger – but he wasn't sure about all the bureaucratic bullshit that came with his silver Captain's bars. He was more comfortable being a "Pipe man," the guy on the nob end of a two and a half inch, double-walled canvas water hose blasting a wall of flames bent on eating him.

Firefighter Frank Droney, on the second of his three-day shift, was sipping coffee at the breakfast table and reading the morning's *Courant.* As usual, he was looking forward to joining his gang at 275 Pearl Street where he was assigned to Ladder 1, a 100-foot, hydraulically-operated metal ladder American LaFrance aerial truck. He liked the work, he liked the guys.

Droney was a cool character with piercing eyes that sized up a man quickly. He labored hard as a firefighter and wasn't afraid to be the first man in on a working fire. But he went about his business calmly and used his brains. He'd learned that fear and stupidity could shorten your career by days or weeks or months, but also could extinguish it forever.

Department Chief Thomas F. Lee was having breakfast with his wife and making small talk about Christmas shopping and the holiday party the couple had been invited to later that evening at the home of Hartford Hospital President T. Stewart Hamilton. He sighed at the thought of having to rub elbows with the city's bureaucrats who would all be attending, but wrote it off as part of the job. Worse, he had a long, boring day ahead of him inspecting new firehouses the city had erected in a realignment effort aimed at combining some stations and cutting costs. He would have to personally sign off on each of the half dozen new buildings. Lieutenant Bob Martin, his driver, would arrive within the next twenty minutes or so in the jet-black Buick sedan assigned to the Chief.

Lee and the car were known synonymously to Hartford firefighters, who referred to him as "The black car." Officially it was known as "Car 1." His two deputy chiefs, assigned bright red Fords, similarly were known as the "red cars."

When Martin arrived, Lee kissed his wife goodbye and spoke the words he left her with every morning.

"Let's hope it's a quiet one, sweetheart."

Richard "Richie" Tajirian, a slightly built young firefighter (only a very brave or very stupid man might have called him "skinny") was still sleeping. Today would be his first day back on the job after two off. The 25-year-old Tajirian had the energy of two men and owed the city nothing at the end of a three-day shift, but when he hit the sack, it was lights out. He'd be up shortly and probably would be the first firefighter at the station at 275 Pearl, checking out the tiller on Ladder 6, his assignment. There wasn't a better tiller wheelman in the city.

Tajirian had only been on the job for three years, but in that time he'd climbed a lot of ladder and was recognized as a most dependable, competent and fearless Trucky. In the one-man tiller seat at the very end of the massive apparatus, he had an instinctive feel for driving the ass end of a 60,000-pound, 45-foot long rig exactly as required: in the exact opposite direction as the front. It was not a skill many could master.

Firefighter John Larkin was up early as usual, making breakfast for his wife and two boys before leaving for work. The morning kitchen of their Mountfort Street flat was always filled with the aroma of fresh coffee and frying bacon, griddled flapjacks or a big pot of fresh oatmeal. In the background, a small radio blared the sound of WTIC's Bob Steele, the gravelly voice of greater Hartford and perhaps its best known media personality, bringing news, weather, gently waking music and the cornpone humor for which he was renowned.

Similar scenes played out all over the city of Hartford.

Firemen with names like Bartlett, Larkin, McInerney, McSweegan, Hart, King, Kelliher, Droney, McCullough, Schaeffer, Walsh and Nolan, and Zazzaro Wolk, Delaney, Slavkin, Attardo, Kieselback, Biancamano, Skehan, Mason, Lombardo and Dicioccio were already awake or stirring with another long day of work ahead. They'd spend it working together either on maintaining fire equipment or battling 'workers' – real, burning fires.

One never knew just what kind of day it would be. It might be filled with so much action that after a 10-hour shift a man might be ready to literally drop into his bed. Or, it might be so quiet that 10-minutes after dinner and settled into his easy chair in front of a small black and white television screen, he'd fall asleep from the boredom of the day. If given a choice, most firemen would pick the former.

These weren't men who enjoyed filling empty hours. Most had been running to put food on the table for their families or fighting to stay alive for most of their lives. Boredom was their enemy, and the knowledge that the bell could ring at any moment, sending them hurtling into unknown danger was always lurking in the back of their minds, creating a certain unspoken anxiety as well as a need to keep their adrenalin flowing. As Chief Lee put it: "If a fireman isn't fighting a fire, then he's probably fighting with another fireman!"

And there was no way to predict what kind of action they would see during their 10-hour shift, if it would be a forgettable day or one they would never forget. So those with wives kissed them goodbye and wondered aloud what would be waiting on the table for dinner that night to avoid talking about anything more ominous. Wives and mothers held on to good-bye hugs for a moment longer, never uttering any sign of fear but pushing it down into a place they never spoke of. Sons and daughters kissed or waved to their daddies, trying not to imagine the unimaginable.

All of this was the Hartford Fire Department's contribution to the quiet and peaceful drama behind the scenes of the city awakening.

Merchants on Main Street were opening their doors. The Police Department day shift had completed its morning briefing on Morgan Street, and cops headed for their beats, twirling their batons and greeting merchants and residents, mostly by their first names.

On Front Street, the fruit and vegetable wagons were serving up the last of their fresh produce and diners were turning on the lights and opening their doors to welcome the coffee and doughnut crowd. Restaurateurs were planning the day's menus and firing up the grilles. The day shift was wandering into the Colt's Firearms factory.

At Hartford, St. Francis and Mount Sinai Hospitals, doctors were making their early rounds and filling operating rooms, nurses were administering morning meds and changing beds and breakfast was being served to the hundreds of patients at each facility. "Candy Stripers," high school age girls with an interest in nursing roamed the halls offering patients books and magazines and other sundries in the red and white striped uniforms that gave them their name. There were an unusual number of girls on today, as schools were out for the Catholic Holy Day.

Doctor Norman Hedenstad, a darkly handsome, 33-year-old assistant resident was roaming the Hartford Hospital halls before dawn, as was his usual practice. The young physician was well liked by both patients and staff, who were always impressed with his genuine smile and gentle manner. He had a particularly excellent bedside manner with the elderly, whom he took great pains to comfort and reassure. T. Stewart Hamilton had personally remarked to colleagues how impressed he was with the young physician, not only for his sharp intelligence and medical skills, but also for his humanity. It was not a trait common among the highly educated resident doctors, and Hamilton had observed many in his career.

This morning, Hedenstad stayed a few extra moments to share coffee with Mrs. Jeannie Dunn, a 73-year-old patient from East Hartford who was anxiously awaiting the results of testing performed the previous day. A severe diabetic, he knew her prognosis was not promising, but did his best to reassure her.

"Now Mrs. Dunn," he said to her softly in her room in the south wing of the ninth floor. "There's no reason to fret, as I've told you," the tall, crewcut Hedenstad comforted her. "It will do you no good to lie here all day being anxious over something you can't control. But no matter what, we will get your diabetes back under control, I promise you."

He peered over his black, horn-rimmed glasses at the elderly woman and tapped her frail arm with a finger. The boyish looking resident wore the heavy framed glasses intentionally to make him look more mature.

"That's a personal promise, Mrs. Dunn," he said, winking at her as he stood to leave. "And with that," he said, downing the last of his third cup of coffee of the early morning, "I'm afraid I must continue my rounds and visit with some really ill people." He winked at her. "I promise to stop in again this afternoon. Ok, dear?" She beamed at his attention.

Acting ninth floor Head Nurse Pat Rinaldi was flipping through charts at the main nursing station in the center of the north wing. She had precious little time to catch up with the overnight activity on the sixty-bed, primarily post-operative ward while keeping a watchful eye on staffing for the day. There was nary an empty bed on the ninth floor, with patients ranging from a 14-year-old girl with appendicitis to the very elderly suffering from a myriad of illnesses. Having enough help to get through the shift would be a challenge. She thought about calling in an off duty nurse for help, then dismissed it. Rinaldi had complete confidence in the staff under her direction, and especially in the energy level of new nurses like Eileen

Gormley Santiglia, not much more than a year out of nursing school. They'd make do, Rinaldi concluded.

Similar activities were going on all over the hospital. The level of energy in the building was enormous. It had to be because Hartford Hospital was a city within a city.

Everywhere in the hospital, someone or something was in motion. Maintenance men and cleaning crews went about assigned tasks. The kitchens were in full operation and dietary aides moved from room to room, collecting menus for the following day. The coffee shop on the third floor was doing a brisk business, as was the florist in the lobby. The line at the lobby entrance on the first floor grew long as visitors stopped to inquire about the room numbers of patients. In the maternity ward, the sounds of mothers in labor, the wails of newborns and the celebrations of families went on endlessly. X-Ray machines went about their mysterious, invisible work, respirators pumped air into the lungs of those struggling to breath, washing machines churned laundry, coffee pots percolated.

The 13-story, glazed white-brick hospital at 80 Seymour Street was an understated, unceremonious source of pride for the city, but one of New England's largest and most respected medical facilities. Just six years before, it had celebrated the 100th anniversary of its licensing. The total campus occupied 35 acres in the south end of the city in an area proudly known as the "Golden Triangle:" Seymour Street at the hospital's front door, with Jefferson Street on its north side and Retreat Avenue to the south.

It was originally intended to be a 20-story structure, but concern was expressed that the building's height would interfere with the flight operations of the only nearby airfield, Brainard Airport, which was situated just a few miles away across the Connecticut River. Two separate buildings were conceived instead. The South Building rose five stories and opened in 1942. It was raised and connected to the new 13-story North Building and opened in 1948.

It took 3,000 tons of structural steel, 10,000 cubic yards of concrete and 2,500,000 glazed white bricks to build what was considered at the time the safest hospital in the country. The two central buildings of the campus, know commonly as the High Building, were linked by a glass-enclosed staircase that looked out over a horseshoe-shaped driveway leading up to its main entranceway and lobby. From the glass staircase, visitors could catch an unencumbered view westward all the way up to the busy Washington Street, just a few blocks from the famed Bushnell Theater for the Performing Arts.

Standing eight blocks south of the downtown business core, it was not only one of the tallest buildings in Hartford, but perhaps the busiest, as well.

On any given day, with nearly 2,700 employees, more than 800 patients, and hundreds more visitors and vendors, Hartford Hospital could easily account for 5,000 people per day working to get well or just plain working at the medical facility. It was bustling with activity seven days per week, 24 hours a day. The lights simply never went out.

Around the clock, sirens pierced the quiet as ambulances raced to the Hospital's Emergency Room. There, specially trained staff calmly treated everything from headaches to the worst kinds of mayhem and accident trauma.

Windowless operating rooms were equally oblivious to day or night, doctors and nurses scurried through the halls tending to patients, and drugs and other medications were dispensed from the pharmacy, non-stop. Full crews labored to keep up with the endless tasks of providing fresh supplies of clean laundry and bedding and incinerating the more than 5,200 pounds of trash that the hospital generated every day. The kitchen prepared enough food to sustain this army, day after day, night after night. The business of treating illness, tending to the living and nursing the dying was a busy one, indeed.

As the whirlwind of life proceeded in the hospital at the center of the "Golden Triangle," firefighter John Larkin, as did so many other members of the brotherhood to which he belonged, kissed his wife and squeezed her hand, then tousled the hair of his sons as he said goodbye. Then, happily whistling his favorite old Irish ballad, *"I'll Tell Me Ma"* he contentedly strolled to Engine Company 6 on Huyshope Avenue and his beloved hose wagon. It was only a few blocks away from one of the city's landmark buildings, the Colt Firearms factory with its famous blue onion dome adorned by gold stars and topped by a gold orb and a rampant colt, the original symbol of the Colt Manufacturing Company.

He had no intention of visiting Hartford Hospital that day. Nor did he anticipate that by the following day, he would have another nightmare to add to the vast collection of things he wished he'd never seen in his lifetime.

# Four

~~~ ❧ ~~~

*When fate chose its victims*

There were others who had no intentions of visiting Hartford Hospital that day.

The first was Mrs. John Ryan, Genevieve, a fetching 22-year-old young woman who had discovered to her wonder and delight that she was pregnant just two months after her wedding. The only person in the world who was happier at his bride's news was her husband, a pipe fitter who upon marrying the stunningly beautiful, red-haired, green-eyed Irish lass had thought his life complete. The prospect of a son or daughter had made the man so proud he thought the swelling in his chest would pop the buttons on his shirt.

John Ryan adored his Genevieve. Every day as he walked to work, deep in thought about the future, he wondered how it would be possible for him to love her more. He vowed to be the best husband and father the Good Lord had ever blessed, and counted each day of
~~~

his wife's pregnancy as one day closer to heaven. The world had never known a happier pipe fitter.

Genevieve, like her husband, had emigrated from Ireland as a child with her family and promptly settled in Hartford to be with relatives. Neither had ever seen the inside of a hospital let alone been a patient in one. They had each been brought into the world with the traditional assistance of a midwife inside a birthing nook common to the small grass roofed cottages that had been home in Ireland. Genevieve, more so than John, was leery of having her baby in the hospital but was assured by her clan that one of the luxuries of living in the new world was extraordinary health care.

"You'll have nothing to fear at Hartford Hospital, darlin'," said an older cousin who'd delivered two children there already. "Why it's a marvel, 'tis, so clean and scrubbed you'll want to stay. And take full advantage of the few days you'll have in bed. Believe me, life will be a bit of a handful with the wee one to care for. For heaven's sake, the nurses will even fix you a spot of tea, if you ask nicely!"

She wasn't due yet for another three and a half weeks, but that morning she awakened John before dawn to share with him the surprising news that her water had broken. The new mother-to-be was terribly frightened at this unexpected turn and John had wasted no time in raising the superintendent of the small apartment they rented to use his telephone to call her doctor.

"Bring her to the hospital immediately, Mr. Ryan," Doctor Mulready had told him. "I'll meet you there. But don't be fretting now, this is not that unusual and I assure you the child will be ready for the world."

The superintendent wouldn't hear of the young mother being brought to the hospital in a taxi and drove them there himself. The Irish took care of each other.

Upon arrival through the Hartford Hospital Emergency Room, Genevieve, with her husband holding her hand, was admitted immediately and as he promised, Dr. Mulready greeted them within the hour.

"You're in labor, darlin', no doubt about it," he told them after examining the young mother in the sparkling clean Maternity Ward at the hospital. "Actually, your little one is coming quite quickly, I don't think it will be more than a few hours." John's smile lit up the room and Mulready laughed.

"By the look of the way your misses is squeezing your hand, I don't think she shares your enthusiasm, John, " the doctor said, grinning. "But I think that will change. With a mother so lovely, I've a feeling you'll be sharing a beautiful child today. Now let's relax as much as possible and let nature take its course for a while."

The second was a 14-year-old Italian girl, a young brown-haired beauty with dark eyes and flawless olive-toned skin, complaining of abdominal pain. She had arrived by ambulance and had been immediately examined by Assistant Resident Doctor Norman Hedenstad, who diagnosed her to be suffering from Appendicitis.

"Louisa, the pain you have been suffering in your belly, along with your fever and nausea, tells me that it is important that we perform surgery, an Appendectomy, as soon as possible," he told the child with her parents by her side. The young girl gasped.

"There is nothing to be afraid of Louisa, I assure you," Hedenstad said calmly to the frightened girl and her worried parents. "This is not an uncommon illness in people of your young age and the surgery is not complicated. Why, we'll have you on your feet and home as good as new in just a few days," he said and reached for her hand.

"You must trust me, sweetheart. Everything will be just fine. I'll watch over you myself, ok?"

The girl smiled at his kindness. Hedenstad was quickly becoming a master of reassurance for the young and old.

"I'm going to go and talk with the surgeon now and get this scheduled as soon as possible. Hopefully, we can do the procedure later this morning and you'll be resting comfortably by this afternoon. You stay here," he smiled, " I'll be right back."

By noon, young Genevieve Ryan had delivered a beautiful baby boy, Liam John Ryan, whom his father refused to share with any of the other two-dozen relatives who flocked to the hospital to see the newest addition to the family. And just a short while later, the young Louisa Papae was wheeled into a room on the south wing of the Ninth Floor after having a successful Appendectomy. She was sleeping comfortably, under sedation, when her parents came into the room. Her mother and father held hands beside her bed, praying there would be no complications. They waited for Dr. Hedenstad, who had promised to visit as soon as possible to discuss their daughter's recovery.

Unfortunately, circumstances would prevent the young resident from keeping his word.

While Louisa Papae was recovering from her surgery in her private ninth floor room, in the ER, located on the ground floor of the North Wing High Rise building, what had been a relatively quiet morning suddenly became frantic with activity.

Just blocks from the hospital, an ambulance driver, escorted by a police car with its lights blazing and siren blaring, had radioed to say he was transporting a bleeding, unconscious hit-and-run victim who would need immediate attention.

The injured, a tall, stooped over middle-aged man who hummed to himself incessantly, had been out walking his dog on Franklin Avenue toward the Park Street Green when he had been hit by a car that blew through a stop light at the corner of Brown Street.

Charles Whitemore, a Korean War veteran who had come home from the conflict suffering from severe emotional trauma, took the same stroll every morning with his beloved pet, a 100-pound German Shepherd named "Sarge." The huge dog was not only Whitemore's only loving companion, he was a friend who filled the mentally disturbed man's life.

Unable to work because of his incapacitation, the two spent every waking minute together, and Sarge slept at the foot of the veteran's bed each night. The great German Shepherd, whom Whitemore had raised from a pup was also his guardian angel. Anyone who gave thought to taking advantage of his master dismissed the idea quickly after one look into Sarge's eyes, which never, ever, left Whitemore. It was if the dog instinctively knew that his keeper fought an uphill battle with life, and consequently was ever vigilant in his behalf.

Unfortunately, on this clear December morning, there was little Sarge could do to protect his owner, who had stepped out from the curb at Brown Street with Sarge leashed by his side after looking both ways for oncoming traffic. But in the middle of the crossing, a car, recklessly speeding through the intersection, appeared out of nowhere.

Whitemore, so startled that he could do no more than freeze in his tracks, still had the instincts to let go of Sarge's leash, which allowed the dog to leap out of the way. But the car caught the man dead center with it's front bumper, actually sweeping him up and tossing him in to the air and over the top of the car where he landed on the rear windshield, smashing it before rolling off the trunk and landing heavily on the pavement. Mercifully, he was unconscious before his head bounced off the black top.

The car never slowed, speeding away from the accident. Although Sarge briefly raced after it, he instinctively knew his friend needed him. He raced back to Whitemore who was lying motionless on the pavement, bleeding heavily from the back of his head and various lacerations. Sarge gently licked the man's face and whimpered helplessly. A bakery owner from across the street who had seen the whole incident, ran towards the body, yelling as he came, "Call an ambulance, somebody call an ambulance!"

The dog saw the approaching shopkeeper and knew only one thing to do: protect the broken man lying in the street. He bared his teeth and the baker stopped dead in his tracks, frightened that the anxious dog would attack him. It was a smart move.

Within minutes, the police arrived and the sound of an approaching ambulance could be heard a few blocks away. A young officer slowly approached the dog, which was nervously pacing and circling his master. He snarled at the intruder, baring his intimidating teeth that gave no doubt of his intentions.

The policeman spoke gently to the frightened animal as he slowly made his way closer to the victim.

The cop, unable to assess the seriousness of Whitemore's injuries, knew that every minute counted. They had to get this poor bastard to the hospital. The thought sickened him, but he was ready, if necessary to put the dog down if he had to clear the way for the ambulance crew to tend to Whitemore. He released the safety strap from his holstered police revolver, ready to do what he must. But once more, instinctively and out of love and loyalty, Sarge chose the right course of action and hesitantly backed off as the officer approached.

As terrifying as the massive dog was, growling menacingly at those who would help his master, the watching crowd felt immense pity for the animal who was heartbreakingly confused. Sarge sat on his rear haunches and warily watched as the policeman rendered what first aid he could. He barked and snarled at the ambulance crew as they carefully loaded the unconscious man onto a stretcher and into the ambulance, but kept his distance.

The policeman made a move towards the dog, hoping to grab hold of his leash, but Sarge wanted nothing but to be with his master. As the ambulance pulled away with its sirens blaring and a police escort to clear traffic to Hartford Hospital's Emergency Room, some ten blocks away, Sarge, still dragging his leash, slowly trotted after the vehicles then burst into a full run chasing after them.

When the ambulance pulled up to the ER entrance, the panting dog was no more than a few yards behind. Again he sat at a comfortable distance and anxiously watched as doctors and nurses began tending to his master even as his stretcher was being wheeled into the hospital. The dog made a move to follow, then thought better of it. He sat again and looked around as if considering his options. Then he got up and walked slowly to the grassy center of the horseshoe shaped turnabout in front of the hospital, a venue that gave him complete visibility of everyone leaving the ER or the Hospital main entrance.

Traumatized to the point of exhaustion, the dog looked around again, then circled several times before lying down heavily on the ground and resting his great head on his huge front paws.

And then he waited… and watched.

# Five

~~~ ~~~

*The fire monster awakens*

Ever so gently, like a feather shed from the wing of a bird in flight, the tiny, nearly weightless cigarette butt sailed down the trash chute against the natural cushion of air trying to prevent it from falling, but to no avail. It fluttered up and down with each gust, dropping a foot, then rising six inches, but even its miniscule weight eventually won out and it landed, still burning, amidst a sea of debris blocking its path somewhere around the third floor.

There was a mountain of trash built up to this level, almost all highly flammable. Cardboard boxes of every description, gauze pads, some soaked in alcohol, bandages of every size and shape, used paper towels, records and files, old mail, newspapers and magazines, copious quantities of discarded x-ray film… the list was endless. The various geometric shapes of the non-compacted trash left a jigsaw trail of open cracks and spaces, narrow highways, streets and veins of room for tiny refuse to fall until it lodged against another object
~~~

that blocked its path. It took little to eventually stop the fall of the cigarette and its glowing ember that finally landed, without a perceptible decibel of sound, atop a dry, crumpled up paper hand towel.

In the ultimate obscenity, the fuse that lit the bomb that would cause so many to die, so many more to cry, and many, many more to never recover from the emotional terror of the next few hours, began it's hideous work in absolute silence.

As the burning tobacco released the last seconds of its fiery heat, the cigarette passed the blazing energy to the paper towel, which accepted its fate without a whimper of objection and began to smolder instantaneously. In a heartbeat, a crimson ring of sparks began to slowly devour the paper, the edges of a burning hole growing outwardly as it consumed the towel. In turn, a wadded newspaper, a folded section containing the daily crossword puzzle that perhaps a patient had labored over to help pass the tedious boredom of hospital stay, was touched by the spreading cinders and also began to smolder. But as wisps of smoke began to rise up the chute, the smoldering trash refused to flame, stymied by a lack of oxygen. Nonetheless, explosive hot gasses, too rich to burn without more fuel, built up quickly and rose to the upper heights of the chute. Minutes passed. Pressure built inside the air-starved chamber. The fire monster waited patiently.

Then, the predictable happened.

Somewhere, on a floor far above the smoldering fire, a nurse innocently opened a trash chute door to dispose of rubbish. The insatiable monster instantly pounced on the resulting surge of oxygen and gorged on it, reveling in satisfying its hunger like a starving wild animal feeding on felled prey. The smoldering wad of newsprint urgently burst into long licks of flame. With rocket-like speed, the blaze began its upward climb, consuming everything in its path in all directions. A massive, unstoppable fireball bullied its way towards escape.

On the ninth floor, the ravenous fire monster found its path to freedom.

And when the inevitable occurred, the beast created by a vindictive fit of anger was free to devour nearly any substance in its path. That would include the inanimate kinds of objects that one hardly notices. A telephone at the reception desk, a framed picture on the wall, spare sheets and towels and blankets in a storage closet. Ceiling tiles and wallpaper. A purse lying unattended beneath a reception desk

And flesh and bone.

# Six

~~~ ∽ ~~~

*The forewarning*

At the corner of Zion and Ward Streets, a scant few blocks from the endless bustle of activity at Hartford Hospital, the five-story brick apartment building was hardly a city landmark. It was a relatively nondescript place with no exceptional architectural presence. Inside could be heard the typical noises that came from a building that was home to 20 families, nearly 60 men, women and children in all. As apartment buildings on the outskirts of the city went, it was a comfortable, if not attractive place to live. But the property was the epitome of the first rule of prime real estate: location, location, location.

On one hand, the building sat squarely in the busy Park Street neighborhood, full of restaurants, grocers and shops. One only had to walk a few feet or a block or two to buy fresh vegetables or flowers off carts parked on the sidewalk, or to visit the butcher's shop. Tailors, shoemakers, grocers and the local garage were
~~~

as close. Downtown Hartford, with its myriad department stores led by the flagship G. Fox and Company, was a 10-minute public bus ride away. The fare was a quarter.

On the other hand, the antithesis of the busy Park Street neighborhood sat a mere block away from the apartment building.

Pope Park, a 73-acre gift to the city from the estate of Col. Albert A. Pope in 1894, was a lushly landscaped oasis of countryside in the busy neighborhood, with tennis and basketball courts, baseball fields and playgrounds that attracted hundreds of local children in the summer. In the cold winter months, ice skating and sledding kept it just as busy. Families flocked to it for Sunday picnics. It was a favorite spot for lovers, young and old to go for long walks holding hands. In spring, the sweet scent of flower blossoms permeated the entire neighborhood, and even wafted through the open windows of the apartments at Zion and Ward Streets.

Unfortunately, sometimes it is the unseen or unforeseen that sneaks up and ruins it all.

The building was old, probably constructed in the mid 1800's. That meant the electrical wiring was old, too. And sometime during that Friday morning of December 8th, a circuit failed in the fuse panel in the basement storage area of the building, sparking a small, smoldering fire amongst the stored belongings of the upstairs tenants, stuffed from floor to ceiling into individual, locked wire pens in the cellar.

As the fire burned, it slowly consumed the available air in the dry, airtight basement, a perfect place for storage, and only the acrid smell given off by the brown, smoky haze gave any evidence of trouble.

But countless boxes of books and rafts of personal papers, old furniture and clothing, rolled up carpets, Christmas decorations, half-full cans of paint, children's cribs and toys, heirlooms and private treasures that filled the more than 1,500 square foot basement were prime kindling for a fire that just needed a little bit of oxygen to explode into an inferno.

It didn't have long to wait.

Just a few minutes before 1 p.m. that bright, chilly afternoon, the building janitor, a nice, older Irish man who had cared for the apartment building like it was his own for more than 30 years, thought he caught the scent of a whiff of smoke in his small, ground floor apartment that was a perk of his employment, and went to investigate. The job had been his first after immigrating to America from the small village of Aglish in the old country and he had treasured it and all the sustenance and stability that it had brought to his family because he had been as loyal to it as it had been to him.

He'd married and buried the love of his life while living in that little two-bedroom apartment and raised three green-eyed, redheaded boys to manhood. There was no place on earth more important to him. It took little to prompt him to take action when the building called – a whispering voice that only he could hear – and the smell of smoke was at the top of the list.

The janitor slipped on the three-button Irish wool sweater with the leather elbow patches that Katherine had hand knitted for him one Christmas long ago. It was his most prized possession. Grabbing a flashlight, he stepped out into the hallway to begin his search for the source, first carefully inspecting the two maintenance closets and the fuse panel on the first floor.

He found nothing. But to his irritation, a tenant caught him in the act.

It was Mrs. Leone, a lonely, elderly Italian woman who had lived in the building even longer than the janitor, who cautiously opened the door to her apartment a crack and peered out to see who was making noise in the hallway. The grey-haired, heavy-set woman smiled. It was just her friend, Mr. O'Neill. She sighed. Someone to talk with. Stepping into the hall, she called out. The old man caught her presence out of the corner of his eye and muffled a curse.

"Why, Mr. O'Neill, whatever are you looking for? How about a nice cup of tea?" she called out hopefully.

Careful to veil his instant annoyance at the interruption of his inspection, O'Neill instead kindly smiled back at the old woman. She was like an old cat, always under one's feet begging for attention, he thought to himself, but recognized well the loneliness she felt. He lived a life of solitude to fight off the hurt of losing his cherished wife some years before, using the free time afforded him to walk in the Park and dig deep into his mind for memories of her. Mrs. Leone, on the other hand, suddenly widowed 10 years before, pounced on any form of humanity to ward off her near phobia of being alone. Not the postman, milkman, door-to-door salesmen or any of her neighbors were able to escape her impossibly warm invitations that only slightly hid her desperation for companionship, but all tried just as desperately to avoid her. So sad, O'Neill thought. Life wasn't so bad with only memories. If only she could come to terms with that.

"Why hello, Mrs. Leone," O'Neill responded to her with as kind a tone as he could muster, even with the smell of smoke growing stronger in his nose.

"I'm afraid I'll have to pass up that attractive offer, dear. I've some work to do that won't hold off," he said, not mentioning his true mission for fear of worrying her.

"Ah, too bad," she replied. "I've just put some freshly baked cookies on the table, too," she added, hoping to change his mind. O'Neill looked up, hesitating at the change in stakes. The woman did make the most incredible sugar cookies. Duty called, but he wavered.

"Well, then," he said, a broad smile coming to his face as he rethought his response, "in that case, let me finish my work and I'll knock on your door a wee bit later, then."

"Why, that would be grand, Mr. O'Neill," she said, already thinking about laying out her prized, hand-painted Deruta ceramic cups and saucers that she had brought with her all the way from Umbria when she left Italy all those years ago. They were one of the few possessions she had now that reminded her of the old country, and there were few opportunities to show off the delicate pieces. She would change out of her housedress, too and thought immediately of the white lace shawl from Burano. It hadn't graced her shoulders in years. The lonely woman reveled at the thought of a visitor.

"Yes, that would be grand, Mr. O'Neill." Mrs. Leone almost sang it as she closed the door.

The janitor just shook his head when he was sure he was alone again and looked heavenward.

"Ah, Katherine, my love," O'Neill thought to himself as he began the short walk towards the outside entrance to the basement. "Now don't be getting jealous on me. It's just a cookie," he laughed in silent apology to his departed wife. "Or two. Nothing sweeter, my sweet." The thought of her made him happy for a moment, but quickly passed. It was like that.

The janitor opened the back door of the building and stepped outside, marveling at what a nice day it had turned out to be. He quickly looked around and up and down the block for signs of smoke or fire. Nothing. He looked up at his building, scanning the windows. Only a few colored electric holiday lights were visible. "There's no Christmas in the air yet, Katherine," he whispered. Then he walked a few feet to the left and down a half flight of stairs to the entrance to the basement, a heavy metal door that was padlocked.

He reached for the ever-present key ring that hung from his belt, a device that held no less than a hundred keys to every door in the entire apartment complex, and located the right one almost by feel. He inserted the key in the oversized lock and turned it, immediately springing it free. Then with the same yank he had given the sticking, windowless door a thousand times before, he pulled on the outward opening door. Oddly, it didn't budge. Perplexed, he dug in his heels and gave the door a mighty wrench. This time the door gave way a half-inch, perhaps slightly more.

Before the old man could take a step inside, he heard the sound of whining, as if an animal was injured and was crying in pain. Unknowingly, by forcing the door open he had broken the vacuum-like seal that the hot gasses had formed after feasting on most of the oxygen in the basement. The noise was the sound of huge quantities of air being sucked back into the cellar. What came next was the whine that almost instantly swelled to a hideous roar, like an orchestra transitioning from a delicate movement to a crescendo of instruments all playing off key and as loudly as possible. In the split second that followed, the thought occurred to him that he was hearing the symphony of the devil. But then the music stopped.

As he stood there, puzzled, a huge fireball raced at him like it was spit from the bowels of hell. The backdraft of flame sped toward the old man with a speed as great as if it had been launched from a great military gun as the sudden rush of air, sucked into the basement by the oxygen starved fire caused it to explode into life.

The flames struck the door with the force of a battering ram that ripped it completely off its hinges and blew it back more than sixty feet. O'Neill was still hanging on to the doorknob and the hundred pound metal entranceway acted as a shield as he flew through the air beneath it. He landed heavily on the ground, the door on top of him as the fireball passed over his head like a shooting star and exploded against a tree, instantly igniting it. Immediately, the casement windows at ground level around the basement exploded outwards, another avenue for the fire to escape. Now fully ventilated and fed by an endless supply of oxygen, the storage area was fully engulfed in fire in a matter of seconds. The entire foundation was ablaze, the fire intent on cooking the building as if it was a pan atop the flaming burner of a gas stove.

O'Neill lay motionless on the ground. His ribs were crushed by the force of the blast striking him full in the chest, which had been protected only by the door, and his left leg protruded awkwardly at a right angle from under it, a compound fracture and third degree burns ensuring he would never walk without a cane again. Despite being nearly deaf from the explosion, he could just make out the sound of Mrs. Leone's terrified screams. His last conscious thought was that the fire had already spread to the first floor. Tears flooded his eyes as shock set in and deliriously he thought how lucky he'd been to have pulled on his precious sweater. It was safe. Then he blacked out.

The janitor's exposed pant leg was still smoldering as strangers strolling by who had witnessed the blast raced to help the old man, four men struggling to lift the heavy door off of him. Another dodged the burning tree and ran to a bright red fire alarm box mounted to a telephone poll at the corner and yanked the handle. Inside, a spring-loaded wheel spun and tapped out a signal on a telegraph wire that sent a signal to a receiver at the Hartford Fire Department's Headquarters and Dispatch Center at 275 Pearl Street. The receiver indicated the box number: 417.

The fire monster was loose.

And hungry.

# Seven

~~~ ঌ ~~~

*"A real snot slinger"*

As Dispatchers Dan Kelley and Dick Walsh were enjoying an unusually quiet afternoon after a busy morning at their post on the third floor of the Fire Department's Headquarters at 275 Pearl Street, both were watching the clock. The shift change at 6 p.m. couldn't come soon enough. Things were quiet. Too quiet. It was unnerving. They shared, but did not speak of a surreal sensation that things were about to change dramatically.

Kelley nervously tapped the end of a pen he was holding repeatedly against the metal top of an Army surplus table that served as his personal office. Walsh watched him, his irritation at the incessant noise building. It was if Kelley was expecting something.

"What the hell is your problem, probie," Walsh mocked his partner as if he was a probationary recruit. "What are you so nervous about?"
~~~

The normally unflappable Kelley didn't respond to the jab immediately, but realized he hadn't been conscious of his behavior.

"Oh, I don't know...we can't all be skaters," he zinged back. "You haven't taken your eyes off that clock in the last half hour. Your wife know you have a date tonight?" Kelley smiled.

"Kiss my ass and remind me to recommend you for the next opening in maintenance, friend," Walsh retorted. "This job is way over your head."

The ostensibly unfriendly repartee was not unusual between the close two friends when things were quiet. Like most firefighters, inactivity made them nervous – and superstitious.

It was a bad combination. Because each knew their instincts usually proved to be on the money.

Almost as Walsh ended his sentence, the alarm bell in the office signaled a box had been pulled. Kelley jumped from his seat and read aloud the Morse code ticker tape signal that indicated the location: Box 417.

Walsh already had his radio transmitter in hand ready to call whichever district chief would inherit command of the call depending on its location in the city.

"What ya got, Dan?" Walsh asked impatiently.

"417. Zion and Ward Streets. Think it's an old apartment building," Kelley responded. "That would be Shortell's."

"Let the district chief know that we're about to transmit the Box," Walsh said.

Kelley nodded. "District 1, Dispatch."

Billy "Festus" Johnson, the driver for District Chief Tom Shortell responded.

"Dispatch, this is District 1," Festus responded, Shortell sitting next to him in the passenger seat of the red Ford.

"Be advised that Box 417 has been pulled at Zion and Ward from the street," Kelley calmly instructed. "No further information is available. You should head in that direction. We will be shipping the Box momentarily."

"Roger that, Dispatch," Johnson responded. "Please provide information as available."

As the District Chief's car sped to the scene, Kelley was already in the process of "shipping" (transmitting) the box number to all fire stations in the city while Dick Walsh searched for information about the building and gathered any information available regarding the situation. Alarm bells sounded in each of the city's firehouses and the Box number 417 came in on the ticker tape.

The station commanders then pulled 417's "Run Card" – an alarm assignment card – out of their filing system that indicated which Engines and Ladder trucks were designated as first responders to the call. Other apparatus scenarios were drawn up if additional alarms were required.

Within seconds, the unusually complacent firehouses that housed the first respondents to the alarm were transformed into meticulously efficient, well-oiled, high-speed machines.

"Here we go," Lieutenant Fred Bartlett announced loudly as he jumped out of his bunk on the upper floor of Company 15 at Fairfield and New Britain Avenue and leapt onto the brass poll that allowed him to slide down in seconds to the garage floor and his waiting turnout gear. Behind him, his four-man crew were also hitting the poles and going to their assigned stations on the running boards, rear steps or jump seats on Engine 15 and Ladder 2 that were housed together in the station. Bartlett and Ladder 2 Captain John Fleming disappeared into the Watch Room where they pulled the Run Card for Box 417. Seeing it only confirmed what both already knew.

"Ok, Engine 15 and Ladder 2, it's ours," Bartlett yelled out to the waiting crews. "We'll have the pleasure of being joined by Engines 8 and 11."

Bartlett donned his heavy gear and stood on the running board below the front passenger seat of Engine 15 while Fleming did the same on Ladder 2.

Quickly both men checked to see that all members of their crew were safely aboard their assigned apparatus. As he knew they would be, Bartlett found John Mulrain and Frank Mangiagli at their stations on the rear steps of the Mack pumper's back bumper, and Ron Forrest on the running board on the right side, ready to go. Driver Tom Whalen was at the wheel, anxious to hit the gas.

On Ladder 2, Fleming performed the same survey and found his driver, Big Joe Rogers ready to go and George Meadows, Jimmy Madigan and Norman Cantin on board. From the time the bell had sounded in the station, the whole exercise had taken less than two minutes.

"Ok, Tom, let's roll, head for Zion and Ward," Bartlett yelled to Whalen and immediately Engine 15 pulled out first followed by the 65-foot ladder truck, the only piece of apparatus owned by the Department manufactured by Seagrave.

The quiet afternoon peace was quickly broken as sirens filled the air with fire apparatus racing to the burning building at the corner of Zion and Ward. In the cab of each truck, Dispatcher Dick Walsh's voice broke through the bedlam with details of the situation that was waiting for the first responders.

Both trucks pulled nimbly out of the station house and merged into traffic, lights flashing and horns blaring. Whalen wove the 25,000-pound pumper through the busy early afternoon traffic with the confidence of a teenager driving a hot rod and blew through the light merging onto Washington Street without incident. Big Joe Rogers was close behind in the giant ladder truck. From the Zion Street firehouse, Engine 8's two pieces, a hose truck followed by a pumper, and Engine 11 from Sisson Avenue had reacted as smoothly and were closing in on Box 417.

"This is a four-story apartment building at the corner of Zion and Ward Streets," Walsh reported. "We have telephone calls indicating heavy smoke can be seen from a block away. There are approximately 60 tenants. There is no elevator in the building." Walsh paused. "Be advised, there are adjacent, occupied structures to the north and west of the address identified."

The radio was filled with dead air as Walsh took another phone call.

"Police just arriving on the scene report that we have a working fire that witnesses claim followed an explosion in the basement. It has already spread to the first floor. There are multiple entrapments although Police report many occupants were able to evacuate from the rear of the building shortly after the explosion. We have one known injured person. Ambulances have been dispatched. Over."

Seconds later, Walsh was back on the radio with more information.

"You have a hydrant on Zion Street, approximately forty yards from the intersection and another on Ward, approximately 50-feet from the corner."

District Chief Shortell pulled up to the fire scene seconds later and began sending Walsh orders to be radio transmitted to the arriving fire apparatus.

"Per order of District Chief Shortell who is 10-2 at the scene, Engine 15 lay into the hydrant on Zion Street, supply a two and half inch line with a straight pipe and begin search and rescue on the first floor," Walsh transmitted, his voice calm and even toned. With the order for a "straight pipe" Shortell was calling for a hose nozzle that would supply a steady stream of water at maximum pressure to knock down the fire.

"Engine 8, take that hydrant on Ward Street and hit the basement," Walsh continued. "Engine 11, assess the situation for occupant entrapments and ladder the building accordingly," he continued. "Ladder 2, raise the stick to the roof, vent the building and then begin search and rescue."

Heavy black smoke and leaping flames were visible to the firefighters from blocks away as Engine 15 approached. Lieutenant Fred Bartlett's pumper was the first unit on the scene and as he instructed, driver Tom Whalen expertly pulled the apparatus within ten feet of the hydrant. Bartlett yelled to the back of the open truck even as Whalen was positioning it. "Alright, you guys, first in, last out, got it? Be careful," he warned. "Let's get the wet stuff on the hot stuff."

John Mulrain raced to the hydrant, uncapped it and spun on a coupling while Mangiagli dragged a length of four-inch diameter, soft suction line to him and connected it to the hydrant and Whalen attached the other end to the pumper inlet. Whalen then connected the two and a half inch hose at a discharge gate on the truck and gave Mulrain the thumbs up to open the hydrant. When he was sure he had pressure, Whalen started the Engine's pump and the line was charged. Mulrain then joined Bartlett and Mangiagli in the arduous task of "humping" the heavy, water filled canvas hose to the front door of the building, 50-feet away while Whalen operated and monitored the roaring pump.

On Ward Street, the crew of Engine 8 was going through an identical drill as they prepared to go into the basement, the source of the fire, but chose to charge their line straight off the hydrant. The city's water pressure was strong enough that boosting it wasn't always necessary unless the fire was at higher elevations. By pumping off the hydrant, the engineer was made available for other duty. The extra pair of hands was always welcome, especially when a crew was faced with going into a blind situation like the black, smoke-filled hole of a burning cellar.

Almost simultaneously, Ladder 2, affectionately known as the "Baby Carriage" because its original 100-foot long ladder had been cut down to 65-feet for just such four-story fires, had been positioned to reach the roof. Ventilating the building before the hose crews entered was vital.

Instructed by the District Chief to "Set it up," Ladder 2's Big Joe Rogers visually assessed the height of the building and angle of attack and gave the order as he set the brake.

"We're gonna raise the stick to the roof," he informed his crew, indicating his intention to raise the hydraulic powered aerial ladder.

Jumping from the passenger seat of the truck, Captain Fleming yelled, "Drop the jacks and pin 'em," to George Meadows and Jimmy Madigan on either side of the rear of the truck. Immediately they manually screwed down the outriggers and set pins to lock them in place to stabilize the truck, then chocked the front and back of the wheels to prevent it from rolling. Even as they were setting up the 20-ton apparatus, Norman Cantin raced to the front of the apparatus and elevated, rotated and raised the multi-section ladder to the roof. He clambered up the ladder with an axe and was quickly followed by Joe Rogers. The rest of Ladder 2's crew was deployed to assist in search and rescue efforts.

With a fury, Cantin and Rogers went to work with their axes opening a four-foot by four-foot hole in the roof to ventilate the structure – effectively creating a chimney for the elevator-less building that allowed gas and smoke on the upper floors to escape before it could explode. It was back breaking work but urgently necessary if there was to be any chance of keeping the blaze from spreading.

Only then did Bartlett and Gurrini give the order for the hose crews to attack the basement and first floor.

With Mulrain taking an iron-fisted grip of the nozzle of the thick, double-walled canvas line with his oversized calloused hands, Bartlett and Mangiagli backed him up, helping to control the pressurized line that wriggled like an angry Anaconda. It took the strength of three men to effectively steer the direction of the water stream.

As they were about to step through the doorway, Bartlett yelled to Ron Forrest, the last man of the Engine 15 crew.

"Ron, strap on a mask and follow us. Kick in the doors." Forrest had already anticipated the order to search for occupants who might remain in the burning building, and was coming up behind the hose team pulling on a Scott Air Pack, the only one the Engine had been issued. The self contained breathing apparatus, with its signature bright yellow bottle filled with filtered, compressed air and equipped with a full face mask allowed a man to concentrate on his job rather than to have to fight for his life just to get air into his lungs. The other guys on his team weren't so lucky. There just weren't enough tanks to go around.

Tommy Fischer from Engine 8 hit the basement entrance on the nozzle with backup from Lieutenant Al Gurrini and firefighter Don Cote. The pumper had two Scott Air Packs aboard and Danny Sullivan and Jack Kelly strapped on the masks. Howie Gillin grabbed a Halligan bar off the truck in the event there were doors or locks to be opened in the storage bins and followed the crew into the black smoke roiling out of the basement.

Flames were rolling over the heads of Fischer, Gurrini and Cote as they crawled into the basement. Virtually everything stored in the cellar was burning and the smoke was so thick that Gurrini could barely see Fischer's back less than eight feet in front of him. He worried about the guys he knew were crawling above them on the first floor. With the basement ceiling burning with such intensity, it was entirely possible the upstairs floors would give way.

"Tommy, hit the ceiling or we're gonna have the guys from 15 in our laps," he hollered to Fischer, struggling to hold the stream of water at an upward angle. The hose crew continued to move forward but was making little progress in knocking down the blaze. He hollered to Sullivan and Kelly, both wearing Scott Packs.

"You guys get out of here and go to number One," he said referring to the first floor. "Give 15 a hand in search and rescue. Tell Bartlett he's gotta get out of there fast. I don't know how long the floors up there are going to last."

On the first floor, Fred Bartlett's crew was struggling to find their way down the hallway with nothing but the spray from the water line keeping the fire off them, trying to stay low below the smoke and superheated air while kicking in doors and screaming for tenants. There were no replies. Bartlett and Mangiagli were getting the crap kicked out of them between the undulations of the hose and the heavy smoke. Fischer, on the nozzle, could get a little air off the tip of the spray by occasionally putting his mouth to it, but the guys backing him up couldn't even find air on the floor as smoke was coming up through the seams in the hardwood floor from the Basement.

Ron Forrest was kicking open apartment doors and hollering out for occupants but finding every unit already empty. Most tenants had fled the building at the rear when the explosion occurred. Some, like Mrs. Leone, had jumped out of her first floor window to safety.

Finally, Bartlett and Mangiagli had no choice but to find air. The Lieutenant yelled to Mulrain to move into one of the apartments and get to a window. Moving quickly, Mulrain maneuvered them through the first open door he saw. Inside, with virtually nothing left in his lungs, Bartlett ripped off his hard, leather helmet and smashed the glass of the nearest window and he and the hose crew stuck their heads outside for air. They spent several long minutes sucking the sweet, fresh air into their oxygen-starved lungs.

Sullivan and Kelly arrived moments later and reported to Bartlett.

"Thanks for the offer to help boys, but we all gotta get the hell out of here," Barlett replied. "Jack, get outside and tell Fleming we've got to pull out. There's no one in here and from the sound of it, the basement is a goner."

"Roger that, Lieutenant," Danny Sullivan responded and ran back down the corridor to report to Captain Fleming that Engine 15 and Engine 8 had been forced to pull out of the building.

"Jack, go back to the basement and tell your boss the good news," a frustrated Bartlett told Jack Kelly. He too was off like a shot. As he ran down the corridor, Kelly could feel the floor beneath his feet beginning to soften. It was similar to running on a hardened sponge. Another few minutes and the floors were going to give way.

On the perimeter of the building, the crew of Engine 11 – Lieutenant Billy Maloney, driver "Red" Nolan, John Walsh, Bob Christiansen and George Brennan—were raising 35 and 50-foot long ground ladders to evacuate the dozen or so tenants who had not escaped the initial blast and had climbed higher to escape the flames.

Ladder 2's Captain John Fleming signaled District Chief Shortell that his orders had been followed but that Engine 8 and 15 had been forced to back out. Shortell quickly gave thought to calling in a Second Alarm, but decided to give his crews a few more minutes. His instincts told him this building was already too far-gone and calling in more men and apparatus wasn't going to make a difference. His decision was ultimately fortuitous. The District Chief instructed his driver to radio Dispatch.

"All Companies are committed and working," Festus Johnson reported to Dick Walsh. "But we've had to abandon the basement and first floor, which is about to collapse. All men are accounted for at this time and will be redeployed for search and evacuation."

"Roger that, District 1," Walsh responded.

Suddenly, spectators in the crowd began screaming and pointing to a young woman standing in an open window on the third floor of the north side of the building. She was holding a toddler, perhaps two, maybe three-years old, and shrieking in panic while waving frantically to get the attention of firefighters who hadn't seen her because of the heavy, black smoke that continued to pour from the building.

Spotting her, Red Nolan and Lieutenant Billy Maloney positioned a 35-foot wooden extension ladder against the window frame of her third floor apartment window. Smoke churned from the opening as the woman desperately held her child, and a terrifying orange glow backlit her slight figure in the window. It was obvious to the horrified onlookers below that there were only minutes left before the fire overcame them.

With the ladder in place, the two men scampered up two rungs at a time, Maloney in the lead. Both were oblivious to the heavy fire resistant turnout gear they wore. At the top, Maloney reached inside to take the child from the woman, but the terrified mother, no more than twenty-five years old, frantically held on to her baby. She was paralyzed with fear.

Looking inside, Maloney, a young man whose lined face misleadingly made him appear much older than the woman, saw with horror that within the next minute the fire would blast through the room in which she stood like a blowtorch. He was already feeling the heat on his face and could barely breath through the smoke pouring from her apartment. There was no time to waste. He locked a leg around a ladder rung and held on.

The fireman's mind raced through the few options available. He could lunge at them to try and drag the woman and her baby to the ladder, but if he missed... forget it. There'd be no time for a second chance and he'd almost certainly lose one or the other. Instead, he used his last seconds to calm her.

"What's your name, honey? I'm Billy," he said calmly. "Billy Maloney."

Nolan, his partner below him on the ladder hollered to him.

"Billy, we gotta get out of here!" the firefighter yelled, watching as the smoke above them began to take on an orange glow, a sure sign the room was going to blow.

"Gimme a minute, will ya?" Maloney barked back at Nolan. He turned to the girl.

"What's you name?" he asked again of the young woman who was holding the baby even more tightly against her chest.

"Maria..." she said haltingly, her eyes wide with terror.

"Listen to me, Maria," Maloney yelled to her, his voice barely audible above the roar of the approaching flames. "We only have a few seconds here or..." He stopped in mid-sentence. There was no more time for bullshit.

"Hell, either pass me your little girl or she's going to die, Maria," he pleaded, assuming the child was a girl by her pink dress.

"No!" Maria implored him, agonizing at the thought of handing over her precious child.

"Then I guess we're all going to die, Maria. And damn it, I can't have that. My wife will be pissed at me and I don't let people die on my shift," Maloney said, forcing his mouth into the shape of a smile. He stared into her eyes, willing her to hand him the child. She hesitated another second, then reluctantly passed the baby to him. The Lieutenant instantly secured the child from the fearful woman and passed the tiny girl down to Red Nolan without hesitation. He trusted anyone from his company, no matter how high the ladder or how bad the situation. Slowly, Nolan descended the ladder, using one hand to guide him and the other to hold on to the screaming child.

As Nolan made his way down the ladder holding the child, Maloney knew it wasn't rated to hold the weight of two more adults, but also that there was no time to wait.

Without arguing with her, Maloney lunged forward and grabbed Maria by the wrist, pulling her towards him with all his strength and heaved the screaming woman over his shoulder. He moved so quickly the mother didn't have a chance to resist and she dangled from his shoulder nearly forty-feet in the air as he struggled to balance himself again on the ladder.

"Hang on, Maria, trust me," he screamed to her. "Just hang on to me and I'll get us down from here."

Despite the thickness of his heavy turnout coat he could feel the young mother gripping his back as he began to descend. With his partner out of the way and the child safely in the arms of ambulance personnel below, Maloney straddled the outside rails with his legs and let himself slide down the rungs several at a time before using his free arm to slow them. No less than eight-feet from the top of the ladder, where they had been just seconds before, a great fireball abruptly blew out of the window just over their heads.

The firefighter instinctively pulled his helmet low over his brow as the intense heat shot out above them and he prayed that the woman holding on to his back was not burned. He heard her scream as he loosened the grip of his legs again and slid a few feet more away from the danger. As they approached the ground, Fred Bartlett sprayed Maloney and the woman with a fog nozzle on a two and a half inch line to cool them down. Steam rose off Maloney's helmet as the cold water cooled the scorched leather.

As he reached the bottom of the ladder, Billy Maloney felt men taking the weight of the petrified mother from his shoulder and knew they had made it. Before his boots could touch the ground, someone had strapped an oxygen mask over the woman's face even while she screamed for her baby. A firefighter handed her the child who was crying from fright and the awful confusion around her. She was blackened from soot, her pretty pink dress ruined. But like her mother, she was safe.

Maloney felt hands slap him on the back as he made his way back to his truck to take a blow. He sat heavily on the running board, gasping for breath but refused treatment from any ambulance staff. A man had to be in dire straights to take oxygen in front of his peers, and he wasn't about to set up himself as a sissy. That's all there was to it. He had done his job and expected no more than a backslap in return. End of story.

As Fred Bartlett walked over to give him one of those silent acknowledgements, Maloney put a finger to one nostril and blew hard, unleashing a torrent of blackened snot from his nose. It just missed his fellow firefighter.

"Heh," Bartlett laughed. "A real snot slinger, hey Billy? Shit, I hate that." It was standard practice for a man exposed to heavy smoke to clear his nose of black soot by forcing it out under blowing pressure. He would still be doing it for days after. Men learned that cleaning out their nostrils in a more gentlemanly manner such as using a handkerchief only led to ruined handkerchiefs. It was a trial and expense of the trade.

Similar if somewhat less dramatic evacuations were taking place on three of the four corners of the building from windows on either the third or fourth floors. Through the herculean efforts of Engine 11's John Walsh, Bob Christiansen and George Brennan, miraculously, every tenant escaped with no more than minor smoke inhalation or burns to show for the horrific ordeal. There was pandemonium on the ground as police continually had to push tenants back from the fire. Some were still determined to try and recover personal possessions. But the battle was over.

Despite thousands of gallons of water being poured upon the inferno, the fire monster was determined to devour its prey. Within the next few minutes, flames began leaching through the tarred roof and the District Chief ordered his men off. There was no way he was going to lose anyone to save a burned out hulk of a building that could never be repaired. In fact, he knew that if the structure didn't collapse on it's own, the city would have no choice but to condemn the remnants and bulldoze them to the ground immediately. The Fire Marshall would have little time to figure this one out.

"Save the basement, pass the word," District Chief Shortell hollered out the order to his men, indicating his decision that the structure was a total loss and he would not allow his men to take any further risks to save it.

Shortell rationalized that every tenant was accounted for, his men had accomplished multiple rescues and no one, with the exception of the janitor, had been seriously injured. Not a bad afternoon's work, he thought. He was not a believer in pushing his luck.

"Festus, alert Dispatch that we are withdrawing," he ordered his driver.

Johnson keyed the transmitter in the district chief's red Ford and relayed the message.

"Dispatch, per order of District Chief Shortell, we are switching modes from offensive to defensive and ordering a tactical withdrawal of the building," Festus Johnson reported as instructed.

"Roger that," Dick Walsh responded and in turn relayed the information to Chief Lee who was being kept informed of the situation status as he inspected the new fire stations.

As the crowd of onlookers a hundred feet or more from the still burning building watched and grew, flames reached higher into the sky and smoke continued to pour from the apartment house. Without warning, the roof collapsed in the north corner and pulled a huge section of the building down with it in a roaring disintegration of the old brick structure. Instinctively, the crowd moved back from the terrifying display, a drama that had only begun to unfold less than 30 minutes before.

"You sure we got everybody out of there?" a shaken Shortell yelled to the two men from Ladder 2 who had just climbed off the roof minutes before.

"Yah… sure, Chief," one of them choked out, his face blackened with smoke.

Shortell turned to the senior officer on the scene, John Fleming.

"Captain, pull all personnel back and knock this thing down. Christ, we'll be here forever," he said in frustration, knowing his men would be pouring water on the flames for hours before they put the fire out completely and hosed down the ruins to be sure there were no flare ups. Meanwhile, there was the constant threat of further sections of the building collapsing without warning. The faster they got this mess cold, the sooner the city could come in and knock down the remaining walls.

"Festus," Shortell called out to his driver, "have dispatch call the Salvation Army, will ya? There are a lot of people here with no place to go to tonight. And you couldn't find a dirty shirt in that mess," he added, nodding his head to the still roaring fire. He took off his helmet for a moment and wiped his brow with the back of a hand.

"How the hell did this thing get going and how'd it move so fast?" he wondered aloud.

A firefighter whose face was blackened with soot stood and turned to the district chief. He had been bent over at the waste, wretching from smoke inhalation. It wasn't the first time. He answered Shortell's question.

"One of the cops told me that before the meat wagon took him to the hospital, the janitor said he smelled smoke on the first floor and the place exploded when he opened the basement door. Must have been smoldering for hours," said Tommy Fischer, who'd been on the nozzle end of the hose team from Engine 8 that tried vainly to penetrate the basement.

Fischer feared nothing. He'd been the first guy through that door holding the nozzle of the two and half inch line, his eyes taking in the whole scene as he tried to knock down the fire. This was about as bad a situation as he'd ever seen.

"The way she ate up the basement and first floor so fast you gotta think it started in the bowels," Fischer said. "Where's the friggin' Fire Marshall?" he asked, looking around. "I'm betting it was electrical, something let loose in the main panel." He looked up at the building, now nearly fully engulfed. "I don't know how anyone can prove that now. But I sure don't remember smelling an accelerant, Chief... any of you guys?" He looked over at the men who'd tried to attack the first floor with him wondering if any of them suspected arson. They nodded in agreement.

"We'll probably never know," the deputy chief said, shrugging his shoulders. "It was a good stop, guys. We could've lost a lot of people in that mess. It's a small price to pay to lose a building."

Shortell turned and walked to his car to personally report the situation to Chief Lee. He didn't like seeing people lose their homes, but breathed a sigh of relief that his guys had saved every man, woman and child in danger. And they'd beaten the beast and hadn't lost a man. The odds were against them today, he thought. A fast moving fire in an old brick building with trapped tenants. If ever there was a formula for disaster that was it.

He turned and looked back over his shoulder at the geysers of water still being trained on the remaining flames of the burning building. It was under control now, but it would be some time before this one died.

The singular bit of good news he had to report was that the only death at this fire was made of brick and mortar.

For Fire Chief Thomas Lee, the next call he received that day would be nowhere near as satisfying.

# Eight

~~~ ঌ ~~~

*The ravenous monster*

Unbeknownst to the District Chief, Lee was already fully preoccupied with other matters.

Even while the fire at Zion and Ward Streets had the attention of nearly two-dozen firefighters and a good percentage of the south end's fire apparatus, the maintenance staff at Hartford Hospital had been working feverishly for at least the last 30 minutes to track down the strong smell of smoke coming from the hospital's trash chute. All over the building and especially on the upper floors, nurses and aides were calling maintenance to report the odor of smoke in the hallways. A nurse on the seventh floor actually saw smoke seeping from around the edges of the closed and locked trash chute. It had happened before. This time, for some reason, the sight sent chills down her spine.

The maintenance men didn't know it, but drastic action was required to stop what was going on inside the 18-inch diameter, unpainted aluminum cylinder that
~~~

stretched the height of the building, 150-feet from top to bottom. Inside, the smoldering fire was desperately seeking a source of air from above. It was a bomb ready to explode, and they were oblivious to the fact that the fuse had already been lit.

In the basement, the maintenance crew were using long-handled hooks and feverishly dragging rubbish out of the chute as high as the third floor, the maximum length they could reach, then hosing it down and carting it away in metal bins to be incinerated later in the furnace some 25-feet away. There was too much trash built up in the chute to incinerate it all immediately.

One story up, a janitor saw smoke leaking from the closed trash door on the first floor, and ran water into it using an inch and a half hose from the stairwell standpipe. Puzzled when smoke continued to escape from the door, he went looking for a supervisor. He wasn't overly concerned. It was a problem they had successfully dealt with before. Nonetheless, he shook his head at how dumb people could be, having witnessed patients, staff, visitors and maintenance people routinely flick lit cigarette butts and empty overflowing ashtrays into the trash chute, not realizing the aluminum cylinder didn't empty directly into the incinerator or that it sometimes became blocked with flammable material. Until now, they'd been lucky, he thought.

But Hartford Hospital's luck had just run out.

With the fire obviously burning somewhere above where they could reach it from the basement, a building engineer rushed to the thirteenth floor to run water into the chute from the stairwell standpipe. He wouldn't make it in time.

Theoretically, the hot gases building up inside the chute should have been released out a recently installed vent pipe exiting out of the roof. Unfortunately, whoever had done the design work had miscalculated the dimensions of the vent that was required. The three-inch pipe was a fraction of the diameter necessary. There was simply nowhere for the gas to go. But that didn't mean the fire monster would stop looking for an opportunity.

Events were escalating as the pressure and heat of the gas inside the chute built up. A nurse on the 12th floor, the hospital's Psychiatric Unit, was alarmed to see black smoke suddenly begin to seep out of the trash chute door near the reception desk. She asked a male aide to wrap adhesive duct tape around the chute door to seal out the smoke. The aide did as he was told, gingerly applying the tape as the door was hot enough to burn his hands.

Patients, many emotionally disturbed, began milling around the hallway, agitated by the sight and smell of smoke. Assistant Head Nurse Nancy Galloway sensed panic building among them and had her staff escort them back to their rooms.

"It's alright Charles," Nurse Leslie Thibodeux said calmly to one of the patients who visibly trembled with fright. She took his arm and placed a reassuring hand on his back then gently guided him slowly back to his room. The man suffered from chronic anxiety and lived in a constant state of turmoil and dread, convinced that his death was imminent. As the odor of smoke built on the 12th floor, she wondered if he knew something she didn't.

Then, with all patients in the safety of their rooms and being cared for, increasingly alarmed Nurse

Galloway decided to take matters into her own hands and pulled the firebox near her station at 2:39 p.m.

Box 5141 registered instantly at the master fire control station in a small room off the lobby, lighting the annunciator panel that indicated the pull station that had been activated. The signal was in turn silently transmitted to Dispatchers Kelley and Walsh at Fire Department Headquarters at 275 Pearl Street.

As the Box was being transmitted, on the eighth floor, a nurse and a male aide were standing in the hallway next to the trash chute door organizing the movement of a patient to a new room, when inexplicably, the door to the trash chute blew open. It had been closed but was unlatched. Black smoke billowed out. The aide instantly kicked it closed and lunged at the latch to lock it down.

"What the hell was that all about?" he said, the calmness of his voice belying his true concern. "We better call this in." The odor of smoke hung in the hallway as the nurse hurried to a phone. But it was too late. It had all happened in seconds, but the damage was done. Just enough oxygen entered the chute to create explosive level pressures inside.

Almost simultaneously, someone, somewhere in the lower floors of the building innocently opened another trash chute door. The oxygen starved fire in the aluminum shaft instantly sucked vast quantities of air inside, the equivalent of dropping a burning phosphorus tipped match into a puddle of gasoline. The embers that had been smoldering from the tiny fire started by the cigarette butt instantaneously burst into great tongues of fire that leapt up the chute and ignited the gases that had been waiting for just such a source of ignition. The result was a huge fireball that raced up the ductwork to the ninth floor where it finally found its escape. It was a latched door that shouldn't have failed. But one of its two hinges was broken, a simple repair that probably was penciled in on a maintenance chart somewhere, but which hadn't yet been gotten to.

With the force of a cannon, the fireball blew unchecked through the weakened trash chute door, ripping it off the wall and hurling it clear across the corridor and into a bathtub in a room on the other side of the floor. A blowtorch erupted from the chute, it's flames taking direct upwards aim at acoustical ceiling tiles made of a sugar cane-based fiber glued to rock lath plaster with a highly flammable adhesive.

An unstoppable chain reaction began. The ceiling tiles ignited immediately and flames rocketed along the ceiling in every direction like a wild, wind-fed prairie grass fire sparked by a bolt of lightening. The upper four feet of wallpaper covering the hallway was set ablaze and flames instantly began spreading. The acoustical tiles burned through in seconds and set alight the adhesive gluing them to the ceiling. Flaming tiles and globs of the adhesive rained down upon gleaming, freshly waxed and highly flammable linoleum floors that exploded into flames and raced to the wainscoting, also made of linoleum that was applied along the bottom four-feet of the wall. From floor to ceiling, the hallway was now a ring of fire that began to advance.

Now the fire monster was unleashed and ravenous. With rocket-like velocity, it began devouring every centimeter of flammable material in the hallway, creating a virtual tunnel of fire. There was no stopping its progress unless the hallway fire doors were closed, a process that required a human being to swing the heavy, one-piece wooden, metal clad door shut and latch it.

As well, the only protection afforded patients, visitors and staff in any room branching off the main or side corridors was a closed door. If a door was open, the enormous cloud of black smoke that rushed in as the fire advanced only preceded the flames. What followed was the horror of suffocation or being burned alive. A closed door meant possible protection from the flames. But closed or not, the black, toxic smoke crept through any crack, any seam or crevice and was capable of killing in minutes.

It took just seconds for the south wing of the ninth floor to become a flaming, death-filled apocalypse and just minutes more for the destruction and death to advance all the way to the fire door at the north wing. But elsewhere in the hospital, only a gray haze and the steadily growing smell of smoke gave any indication that something was direly, and perhaps deadly wrong.

On the 12th floor, Nurse Galloway, unaware of the events three floors below, grew alarmed that there had been no visible or audible response to pulling the fire alarm box. She pulled it again.

And waited.

Finally, a voice came over the public address system, hospital-wide.

"Calling Dr. Rover. Calling Dr. Rover." It was the staff code for fire somewhere in the building. Unfortunately, few of the hospital's personnel knew how to react to the announcement or what to do. Those who did followed emergency procedures but assumed the situation was not serious because fires had occurred in the trash chute before. There were no further directions or indications of its seriousness. But within minutes, it was clear this was a different situation.

The alarm bell startled dispatchers Kelley and Walsh, still concentrating on the Zion and Ward Fire, as Box 5141 came in over the tape. Kelley jumped up from his desk and read it to his colleague.

"Oh, shit," he said staring at the tape, "it's 5141, Dick... that's Hartford Hospital." He stared at the Box number in his hands for a moment, thinking about the implications of the call.

Hartford Hospital was a designated "Target Hazard," code for a highly threatening fire that required an unusual initial response of apparatus and men: three Engine Companies, two Ladder trucks, and both deputy chiefs. This was rapidly becoming one dangerously busy afternoon, Kelley thought. Behind him, the phones were ringing incessantly and Dick Walsh was recording complaints by hospital staff of heavy smoke in the building and neighborhood residents who reported seeing black smoke coming from what appeared to be the roof.

"Seems to be a lot of smoke showing," Walsh said, hanging up the phone. It began ringing again almost at once. "I'm letting Bob Martin know. He's driving the 'black car' today. The Chief is somewhere doing an inspection and Shortell is already off line."

"Poveromo is in quarters," Kelley responded. "He'll pick up the Box transmission but I'll give him a heads up," Kelley responded. Jim Poveromo was a deputy chief responsible for District 2 and would be second in command at the hospital under Chief Lee. Lee was required to respond to the Target Hazard in lieu of District Chief Shortell's absence commanding the Zion and Ward Street fire.

Walsh radioed Chief Lee's driver, while Kelley contacted John Stewart, who drove Poveromo's red Ford.

"Car 1," Lieutenant Martin responded as he answered his radio.

"Car 1, Dispatch. We just had Box 5141 come in and you will be responding. It's Hartford Hospital. You'd better head in that direction. We've had several calls from inside and outside the building indicating heavy smoke. Over."

"Roger that, Dispatch," Martin answered. "I'll inform the Chief. We're at Company 10 on Franklin Avenue. Over."

"Roger that, Bob. Please be advised that District Chief Shortell is off line at Box 417. Over."

Down a man to start, Martin thought. Not good.

"Roger. Will advise when we're rolling. Over." Martin ended the transmission and hurried inside to converse with Chief Lee who was discussing some minor changes required in the new station house with a contractor.

"Chief, Box 5141 is being shipped," Martin told Lee. "Hartford Hospital. Dispatch reports heavy smoke is showing. We need to roll. Shortell is at the Zion and Ward mess."

"Shit," was all Lee could think to say, his mind already whirling. "Let's go," the Chief responded, knowing that with District Chief Shortell off line, he was required to respond per the Run Card. It didn't matter. Being Hartford Hospital, he would have gone anyway. He and Martin headed for the chief's black Buick.

"Let the 'red cars' know we are in route," Lee instructed Martin.

Martin keyed the radio transmitter already in his hand. He knew his Chief.

"Dispatch, inform the district chiefs that Car 1 is in route to Box 5141. ETA is eight minutes."

Even as Martin was relaying the chief's position, Kelley and Walsh were transmitting the Box to all of the city's stations.

As the bells began chiming in the firehouses, men immediately began sliding down the brass poles to stand by their assigned locations on the apparatus that would take them to the call, awaiting further orders from their officers who were busy checking the Run Card box. It didn't take them long. There weren't many officers in the department who didn't know the location of Box 5141.

On the First Alarm, the Run Card called for response by Engine 1 and Ladder 6 out of Company 1 at 197 Main Street, Engine 4 out of 275 Pearl, Ladder 2 out of Engine Company 15 on Fairfield Avenue and Engine 6 from the Huyshope Avenue station. Ladder 2 was already working at the Zion and Ward Street fire, so the deployment alternative called for the seven-man, 100-foot Ladder Truck 1 from 275 Pearl Street to respond – a fateful, if unintended stroke of fortune on a day that would see little in the way of good news. Ladder 2's 65-foot reach would have been nearly worthless at this high-rise fire. Within minutes, the three fire companies indicated on the Run Card plan were in motion and apparatus was flying toward the scene. Some 27 men were on their way.

Several minutes later, Walsh's voice broke through the din of horns and sirens with an ominous report. "Be advised, responding companies are seeing heavy smoke from several blocks away."

District Chief Jim Poveromo, who had been in quarters at the station house at Main and Belden Street was flying towards the scene in his unmistakable red Ford.

"Put your foot in it, John," Poveromo said to his driver, John Stewart. "I've got a feeling about this one..."

Chief Lee and Lieutenant Martin raced down Franklin Ave towards Retreat Avenue. As they approached the scene, they could see the black smoke that was already billowing into the afternoon sky from the upper floors of the hospital's High Building and also pouring out of the elevator penthouse on the roof.

Walsh and Kelley were continually radioing details of the Box and the structure to all responding units.

"This is a confirmed working job, with fire visible on the upper floors," Walsh reported. "The building is 13-stories high and of steel frame and brick construction. There are standpipes on the ground level and in the stairwells on both ends of the building. Note that there is oxygen in use throughout the structure. Over."

Kelley added information.

"Police on the scene report multiple entrapments on the upper floors, but they are uncertain as to the exact location. This building is elevatored with eight public entrance cars. Repeat, we have multiple hoistways in the building. It is unknown if the public elevators are operable.

"At the current time, the building supervisor reports that there are as many as 2,000 people occupying the building and they have initiated an evacuation. The exact location of the fire is still undetermined, although the master fire control station indicates number twelve, repeat, number twelve.

"Hydrants are located in six locations around the complex," Kelley continued. "Two on Seymour Street two on Jefferson and two in the rear of the main building. All have been tested and are operable."

Lee assessed the situation from his speeding car and didn't hestitate after studying the massive plume of smoke reaching into the clear afternoon sky.

"I don't like the looks of that even from here," he said. "That crap is black, too. I wonder what the hell is burning?"

He thought a moment more but had already made up his mind.

"Bob, call in the 2-2," the Chief ordered, a decision that would launch a Second Alarm, putting in motion Engine 2 and Ladder 3 from the Belden Street house, Engine 3 out of 275 Pearl and Engine Company 10 from Franklin and Bond Streets.

Martin immediately radioed Kelley and Walsh who transmitted the Second Alarm.

"Per order of Chief Lee, a Signal 2-2 has been issued for Box 5141," Martin instructed the Dispatchers.

"Roger that," Walsh responded, surprised that Lee was calling the Second Alarm before even getting to the scene. He could feel what was coming next.

The alarm bells hit in the firehouses all over the city and across the tape came a "Signal 2-2" – a Second Alarm that would send even more equipment and manpower to the scene even before the first fire truck had arrived.

Lee's instincts were correct but came with a price. Normally, the dispatchers would have sent a "Signal 1-1-2" to indicate a Second Alarm on a Box. But with two major working fires within blocks of each other, and now one upgraded to a Second Alarm, the signal was shortened to the dreaded "2-2." It was a call the Chief hated to hear, recognizing that it committed the majority of the City's fire fighting men and apparatus to two fires in a small radius and left a large proportion of Hartford in danger with severely limited fire protection.

But it was not a situation that the department's leadership hadn't anticipated. Years of pre-planning for just such an event set in motion a whole series of actions.

Immediately, all men who were due in for the night shift starting at 6 p.m. and all who were scheduled to work the following day and were designated "On Call" were contacted by headquarters and ordered to report for duty immediately. Those firefighters whose Companies had been called as responders under the first two alarms reported to their units at the fire scene.

Several fire companies not called under the first two alarms were repositioned to other firehouses in the city, providing a modicum of protection to neighborhoods left bare by the demands of the two working fires. As the night shift and "On Call" personnel reported to sometimes empty firehouses because their apparatus had been relocated, they were redeployed. When a full crew became available, the men commandeered one of several spare engines and trucks available for just such an emergency. The ultimate objective was to utilize all available manpower and spare apparatus to triangulate the fire protection over the City. That meant providing at least the minimum number of trucks and men to make operational Company 1 at 197 Main, Company 2 at 1550 Main and Company 5 at 129 Sigourney Street.

Theoretically, any box alarm in the city could be responded to by these remaining available assets, but it would take more time to reach outlying neighborhoods.

Special units, under the command of deputy chiefs, were also called to the scene. The Signal Division, which engineered dedicated communications links at a major fire, immediately reported on the Second Alarm. The Maintenance Division also sent a truck dedicated to on-site repair of equipment. Half the men of the unit went to the fire location while the other half manned the maintenance shop located behind Company 1 at 197 Main Street for larger scale repairs that were urgently required.

In the Dispatchers Office, Dick Walsh and Dan Kelley were maxed out relaying information and instructions and information to and from the chief and providing support in contacting the men to be called in. They were quickly overwhelmed with the simultaneous calls, and as the pre-plan called for, the night shift dispatchers were called in to assist. On this helter-skelter afternoon, night shift Dispatchers Charlie Dorris and Zeke Emmons reported for duty.

As well, deputy chiefs in staff positions temporarily assumed line responsibilities. Deputy Chief Larry Meade, who ran the Department's Training Division, assumed temporary responsibility for District 1 from Tom Shortell, off line at Zion and Ward. Meade's number two man in the Training Division, Captain John O'Meara similarly assumed line command for District 2, relieving Jim Poveromo to concentrate on the critical situation at the Hospital. Deputy Chiefs Ed Mullins and Ed Curtin, normally assigned to the Chief's Office at Headquarters, reported to the fire scene to assist Lee as needed. Every man was an asset, from the newest "Probie" to the department leadership.

The pre-planning was in place and the response was immediate once the 2-2 was issued. But that gave Chief Lee little comfort as he got closer to Hartford Hospital. He knew in his guts that this one had gotten a real head start on them.

From everywhere, the city was awash in the sounds of screaming fire apparatus racing towards Hartford Hospital. There was literally nowhere in Hartford or neighboring Wethersfield, bordering on the south end, where the smoke couldn't be seen, and even traffic on River Road on the banks of the Connecticut River in East Hartford had a clear view of the horrific sight.

From a distance, it was impossible to know exactly where the fire was. It was clearly in or near the downtown area and serious, but the exact location and how bad was anyone's guess. But the last place in the world they would have thought of was Hartford Hospital.

Golfers on the course at Wethersfield Country Club looked northward and saw the heavy, black smoke rising in the air. It brought back memories of the Circus Fire in 1944, the great lumberyard fire on the Silas Deane Highway in Wethersfield in 1955, and the firestorms that caused the loss of St. Joseph's Cathedral in 1956. Some Wethersfield Volunteer Firemen went to their stations in the event they might be needed. Other volunteers in the Greater Hartford area did the same – in 29 Connecticut towns, to be exact.

On the Silas Deane Highway, the six brothers who were partners in Hughes Bros. Inc., a gas station and repair garage on the Hartford border intersecting with Wethersfield Avenue, stood outside and looked northward. All War vets, they had pooled their money from GI Bill loans and opened the garage in 1946. Three had joined the Wethersfield Volunteer Fire Department shortly after. By 1961, Clinton "Jiggs" Hughes had been named deputy chief of the department and his brother Richard "Spec" Hughes was an engineer for Company 2. They each remembered well that the Hartford Fire Department had not hesitated to stand by and come to the aid of the Wethersfield Volunteers when the 1955 lumberyard fire had commanded every firefighter and piece of apparatus the town could muster to fight the Four Alarm blaze.

"We ought to keep an eye on that," Spec said to his brother, the deputy chief. "I'm not sure where that is," he said, eyeing the huge plume of black smoke climbing higher in the sky, "maybe somewhere south of downtown. Wherever, it doesn't look good."

"Yah," Jiggs replied. "If they don't knock it down soon, I'll put a call through to Hartford Dispatch and see if Tom Lee might need an extra hand or two. At the least, we can station a piece and give them a hand in covering the south end of the city. I'm going to call Al Knapp now to clear it," Hughes said, referring to Wethersfield's Fire Chief, Albert Knapp.

Word was spreading fast, even beyond the brotherhood of firefighters that there was a serious fire at Hartford Hospital, even before the first men or apparatus had pulled up to the front or back of the building.

But inside, there were people who knew exactly how bad it was – and that it was getting worse.

# Nine

~~~ ୨ ~~~

*"Calling Dr. Rover "*

Dr. Norman Hedenstad was chewing on the last bite of a tuna salad sandwich in the coffee shop on the third floor, gulping down his working lunch as he did every day. He pored over patient charts as he ate before beginning afternoon rounds each afternoon. Yawning, he shook off the urge for a nap. The struggle was always the same. He was fine so long as he was moving at his accustomed non-stop pace. But relax so much as even a few minutes for a bite to eat, and the constant exhaustion that was the life of a resident doctor hit him like a hammer.

He drank down the last drops of his second cup of black coffee as he finished the sandwich, resisting the temptation for a piece of lemon meringue pie that was calling his name. Skipping the dessert wasn't only to avoid the calories, but more because he knew the instant sugar rush it would give him would make the afternoon
~~~

that much more difficult to weather when it wore off later in the afternoon. His shift ended at 7 p.m. Then he'd get six hours of sleep before starting another eighteen-hour day. There were times when it hardly seemed worth it, he thought to himself, then shook off the doubt. There was nothing else he'd rather do than medicine, nothing that gave him greater satisfaction. He'd come so far. No turning back now.

He had just picked up his napkin to wipe his hands when he first heard the announcement over the public address system.

"Calling Dr. Rover, calling Dr. Rover. Calling Dr. Rover, calling Dr. Rover..." the anonymous recorded voice droned on. He looked around, startled to see more than a few staff faces with the same look of surprise. The men dressed like him in blue scrubs and nurses in white had recognized the announcement for what it was: the emergency code for a fire in the Hospital. That's how it was supposed to work. Visitors in the coffee shop had no idea what was happening. For that matter, neither did Hedenstad or the other hospital personnel who all calmly walked out and went searching for an answer.

The resident went to the nearest nurses reception desk and called into the lobby security console.

"The alarm was pulled on the 12th floor, Dr. Hedenstad, that's all I can tell you," a guard informed him. The Fire Department is on the way." The young Resident was relieved. He had no patients on twelve.

No, they were mostly on nine and all in the south wing.

He walked quickly to the lobby intending to take an elevator to nine and start his afternoon rounds there, just to be sure his patients were safe. Then he would tend to those on the lower floors. But afternoon visiting hours had just begun and there was a large queue gathered. He waited impatiently but finally got aboard the last elevator car on the south wing side of the lobby and pressed the call button for the ninth floor. The trip took forever with the packed elevator stopping at nearly every floor in between. Finally, it arrived at nine.

As the elevator glided to a stop, he immediately smelled smoke. When the center opening doors slid open a thick haze of gray smoke was clearly visible in the air and a blast of hot air surged into the cab. Passengers screamed and someone frantically pushed the call button for the 10th floor and someone else the button to close the doors. Miraculously, the elevator doors closed and the car proceeded to the 10th floor where terrified passengers ran to the north wing exit stairwell and began the long descent back to the main lobby on foot.

Everyone, that is, but Dr. Norman Hedenstad.

When the Resident saw the smoke on the ninth floor, he knew the fire was not on twelve, but in the very place where he had so many patients. Without hesitation, he stepped out of the elevator and turned the corner to head for the south wing. He never looked back as the elevator doors closed and the car proceeded upwards.

Until that moment, Norman Hedenstad had made good decisions in his life and was well on his way to a very promising professional career and probably a more than satisfying personal life. Unfortunately, fate had other plans for him.

He took two steps down the corridor and stopped dead in in his tracks. The resident blinked, then looked again.

Unbelievably, a cloud of black smoke was rolling towards him and behind it he could make out a blast furnace of flame shooting out of the wall. He realized that the flame was coming out of the trash chute and there were only two obstacles to it engulfing the entire ninth floor: the south wing fire door— which was still open – and him.

Norman Hedenstad was a doctor, not a fireman or an outwardly heroic man. He could have turned and run to the safety of the north wing and the stairwell exit, but to do so would be to abandon his patients, some of whom, unfortunately, occupied beds on the other side of the fire door. Hedenstad never even considered saving himself.

With the ceiling, walls and floors adjacent to the trash chute ablaze just feet behind the south wing fire door, he could already feel the heat blistering his skin and there was no air to breath. But his mind was still working and he knew that he only had seconds to reach and close that fire door to stop the conflagration from progressing any further into the south wing and beyond. If he could manage to shut the fire door, then he could close the doors to his patient's rooms and wait for help. Without regard to his own safety and the agony of his already gruesome burns, he leapt for the door, grabbed the handle and pulled with all his strength against the tremendous pressure of the superheated gasses that were being produced by the fire. But the pressure from the heat and flames was overwhelming and it slammed the door back against the wall – and Dr. Norman Hedenstad with it.

At once, the fire monster was upon him, his lab coat bursting into flames a half second before his hair and skin spontaneously ignited. He frantically began slapping at the searing tongues of fire that were devouring him with hands that were already charred. He screamed in agony and involuntary jerked and danced like a macabre puppet as the fire burned through the epidermis, then quickly the dermis layers of his skin.

Mercifully now in shock, the flames finally consumed all layers of his body tissue and he no longer felt any pain as he died. His charred corpse fell to the floor against the fire door that he had so valiantly tried to close, yet still continued to burn as his skeletal remains were all but incinerated.

It would be hours before firemen even recognized that the charred pile of rubble leaning against the south wing fire door were the remains of Norman Hedenstad – a doctor and a hero.

# Ten

~~~ ∽ ~~~

*"There was nowhere to hide"*

Just moments after Hedenstad succumbed, male aide Bob Maher exited an elevator of which he was the only remaining passenger on the north wing side of the ninth floor lobby. He had been summoned to assist a double amputee in getting out of bed.

Maher was deep in thought about the football game scheduled for that Sunday, the New York Giants versus the Philadelphia Eagles, a bitter rivalry, and never looked up as he stepped out of the elevator. As the doors closed behind him, he was abruptly shocked to find the air full of smoke and the air so hot it was hard to breath.

"What the bloody hell…" he thought, suddenly aware that he had walked into a world on fire.

Maher hesitantly turned the corner towards the patient he'd come to assist in a north wing room, but then stopped. Something made him turn around and look. What he saw was a wall of black smoke and fire
~~~

racing towards him from the south wing. It was nearly on him in seconds.

With the inferno snapping at his heels like a rabid dog, Maher sprinted to the north wing fire door, and with the assistance of Nurse Eileen Gormley Santiglia, who had seen the fireball at virtually the same instant, pushed it closed and latched it shut.

The assistant head nurse on the wing saw the smoke and what Maher and Santiglia had done and screamed to other nurses to close the doors of patient rooms on the north wing and the intersecting east and west corridors. It appeared they were safe for the moment.

Then, shockingly, as they slowly backed away, the pair watched as smoke began to seep from above the closed fire door. It was all too clear that the hallway divider walls to which the fire doors were hinged had open lintels. The space above the ceiling was open and smoke would continue into the north wing unimpeded. Soon, enough smoke had seeped through to make the fire door all but invisible.

Unfortunately, on the south wing, even the same quick action by nurses couldn't prevent what was about to happen.

Unaware of Hedenstad's failed effort to close the south wing fire door, they raced from room to room, just feet ahead of the roiling smoke and fire spreading like greased lightening in every direction, slamming shut patient rooms all along the south wing and on the adjoining east and west corridors. Nurses who managed to reach the end of corridors on the south wing ultimately had nowhere else to go but to lock themselves in with patients, doctors and visitors in the last rooms and wait for help.

Most of them thought it would arrive in minutes. In fact, it would be quite sometime before anything could be done to rescue them.

And not all would live to see it.

The flames spewing from the mouth of the open trash chute just south of the elevator banks and the center wing fed the fire that was speeding along the ceiling, floors and walls in all four directions. Within seconds, the wall of fire had spread more than 275-feet along the entire corridor, stopping only at the closed north wing fire doors. Hedenstad's tragic inability to close the south wing fire door allowed the flames to travel unchecked through the elevator lobby.

The temperature of the racing fire quickly rose to over 1,200° F, producing immense pressure that blew open even closed doors. Any human being caught in the lobby or the center wing had nowhere to run.

A nurse at the center wing desk saw the fireball coming at her, leaned under the desk to grab her pocketbook and before she could stand and run was overtaken by the flames.

A dietician, who worked in the kitchen in the center wing, saw the wall of fire coming and ran to her station, slamming the door behind her. With explosive force, the flames blew through the door and were upon her before she could discharge a fire extinguisher she was holding.

Two women visitors, choking in the thickening smoke didn't think to run for the north wing exit stairwell but waited for an elevator. They were caught in the full fury of the fireball as well, and fell where they stood. Like Norman Hedenstad, it would be hours before anyone even knew they were casualties, their remains nearly reduced to ashes.

Those who died, caught in the open, did so quickly, but horribly. There was simply nowhere to hide. For patients, visitors and staff who had managed to take shelter in rooms on the south wing, time was running out as the fire continued to seek out anything consumable to extend its brief but fiery life.

And although the trapped could now clearly hear approaching sirens, no help was in sight.

Mercifully, they were unaware that it was also out of reach.

# Eleven

~~~ ⁂ ~~~

*"God help them"*

T. Stewart Hamilton was on the phone with his wife when his secretary, Marjorie burst into his office, swinging the door open without so much as a knock. He saw the look of dread in her eyes and abruptly interrupted his call. It was so unlike his usually very proper and in-charge secretary.

"Hang on a minute, dear," he said calmly, carefully hiding his aggravation that she would call him at the office to chat about last minute plans for the Holiday Party later that evening. The problems lying in files and memorandums all over his desk would not go away by themselves. Yet today, already, he had wasted valuable time on a ridiculous staff presentation and now— he swallowed hard to keep from screaming aloud— Amy's "urgent" questions regarding seating arrangements for a cocktail party were occupying his precious attention.
~~~

"What...?" he said tersely to Marjorie but never got a chance to finish his sentence.

"There's a fire, Dr. Hamilton..." she stammered, genuine terror reflected in her eyes. "I don't know where, just that it's somewhere on the upper floors. I think it's bad, Stew," she added, unconsciously dropping the formality with which she typically addressed the Hospital CEO.

Hamilton, stunned, stared back at his secretary as if he was trying to comprehend the words that had just come from her mouth. It took him several long seconds to process what the normally composed Marjorie had told him. Without thought, he abruptly hung up the phone on his wife, forgetting she was even on line.

"Has the Fire Depart..."

"Yes," Marjorie interrupted him, anticipating the question. "Security just told me the Hartford Fire Department is on the way. They also said there's a smell of smoke throughout the building to varying degrees."

"What does that mean?"

"It's apparently strong on some floors, not so bad on others. But it's spreading throughout the whole building."

Hamilton jumped up from his desk and literally ran to the lobby. There he found Tom Devanney, the Hospital's Fire Marshall entering the small room behind the main reception desk where the master fire control station was located. He followed him inside.

"It's 12. It came in from the 12th floor," Devanney said aloud after reviewing the annunciator panel and checking the black indicator switches for each floor, unaware of Hamilton's presence. Security guards were already racing to the floor. Another guard stepped in to the room all but ignoring the hospital president.

"Yah, but I think the fire is lower, Mr. Devanney," the guard said. "I was just outside. We've got heavy smoke on nine and maybe ten and there are nurses and patients who are screaming and waving from the windows. They appear to be trapped. We can't contact the people on nine. The phone lines are not working."

"God help them," Hamilton finally spoke.

Devanney turned when he heard Hamilton's voice.

He paused momentarily before responding.

"Perhaps…yes, God… but I think we better put our faith in the Hartford Fire Department, Dr. Hamilton," the Fire Marshall said. He turned to the security guard. He only knew him by his first name.

"Rick, meet the first guy who shows up at the door in turnout gear and a helmet and escort him in here. And have two guards outside to show the others the way to the north and south wing stairwells. Tell the rest of the guys on duty to begin escorting visitors and contractors out of the building, including the lobby. And have Henry at the main reception desk start calling in every off duty guard he can reach. I want the whole department here, ASAP. Got it?"

"On it," the young guard responded and walked quickly from the room. Outside, a handful of guards had already gathered and were awaiting instructions.

Devanney turned to Hamilton again.

"First thing we gotta do is find out where this mother is and if it's spreading, Dr. Hamilton."

The hospital president shook his head in disbelief.

"I'll have the nurses stations on every floor polled immediately as to their status," he said.

"Good," Devanney said. "And can you instruct the head nurses to quietly and calmly ask visitors to immediately exit the building? I think we need to get as many non-essential people out of the way as we can and to move them as quickly as possible without creating panic. Just have your people explain that it's a drill." He paused, sniffing the air.

"Forget I said that. Within a few minutes it's going to be quite clear to everyone that this is no drill."

Hamilton thought for a moment, not used to taking instructions.

"Why don't I just make an announcement that all non-patients are to evacuate the building at once?" Hamilton asked, the stress of the moment causing him not to think the process through.

"Because that will do exactly what I said – create panic. No mom or dad is going to leave their child if they know there's danger anywhere in the building and the same goes for spouses. This needs to be done calmly, Dr. Hamilton."

Hamilton shook his head at his own naiveté. He had learned in the military that sometimes the power of rank got in the way of ones brains.

"I'll get on it." He turned on his heels without another word and headed back to his office where he would give instructions to Marjorie and everyone else from his staff to begin calling the nurses stations in every wing of every floor. As he ran down the first floor corridor towards the administrative offices, he passed James Anglan who had just left a very contentious meeting with Hamilton's assistant, Tom Markus. The two nodded but didn't speak.

"Good," Anglan murmured to himself on seeing Hamilton go whizzing by, thinking he had established his whereabouts for the last half hour or so.

"I wonder what his problem is," he mumbled, a smirk on his face. Then the thought struck him.

"No, it couldn't be, " he whispered and grinned slyly. As he approached the lobby he suddenly noticed a certain commotion. It seemed people were exiting the building in greater numbers than usual. Then he realized that a guard was preventing anyone from entering the lobby.

He stepped outside through the first exit door and reached for a cigarette. "That's strange," he thought to himself before lighting it, as an acrid odor of smoke filled his nostrils immediately. That was when he saw dozens of people pointing to the sky.

The hospital administrator turned and looked upwards.

James Anglan's heart nearly stopped at the sight of a thick plume of black smoke curling around the upper floors of the hospital's High Building. With his intimate knowledge of the complex, he searched for the source of the smoke, but could not find it.

Then, so startled by the shocking thought, he sucked in a deep, quick breath at the possibility of what he was seeing.

Was this the product of his vengeance?

It can't be, his mind reasoned, frantic for escape from the truth. He had been on the 13th floor. At most, his conscience argued, he had started a little fire, just enough to ruin Hamilton's afternoon. Then a gust of wind swept across the front of the building from the west and for a moment, the smoke gathered and rose upwards in a spiraling plume and uncovered what it had been hiding.

The sudden shift in wind exposed the nurses, doctors, patients and people of all sorts at the south and north wing windows of the ninth floor, desperately waving and screaming for help. Oddly, there were no people visible in the center wing, only an ominous orange glow in some places.

He gaped at the nightmare in disbelief, refusing to accept what his eyes were telling him, desperate to deny what he knew to be the truth.

"Impossible," he said, his lips barely moving as he uttered the word. Then he did the only thing a coward can do in such a situation.

He turned his back to the hospital and ran.

But on the ninth floor, there was nowhere to run.

# Twelve

~~~ ~~~

*"There was no safe place"*

As they raced to close all the patient room doors while running down the corridor, finally gathering into the last rooms on the south wing in desperation, the nurses and doctors who acted so valiantly could not have known that the tremendous pressure of the hot gasses preceding the smoke and flames was just as quickly undoing their work.

Just as it had tossed aside Norman Hedenstad like a rag doll as he attempted to close the south wing fire door, the pressure also blew open the doors of some of the patients rooms, allowing the beast and its inferno to pounce on the bedridden innocents within.

For the most part, those patients and visitors who found or remained sheltered behind closed patient room doors survived. But it wasn't quite that simple. The doors of each room were equipped with friction latches
~~~

– a type of closure system that allowed staff to simply apply pressure to an entryway to open it for ease of moving beds and stretchers or to back in a wheelchair-bound patient. There was no sort of positive latching hardware, such as a doorknob with a striker that had to be manually turned to open it. As a result, the gaseous pressures that built up in front of the fire actually pushed back open some of the doors that had been slammed closed.

Consequently, there was no absolutely safe place anywhere on the ninth floor. And the fire monster was undiscerning. The young, the old, the recovering, the dying, all were victims to its ravenous and merciless appetite. Some died quickly in the flames, some slowly, suffocating on the black smoke that filled their rooms.

Frederick Greenberg, a retired Pratt & Whitney machinist was visiting his wife of 47-years who was a patient in a private room in the far section of the south wing. The 75-year old man was distraught over his wife's illness and would only leave her side when visiting hours were over. He always brought his Laura fresh flowers when he returned in the morning and would force a smile upon his face upon seeing her, despite his breaking heart. They would hold hands for hours, usually not speaking, but taking quiet peace and comfort from just their nearness to each other.

On this afternoon, while Laura slept, Greenberg heard the tremendous explosion as the trash chute blew off its hinges and the roar of the savage blowtorch as it began to consume the south wing. He leapt from the chair in which he had been dozing, calming his wife who had been startled awake.

"Fred! What…" she cried, her voice trembling.

"I don't know darling," he said calmly caressing her face, although completely unnerved himself. "Let me go and see what the trouble is. I'll be right back."

"No," she begged him, looking into his eyes. "Don't leave me."

"I never would, my love," he replied, smiling to reassure her.

Greenberg opened the door and stepped into the hall. Astonished, he saw a tidal wave of dense black smoke surging towards him, chasing nurses down the corridor who were ordering people into the nearest room. He felt a tremendous surge of heat on his face that caused him to instinctively raise his arms for protection. One of the nurses pushed him back inside his wife's room and told him to close the door. He didn't bother asking questions. The problem was obvious.

Greenberg quickly stepped back inside, closed the door and pushed against it, noticing the slight give of the friction lock. Then he rushed back to his wife's bedside and held her hand.

"There appears to be a fire," he said to her calmly, trying to hide his own fear, but the look in his eyes gave away the truth.

"Is it bad, Fred?" she asked in alarm, reaching for the hand she had held for so many years. His silence answered her question. "Oh, no, my God… this can't be happening," she whimpered. Tears welled in her eyes.

Black smoke suddenly began drifting under the door and in minutes the elderly couple were choking on the fumes. Greenberg grabbed towels and stuffed them under the door trying to stem the flow of the noxious fumes and then hurried to the telephone on the nightstand. There was no connection, not even a dial tone. The line was simply dead. Fred Greenberg knew at that moment their situation was hopeless.

"It's all right, sweetheart," he lied to his crying wife who was already having trouble breathing through the smoke. "We'll get out of this. I can hear the fire engines already. Just hang in there…I'm with you."

"I can't breath, Fred, can you open the window?" she begged. Immediately, he went to the windowsill, unlocked and pushed it open. The action sealed the couple's fate.

At once, Greenberg felt a rush of cool air on his face. But in the same instant, behind him he heard a loud sucking that sounded like a gigantic vacuum. He spun around and watched, puzzled, as smoke was rapidly drawn out of the room beneath the gap between the door and the floor. Almost simultaneously, a ball of fire exploded through the door, disintegrating it in a massive backdraft. In seconds, the entire ceiling was ablaze in a sea of churning flames. The highly flammable acoustical tiles began dropping from above and set fire to the floor and Laura Greenberg's bed.

With superheated air now igniting everything in the room, Fred Greenberg watched his own clothes burst into flames and felt his skin begin to blister. He ran from the window and leapt on to his wife's body, already ablaze, in an effort to smother the fire that now engulfed her. He held her as she thrashed beneath him, and screamed not from his own pain but in frustration from his inability to take away her agony.

"I love you…" he whispered to her in the final seconds of his life, but she was already gone. Then Fred Greenberg died too, holding the woman he could not save. The beast fed on them and everything else consumable in the hospital room.

Still the fire monster was not satiated.

Across the hall, Louisa Papae was heavily sedated, sleeping after her Appendectomy surgery earlier that morning. The 14-year-old Italian girl had come through the surgery with no complications and would probably be back at school again within a week. Her parents, Genny and Salvatore waited patiently with her and for Dr. Hedenstad who had promised to visit in the afternoon to examine their daughter. The whole family was exhausted from the anxiety of the morning and Louisa's parents were napping as well when the explosion occurred.

They both jumped at the shocking noise and Genny hurried to her daughter, still unconscious from the sedation. She remained asleep despite the deafening commotion.

"I will go and see," Salvatore whispered to his wife, alarm in his eyes, but shrugging his shoulders in bewilderment. "It's probably nothing." But before he could reach the door, someone banged on the closed door of their private room and told them to remain inside. "And keep the door closed," whoever it was hollered while racing past.

Papae smelled the smoke seconds later. "Genny, there must be a fire. We are to wait. Help will come, I'm sure. "

"No," Genny replied, terror in her eyes. "We don't wait here. Let's go home Salvatore," she implored.

"We cannot, woman, she is sleeping." The grey-haired man pointed to Louisa. "The Dottore, remember he promised to come and see us, yes? He will be here soon, I know, Genny. Essere paziente e non temere!" he said, urging her to be patient and not to fear.

Genny Papae began to cry and then to wail as she saw smoke begin to billow into the room from under the door. Salvatore was also frightened but did his best to hide it.

"Come, Genny, we hold hands and pray… Si, il mio amore?" he begged her.

Weeping, the Italian woman held her daughter's hand and shook her head in fear. This nightmare will never end, she thought. She shook her head.

"Si, il mio amore…" she answered her husband. "Yes, my love."

The husband and wife carefully lay beside their daughter on the bed and placed their hands over Louisa's. Then they began to recite the Rosary and faithfully waited for Norman Hedenstad. Smoke began to cloud the room but still they prayed as the roaring sounds of fire in the corridor and the blaring sirens, ever closer, filled their ears. Within minutes, the room was full of smoke and they could not breath.

Genny and Salvatore locked their eyes on their beautiful young daughter, mercifully still unconscious, and prayed that salvation would come. At the end, they held each other more tightly, gazing into each other's eyes and whispering "Ti amo," – "I love you" – to each other just as they had on their wedding day. Salvatore hugged his sleeping daughter and caressed his wife's hair as she fought back tears through the choking smoke and waited for the help that never came.

Salvatore's last thought, after a prayer that his wife and daughter would suffer no more, was one simple word. He looked towards the heavens.

"Perché?"

Why?

The light gradually faded from their eyes as they slowly suffocated from the smoke. They died together in an eternal embrace, the couple's hands clasped together over their daughter's sleeping body.

# Thirteen

~~~ ~~~

*"One way or another"*

Driver John Stewart followed District Chief Jim Poveromo's orders to "put his foot into it" and pulled the red Ford to the curb on Jefferson Street minutes later. They were the first unit on the scene. Stewart radioed Dispatch to report they were 10-2 at the fire scene. Poveromo jumped out of the sedan and eyeballed the situation.

"My god, John, this thing is already going like a bat out of hell," he said as dense, black smoke poured from somewhere on the upper floors of the Hospital. A strong easterly wind kept much of the smoke from rising, instead creating a ring around the top floors that would occasionally clear when a strong gust hit. The first time that happened, Poveromo blinked twice to be sure his eyes weren't deceiving him. What he saw made his stomach churn. Hanging out of open or smashed windows on the ninth floor were dozens of people, obviously trapped by fire.
~~~

"We need to get ladders to nine, at least," he yelled to Stewart who was already reaching into the car for the radio transmitter. "Maybe higher, I can't tell yet."

"The Chief just shipped the 2-2, boss. We're gonna have a lot of people and trucks here soon," Stewart responded.

"It ain't how many we're going to have, John, it's how we use 'em and how fast," he reminded his driver.

Behind him, the sounds of screaming sirens were come closer.

"That should be Engine 1, Jim," Stewart said. "I imagine Ladder 6 is right behind them."

Poveromo scanned the front of the building again looking for the best point of access to the ninth floor. At the moment, there was no smoke showing at the north wing at the far end of the Hospital. The district chief made a decision and turned to Stewart.

"Tell Dispatch to have Engine 1 pound into that first hydrant on Seymour and get water to the building at the front portico. There's a standpipe there, I'm sure of it. Then have him instruct Ladder 6 to pull right up under the portico and pull his nose in tight. We want to raise the stick to that last window on the east extension of the north wing. Got it?"

Stewart only had to nod.

"Dispatch, per order of District Chief Poveromo," Stewart began, "instruct Engine 1 to hook up to the hydrant on Seymour Street and lay into the standpipe at the front of the building at the entrance portico. Have Ladder 6 pull into the horseshoe to the far right and put the nose of the truck as tight to the front of the building as possible under the portico. Raise the stick to the last window on the east extension on the north wing of number nine. We need to get a man inside quickly. Acknowledge. Over."

"Roger that, District 2," Walsh responded immediately. "Transmitting."

Walsh was still relaying the instructions as Engine 1 raced up to the hydrant on Seymour Street, 150-feet from the front entrance to the hospital. Driver Robert Coyne set the brake and jumped out of the truck to grab a 12-foot length of soft suction, four-inch diameter supply hose. Firefighter Marty Conroy leapt off the back bumper, quickly uncapped the hydrant and hooked up the line Coyne provided.

Simultaneously, Jack Hull and Jay Flanagan began pulling 50-foot sections of two and a half inch diameter lines from the hose bed of the Engine and started the grueling task of "humping" them to the standpipe half a football field away. Coyne connected the four-inch supply line to the pumper followed by the two and a half inch hose to one of the four discharge gates standard on a 1,000 gallon pumper. Within minutes, Flanagan had the line connected to the standpipe and Hull gave the signal to charge it. After Conroy opened the hydrant, Coyne started the truck's pump and water surged through the 150-foot length of canvas hose at a pressure of some 200 gallons per minute. The supply line wriggled to life as the water rushed towards the hospital's standpipe. They now had water to the building. The only problem was getting it to the upper floors. Captain Bill Kenney called in to Walsh.

"Dispatch, Engine 1. The standpipe at the entrance is charged. But we don't have an option here. We're going to need to do a three-inch hose pull up the center section to the upper floors. We gotta pump the wet stuff up at least nine floors and the standpipe alone will not provide sufficient pressure. Please advise the district chief that we need to ladder the portico and begin a hose pull."

"Roger that, Engine 1," Walsh responded. A moment later, Walsh confirmed Poveromo's approval. Kenney instructed Flanagan and Hull to pull a 24-foot extension ladder off the Engine and position it to reach the portico. Robert Coyne spun a three-inch line onto another discharge gate at the pumper with a two and a half inch connector while Conroy began pulling the amount of hose he estimated it would take to reach from the truck to the eighth floor of the hospital, "flaking" it, serpentine like, along the ground.

Flanagan grabbed the end of the heavy line and made another exhausting pull to the ladder at the portico. He handed the hose to Hull who dragged it the last few feet up the ladder to the portico roof. Marty Conroy grabbed a hose roller and a long coil of rope off the truck and ran for the hospital's center stairwell where he began the long climb up 16 flights of stairs that would bring him to the eighth floor. While waiting on the portico roof, Jack Hull spun a gated Wye connector on to the hose allowing for the attachment of two attack lines when the hose was finally in place on the eighth floor.

Close behind, Lieutenant Dan Nolan, sitting in the passenger seat of Ladder 6, watched as Engine 1 finished laying into the building then turned to his driver, Joe Skidd.

"You heard the man," Nolan said. "We're going to raise the stick to the last window on the right on number Nine, Joe. Pull to the right of the driveway and

I want the bumper of this piece touching that front wall. Got it?"

"You got it boss," Skidd responded.

" You get one chance at it, kid. Get it right."

Skidd hit a lighted button on the front dash to alert the tillerman, Ritchie Tajirian of his intentions and swung the nose of the big truck to the right, sneaking it up as close as possible to the building. Tajirian turned the rear wheels of the back end of the rig sharply to the left. The two drivers could practically read each other's mind.

The second Ladder 6 came to a rest, expertly pulled up so tight to the building a sheet of paper wouldn't fit between the trucks front bumper and the white brick, the rest of the crew bailed out and began preparing to raise the huge aerial ladder.

Ritchie Trajirian squeezed out of the tillerman's seat and ran forward to the turntable for the 2,500-pound ladder. Ken O'Connell and Joe Kelley hurried to each side of the rear of the truck and began screwing down the jacks that would stabilize the giant machinery, while Sammy Booth chocked the wheels. Dan Nolan jumped out of the passenger seat to get a better view of the window they were going to attack on the ninth floor.

"This is gonna be a son of a bitch," he said to himself, shaking his head.

Inside the truck, Joe Skidd picked up a call from Dispatcher Dick Walsh.

"Ladder 6, Dispatch. Car 1 is in route with an ETA of less than three minutes and is inquiring your status. How long before you can raise the stick? We need you in that building. Over."

Nolan grabbed the transmitter from Skidd. "Roger that, Dispatch. We're screwing the jacks down now and are about to elevate. We'll have a monkey on the ladder in a few minutes," Nolan responded. He looked upwards. "Per the district chief's instructions, we will attempt to put a man into the last room on the east corridor of the north wing. Over"

"Car 1 is inquiring if the ladder will reach number nine," Walsh continued. Nolan eyed the height again. His gut told him the 100-foot ladder would not be long enough to reach the fire floor.

There was a long silence before the Lieutenant replied.

"Dispatch, Ladder 6. Inform Car 1 we will get it done one way or another," Nolan said. "God help us, one way or another. Over."

Walsh hesitated, understanding what Nolan was telling him.

"Roger that, Ladder 6," he said without comment and relayed the information to Chief Lee. There was no response from Car 1.

At that moment, Bob Martin pulled Chief Lee's car to the curb onto Seymour Street, screeching to a halt on the blacktop. The two men jumped out and were shocked to see the number of people that were frantically waving for help from the ninth floor. Lee, seeing the immense amount of smoke knew the fire was big but had no idea of its exact location and if it was spreading. He asked himself the first question he always did when coming upon a fire scene.

"What have I got and where is it going..."

He looked again at the men and women at the windows on nine and scanned the upper floors for others. There were none. The fire floor was nine, he was certain of it. Somehow they had to get those people out of there and hold it to nine. But it was all a guess until he got men into the fire scene. Poveromo had done a good job positioning the first two arriving pieces, he thought, two good calls. But he knew every decision they made from here on out was going to be just as important. Instinctively, the longtime firefighter and officer knew they had a very serious situation on their hands.

Lee spent a few minutes taking in the scene before issuing any new orders. He watched as firefighter Marty Conroy smashed out the eighth floor window in the center wing, mounted a hose roller on the windowsill and dropped a rope line down to Jack Hull on the portico roof to tie to the three-inch line they were getting ready to haul up. The hose pull was about to begin. It was going to be a long, hard tug of war to the top floors of the building with the heavy canvas hose and only a single five-man crew working the job.

Then Lee turned to see the crew from Ladder 6 frantically readying their truck to raise the aerial ladder, another agonizingly slow process. Speed was of the essence, the Chief thought, but getting to a fire as high up as this one was going to take time. Way too much time.

Martin informed Dispatch that Car 1 was 10-2 at the scene and assuming command as apparatus and crews were arriving from every direction.

Engine 6 flew up Jefferson Street, a red blur of screaming sirens, blaring horns and flashing lights. Lee saw the Engine approaching and having absorbed as much as he could of what was happening around him, began making decisions and barking orders.

"Dispatch, Car 1," Lee radioed. "Instruct Engine 6 to steer to the front of the Emergency Room entrance and hose up. Have the crew grab every donut roll they have and all their standpipe equipment and proceed to number nine by the north wing stairwell. We have entrapments, and the exact location of the fire is unknown at this time. Commence search and rescue if possible."

Lieutenant John Larkin, hanging on for dear life in the front passenger seat of the Mack Engine saw the black smoke pouring from the upper section of the Hospital's High Building and knew immediately they were in trouble. He hoped that someone had already called in a Second Alarm because this was more than a working fire. It was going to take them at least 20 minutes to even get water on a fire that high up, he thought. That's when he saw the people screaming and waving hysterically from open windows on the north wing of the ninth floor. His stomach churned in a way he couldn't remember since hitting the beach at Anzio.

Dick Walsh transmitted the Chief's instructions for Larkin's crew just as Engine 6 turned on to Seymour Street.

"Roger that," Larkin responded. "Engine 6 is 10-2 at Box 5141 heading for the north wing stairwell on number nine."

Driver George Murphy made the hard left turn in to the horseshoe and carefully pulled the pumper around Ladder 6. Larkin jumped out of the truck even before it rolled to a stop and yelled to his men.

"You heard the man, guys. Grab a roll and let's go." Firefighters Murphy, Ed Grady, Joe Edmunds, Frankie Zazzaro and Joe Curtain followed Larkin's lead and grabbed "donut rolls" – hundred pound rolls of two and a half inch hose – and slung them over their shoulders for the long tedious hike up 18 flights of stairs to the ninth floor. Larkin slung a roll over each shoulder and hollered to his guys to grab the two Scott Air packs assigned to the engine and whatever other standpipe equipment they might need including a fig nozzle and gate valve handles.

He looked up and saw a lot of nervous faces.

"Come along boys, this is going to be a bad one but we know what we gotta do," he said to them, looking each of his men in the eyes. "Let's get some water up there. There's people in need."

As the crew of Engine 6 jogged toward the north stairwell, Engine Companies 3 and 4 pulled in almost simultaneously with orders from Deputy Chief Jim Poveromo to take the hydrants on Jefferson Street and lay into the building's standpipes. The men on those trucks saw the heavy black smoke pouring out of the south wing and instinctively knew what they were up against.

"Engines 3 and 4, hook up, grab every donut roll you got, standpipe equipment and breathing apparatus and take your crews to the stairwell landing on number nine on the south wing," Walsh said, repeating Poveromo's instructions, "but hold your position until you can assess the situation. We do not – I repeat – we do not have eyes on the fire location but it appears to be focused in the south wing."

Engine 3 Lieutenant Frankie Burnes and Engine 4 Lieutenant Joe McSweegan exchanged anxious glances as they jumped from their rigs. There was nothing worse than looking up at a high rise and seeing a fire-storm except knowing that you were going to have to lead your men into that living hell. The burden of leadership was never greater than when you had to give orders that put the men in your charge, guys you knew not only as subordinates, but as friends, directly in the face of death.

"On the double," Burnes yelled to his team while McSweegan rallied his crew. Within minutes, both hydrants were charging the hospital standpipes for the south wing and the ten men who made up the crews of Engines 3 and 4 were hurrying to the south stairwell, the brutally heavy donut rolls slung over their shoulders.

Deputy Chief Jim Poveromo had made his way inside the building and radioed the chief with new information. He had just come from the master fire control room and a meeting with hospital Fire Marshall Tom Devanney.

"Chief, we are at the lobby location. There is reason to believe there has been loss of life on number nine. There is no communications available with hospital personnel at that location," Poveromo said flatly.

"Do we have land lines jacked in yet?" Lee asked, inquiring if the Deputy Chief of Communications in charge of the Signal Division, Patrick Garrahy had arrived at the scene. Garrahy was the department's chief electrician in charge of the operation of all of the City's fire Boxes, communications and establishing private telecommunications lines at major building fires. The first person he sought out upon entering the building was Linus Steck, a hospital employee who served as an electrician in the Maintenance Department. With Steck's help and knowledge of the hospital's telecommunications system, Garrahy made short work of setting up a telephone network for the private, secure use of the fire department.

"Deputy Chief Garrahy just jacked us in, Car 1," Poveromo responded. "We will have working phones on each floor momentarily."

"Tell Pat good work, chief," Lee responded. "Jim, move to Forward Command on north Nine and make sure you've got a runner with you to keep me informed," he instructed Poveromo.

"Roger that, Car 1. I am moving to Forward Command now. Over," he responded, already heading for the north wing stairwell that would bring him to what was believed to be the fire floor.

Lee pondered the situation. The good news was that they now had at least a minimum of communications. The bad news was they also had bodies. People were already dead from this fire. How many, he wondered. He rolled the dice. They needed more help, but it would come with a price.

"Bob, call in the 3-3 immediately," he told his driver, ordering a Third Alarm even before most of the first responders had arrived at the scene. But now they were nearly bare assed naked if another Box came in. "And have Dispatch confirm that all elements of the pre-plan are in effect. I need every man I can get."

"Roger tha…" Walsh began, but Lee interrupted. The Chief was giving orders so fast, the dispatcher didn't have time to acknowledge them.

"Also, instruct Deputy Chiefs Mullins and Curtain to report to District Chief Poveromo at forward command as well, ASAP. They are to assume command of the evacuation of all floors above number nine."

Even as Martin keyed the handheld microphone on his car radio to call in the Third Alarm, Dan Kelley was taking a quick call from his daughter, Nancy, at Headquarters. She had stayed home from school that day, convincing her father that she was ill, and was checking in with daddy as promised. He hadn't been convinced.

"Can't talk right now, honey, kinda busy," Kelley said as calmly as he could muster.

"Why, what's up Daddy?"

"There's a fire at Hartford Hospital. Two Alarms. Wouldn't be surprised if it went to a Third. Gotta go."

He put the receiver down just as Martin called in.

"Wow!" the teenage Kelley thought as the phone went dead. Talk about a story. She quickly dialed Hartford's most popular radio station, WTIC and spoke to a reporter.

"Say that again... Where was that fire, honey?" the reporter asked the young girl, not sure he had heard her correctly.

"Hartford Hospital," she said.

"How do you know? Are you there?" the reporter asked.

"No. But my Daddy is a dispatcher for the Hartford Fire Department."

"Oh," the reporter said nonchalantly. "Oh!" he repeated a second later, suddenly recognizing the quality of his source.

The news was out. WTIC, owned by the Travelers Insurance Company, had the strongest transmitters and largest share of listeners for their television, and AM and FM radio broadcasting channels in the state. Within minutes, news bulletins were being broadcast on all three venues and anyone within view or earshot of a TV or radio was glued to the unfolding drama. Crack WTIC reporters Dick Bertel and Dick O'Brien sped to the scene. The Bulletins alerted reporters and photographers from the City's two newspapers, the morning *Hartford Courant* and the evening *Hartford Times.*

Word of the fire spread fast throughout the City. The black, billowing smoke pouring from the upper floors of the Hospital could now be seen for miles around. The south end air was filled with the sounds of sirens coming from every direction, replacing the festive echoes of downtown carolers and the bustle of Christmas shoppers. Suddenly, all the cheery holiday decorations, quaint, snow-covered North Pole window sets, mechanical ice skaters, snowmen and Santa's seemed almost indecent in their levity.

A wave of spectators began moving toward Seymour Street, some out of morbid curiosity, others out of concern for loved ones. The steady stream of ambulances and hearses that flew by after being ordered to the scene by Governor John Dempsey, their sirens blaring as loudly as the fire trucks, did nothing to ease their concerns.

The city's Public Schools were just letting out as fire apparatus began screaming toward the hospital, and students hurried to watch. Parochial school students, who were excused from classes because of the Holy Day for Roman Catholics, began spreading the news to their friends as they heard the excited radio reporting or saw the television news bulletins while waiting for the afternoon kids programming of the "Mickey Mouse Club" and "The Ranger Andy Show." Some went outside in search of the reported heavy smoke.

On Cheshire Street, nine-year old Carla Miano tore herself away from the television and wandered outside into her front yard. She looked upward to the north, wide-eyed at the huge plume of black smoke that was reaching high into the afternoon sky. Likewise, crowds of kids on Grandview Terrace and in Goodwin and Highland Parks also stood, transfixed by the sight. Peter Larkin, son of Lieutenant John Larkin on Engine 6, sat glued to the television, frantic for information. In every south end neighborhood, people came out of their homes to look towards the sky over Hartford Hospital, filled with spirals of black smoke.

"How bad is it?" they wondered.

The sickening irony was overwhelming. Wasn't a hospital a place dedicated to saving lives? Wasn't it a refuge from illness, a place to be cared for, to heal or die in peace? Hospitals were immune to danger —weren't they?

This couldn't be happening.

But the Hartford Fire Department didn't have time to worry about what was or wasn't supposed to happen. It was happening right before their eyes.

Chief Lee resumed transmitting orders to the dispatchers as additional apparatus from the respondents to the first two alarms continued to arrive. The Third Alarm men and machines would be just minutes behind them.

From the Blue Hills Avenue firehouse, Ladder 4 and its six man crew was on the road in minutes. Engine 7 was right behind out of 2384 Main Street and Captain Tim Kelliher Sr.'s Engine 12 rolled out of it's South Whitney Street barn. Walsh and Kelley were briefing the senior officers of each company as they raced to the scene. Instructions were pouring out of Dispatch as Lee and Poveromo directed the fight.

"Per instructions of Car 1," Walsh transmitted to the racing apparatus, "Ladder 3, go to the front of the building at Seymour and raise your stick to the south wing of number Nine. Ladder 4, go to the front of the building at Seymour and raise your stick to the center wing of number Nine. Engine 7 and Engine 10, hose up and take your crew to the south wing of number 10 and assist in the evacuation of the floor. Report the situation to Forward Command if smoke or fire is showing. Over."

Within 20 minutes of the nurse on the 12th floor of Hartford Hospital pulling Box 5141, some 70 firefighters and more than 20 fire trucks were engaged in preventing a disaster at Hartford Hospital from becoming a bigger one.

Without knowing the cause or source of the conflagration, Lee knew instinctively that even with nearly all of the department's available resources at the scene, it still probably wasn't enough. But he had few choices. Already, with the fire at Zion and Ward Street still blazing and a huge percentage of the department engaging the Hospital situation, Hartford was dangerously exposed to emergency calls in wide sections of the City. There simply weren't enough men or apparatus to go around.

But the Chief wasted no time in getting creative.

"Dispatch," he radioed," move Ladder 5 from South Whitney Street to 275 Pearl on standby," he ordered. "Have Lieutenant King organize Scott Air Pack replenishment. This is going to be a smoky son of a bitch for a long time. Coordinate with Lieutenant Martin and District Chief Poveromo's driver for shuttling the bottles. God knows we don't have enough as it is."

Tim Kelliher Jr., "a fire house rat," arrived at Company 5 just as Lieutenant Bob King, a close family friend, was instructing his driver, Eddie Sullivan, to move Ladder 5, an 85-foot straight truck to 275 Pearl.

"You're dad is rolling Engine 12 on a Third, Timmy. He just pulled out," he told the wide-eyed teen. "If you want to catch him, take the bus to Main and Pearl and then you can run through Bushnell Park to the Hospital." King didn't have to say it more than once. Timmy was off like a rabbit. A city bus pulled up moments later and he hopped aboard, excitement at the thought of seeing a big fire sending adrenalin coursing through his veins. He looked out the window of the rolling bus and stared, his mouth agape, at the cloud of smoke overwhelming the mid-afternoon sunshine. Suddenly, the thought of his father in the middle of the conflagration made him feel like he was going to be sick to his stomach.

At the hospital, Lee was still playing a chess match with his men and equipment, trying to head off the fire monster at every turn. But the beast hadn't given up yet.

Apparatus was now beginning to surround the building and Lee directed pumpers and ladders to the rear of the Hospital as well.

The radio crackled in Ladder 1 with orders relayed from the chief.

"Ladder 1, go to the back of the building and raise your stick to number nine," Walsh relayed the chief's instructions.

"We'll be 10-2 in the rear in less than five minutes, Dispatch," came the immediate response from Captain Dwight Schaeffer.

Frank Droney heard the banter between Dispatch and Schaeffer.

"Begging the Captain's pardon, that's a fecking waste of time," the crusty Irishman said to Schaeffer.

"Why?" Schaeffer responded, perplexed at the opinion of the man he'd most want at his back if they ended up in the middle of this disaster.

"Because the god damned ladders won't reach number nine, you'll see," he predicted. "The hundred footers are going to be useless for entering the building."

Schaeffer trusted Droney with his life and grabbed the microphone to call Dispatch and pass on the thought. But instead, he tucked it away.

"We'll follow orders for now, Frank," he said. "But God help us if you're right."

At the fire scene, Lee scanned the top of the High Building looking for smoke coming from the roof or the elevator penthouse. Sure enough, there was dense, black smoke as thick as mud pouring from the heavily ventilated elevator machine and control room. The elevator penthouse sat directly over the building's eight hoistways, which, extending the height of the structure, essentially acted as chimneys providing critical ventilation. There was fire in at least one elevator, or maybe several.

"Dispatch, Car 1," Lee radioed Walsh. "Have Engine 2 hose up and take the south wing stairwell to the elevator penthouse on the roof. Tell them to send a man to report the situation. I need to know which elevators are running."

"Roger, Car 1," Walsh responded and transmitted the Chief's orders to Engine 2.

Lee's plan of attack was formulated from his experiences in fighting big building fires. All the bases had to be covered. It was easy to make the mistake of assigning all your resources to one location, then get blindsided when the beast snuck out in the last place you'd expect. That's how you lost guys in fires like this, he thought, and he'd be god damned if he was going to be making any family condolence calls tonight. Every man was going home after they beat this thing to death. He shook his head wondering what kind of grief was already waiting inside.

Lee had dispatched every man available and did his best to cover all possible scenarios. But until they had someone at the location – someone inside at the source – they were as good as a blind. They had to get eyes on the fire quickly, but climbing 18 flights of stairs while carrying hundred pound donut rolls of hose and wearing forty pounds of turnout gear took time. And time was something they couldn't spare. He was painfully aware of how long it was going to take to get water on the fire and reach survivors and watched in growing impatience at the slow progress Engine 1 was making on the hose pull. He quickly made a decision. What he needed was an experienced man to take over the job.

"Dispatch, Car 1. Instruct Engine 12 to pull in behind Engine 1 at the portico and take command of the hose pull in the center section as soon as they arrive."

"Roger that, Car 1," Walsh replied and relayed the Chief's instructions to Captain Tim Kelliher Sr. riding shotgun in Engine 12. Kelliher was the guy the Chief had in mind.

The captain groaned. The job of hauling a two and half inch line up nine floors, snaking it up the building through smashed open windows was huge. They'd need help.

Over the roar of the screaming truck, Captain Kelliher responded. "Dispatch, Engine 12. Please inform Car 1 that we're going to need a hand with that. It will take us forever with a single engine crew. Over." Kelliher knew that it would take him far too long with only five guys and that the chief was probably fighting the clock.

"Roger that, Engine 12, standby," Walsh responded.

There was a momentary silence, then the radio crackled back to life and Kelliher listened.

"Engine 12, Dispatch. Car 1 advises that Engine 1 has already begun the job and will assist with the hose pull, " Walsh transmitted. But there was more.

"Also Engine 12, Car 1 has instructed you to muster up some volunteers among the hospital staff to assist in the pull."

"Roger that, Dispatch," Kelliher responded. He hid his irritation at the orders. Where the hell was he going to find "volunteers" for such a brutal job?

No matter the reality of his assignment, Kelliher understood the chain of command and immediately began thinking through the problem. He was intimately familiar with the hospital layout and knew what this effort was going to entail. He also knew that Chief Lee must be desperate to get water up through the center section if he was assigning two full crews to get it done.

The Captain had no idea that it wasn't only the chief who was desperate. Lee wasn't nearly as anxious as those waiting for help.

They were rapidly losing all hope.

# Fourteen

~~~ ❧ ~~~

*"Pandemonium"*

Inside, order was quickly turning into chaos.

On the ninth floor, the fire monster continued its rampage in the south wing. There was no possible route of escape for the dozens of patients, staff and visitors who had made it into the last rooms of the wing. They were safe if they stayed behind a closed door and prevented smoke from entering the room. But the intense pressure of the heat had blown some of the doors open, either enough to allow the flames to quickly engulf helpless bed-ridden patients and anything combustible, or just enough to allow suffocating smoke to fill the room with deadly, superheated gas. Either way, the outcome was not survivable.

Two elderly patients died in their beds as the flames pounced on them. Four others, all helpless to leave their beds in the one room they shared, died of suffocation as the noxious, black cloud of smoke descended on them. How many more would die was
~~~

now completely dependent on how fast help could arrive and how many were willing to push their own safety aside to save the life of a stranger. The situation came down to two unknowns: speed and heroes.

In one south wing room, where four patients, a young intern doctor and a nurse had managed to find shelter, the doctor shoved pillows and sheets under the crack between the door and the floor to keep out smoke. As he and the other trapped occupants of the room watcher in horror, the pillows and linens began to burn. He instructed everyone who could to fill up bedpans, basins and any vestibule that could hold water to keep filling them and throwing them on the burning materials. It worked, preventing the deadly smoke from entering their room until the fire had passed. In other rooms, nurses did the same, shoving bedding into any crack that was seeping smoke. Where there were cool heads and closed doors, people survived.

But still there was no rescue in sight. Those who were ambulatory stood at open windows, screaming to firemen and spectators below to do something, anything to save them. But looking down from where they stood, it appeared as if nothing was happening. They could not know that help was coming from every direction. It didn't help that someone turned on a patient's portable transistor radio only to hear speculation by a reporter that the Fire Department's ladders might not be high enough to reach them. Ladder 3 and Ladder 4 were pulling into position even as reporters guessed at the outcome.

In the north wing, smoke had managed to squeeze by the closed fire door and was rapidly filling the corridor. But nurses were instinctively resolute that fear would not stop them from doing whatever they could until help arrived. Some, whose patients could walk, wet towels and covered their faces to help them breath through the smoke and began escorting them down the north stairwell to the eighth floor and safety. Incredibly, despite the smoke, some nurses on the lower floors continued to believe the whole thing was a drill until they were suddenly confronted by patients whose faces were blackened with soot being escorted by nurses carrying their intravenous lines and Foley bags.

The stress was too much for some of the ailing patients. An older woman, having survived the walk down the north stairwell to the seeming safety of the eighth floor experienced a heart attack from the stress and her limp body was dragged into a Croup room in the Pediatrics unit, where two doctors quickly opened her chest and performed open heart massage until they could move her into surgery.

Nurse's Aide Bob Maher, who's quick thinking with Nurse Eileen Gormley Santiglio had managed to shut the north wing fire door just as the fire monster was about to burst into the wing, was also working feverishly to evacuate those who could be moved. The fire door had long since disappeared in the smoke and was no longer visible at the end of the corridor. But the cloud of black smoke was creeping toward them at an alarming pace.

Suddenly, Maher heard what sounded like scraping and someone crying on the other side of the door. He got as close as he could to listen.

"Help me, please help me," a weak, barely audible voice repeated over and again.

Maher called back through where he knew the fire door to be.

"Come to the door," he yelled. "I'll get you. Just come to the door!"

The response was heartbreaking.

"I can't. I can't see it, I can't find it," the anonymous voice answered weakly. "Help me, please."

Maher knew that opening the latched fire door was high risk. But he could not ignore the plea for help.

He took a deep breath, and feeling along the wall, finally found the fire door and the latch to open it. The door was hot, but he gambled. He unlatched the eight-foot wide metal clad door, opened it a crack and went to peer around it. Instantly, a surge of superheated air sprang upon him and burned all the hair off the side of his head and the skin on the exposed portion of his face.

He couldn't know it, but the temperature inside the south wing and central corridor was now well in excess of 1200° F. The pressure built up inside the wing threatened to blow the north wing fire door completely open.

Despite his burns, Maher pushed back against the beast with everything he had. He knew he could not open the door any further and to even attempt to rescue the person on the other side. To do so would put the more than 100 staff and patients still in the north wing directly in the path of the blowtorch that was already trying to eat its way through the fire door.

Heartsick, he knew he somehow had to latch the door locked again. Agonizingly, badly burned and almost out of air from the smoke, he made progress, moving the door a millimeter at a time. Finally, his strength nearly gone, he was able to reach up and latch the door. With the last of his resolve, he ran for safety.

He tried not to think about what was happening to the person on the other side of the door.

By now, the acrid smell of smoke had filled the hospital. In some areas, one could just detect a faint odor; in others, the smoke actually cast a grey pall over the corridors. T. Stewart Hamilton's efforts to contact the nurses stations on each wing thankfully had revealed that fire was evident on only the ninth floor. But the pervasiveness of the smoke was giving everyone the jitters, whether they were in harm's way or not.

To their credit, staff remained calm, doing their jobs and their best to reassure patients that all was well when the truth was they had little knowledge of what was happening. If anything, the lack of information was more worrisome and they couldn't help but pass nervous glances between each other. Their question was the same one that was going through Chief Thomas Lee's mind at that very minute: "What have I got and where is it going?"

On the 10th, 11th and 12th floors, patients were clamoring for information as the smoke from the ninth had not only made it uncomfortable to breath, but was quite visible. Pandemonium was building. The patient call button panels at the Nurses Stations in nearly every wing on every floor, but particularly on the 10th, were lit up like holiday displays. Every light signified a patient whose anxiety was growing by the second. On the eighth floor, nurses began walking patients who could get out of bed down the stairwell to the lobby.

Even as far down as the fourth and fifth floors of the south wing where the Maternity Ward was located, the heavy smell of smoke was quite evident.

That very morning, the young Irish girl, Genevieve Ryan had given birth to an infant son, Liam, and was now resting comfortably in a bed on the fourth floor. Her husband John, elated at the birth of his first son, was on the fifth, gazing through the large viewing windows of the Nursery at his newborn. A smile seemed to be tattooed on his face.

"That's the little one, that's him alright, he's mine," he said repeatedly to any one who would listen and he would knock on the glass until a nurse would hold up little Liam for the world to see.

Even in his excitement, John Ryan sensed the tension amongst the staff and could smell the smoke. He stopped a nurse's aide and asked.

"I'm sorry, Mr. Ryan. There really should be an announcement explaining the problem," the aide responded. "I'm sure it's just a minor fire in one of the trash chutes, which happens from time to time, and there should be nothing to worry about," he explained. "Believe me, if you and your wife and son were in any danger, we'd have you out of here." Ryan smiled at the explanation and went back to celebrating his son's birthday.

But in his wife's room, the mother who had just given birth was nearly hysterical. Out of sight of her husband and new son, she could not get a nurse to answer her repeated calls. Finally, she struggled out of bed and forced herself to walk to the nearest nurses station.

"Dearest," she said to the first nurse she could find, "could you kindly tell me what will become of us with all this smoke? And I would like to see my son, I'm very worried."

"Now, now, young lady," the nurse responded. "I assure you there is no danger. We have experienced minor smoke like this in the past from fires in the trash chute, and there is no cause for worry." She smiled trying to assure the frightened Irish woman that all was well.

"I will go and find your husband for you, Genevieve. I'm sure he will tell you there is nothing to worry about. How much would you bet that he is upstairs at the nursery doting over that beautiful new son of yours?" the nurse laughed. "In fact you'll be needing to feed him soon. Now let's get you back to bed so you can get some rest."

Genevieve did what she was told but the churning in her stomach would not go away and try as she might, she could not sleep. Soon, her husband appeared at the door.

"Hello, my darlin', I'm sorry to be off and about so long, I just couldn't take me eyes off the lad! " he said, unable to hide his elation. "Why, it's a bloody miracle what you've done, Gen. My little... excuse me ... *our* little boy, is just the handsomest creature those lovely green eyes of yours have ever seen, sweetheart."

"But John, the smoke..." she said with worry.

"Yes. Tis' a bit stronger now, it is," he replied, a deep frown of worry crossing his brow. I think I'll be poking a nose down the hall to speak with the nurses. All right my lovely?" He turned and hurried out the door, only to poke his head back inside a second later.

"Trust me I would never let anything happen to either of you, sweetheart. You know that, don't you? I'm going to go find someone who will tell me what's happening here. I'll be right back."

A minute turned into ten. Ten turned into twenty. Suddenly John Ryan reappeared in his wife's room, their precious Liam wrapped in a blanket, in his arms.

"Here you go my love," he said to Genevieve. "Hold on tight to the little one."

"What's wrong, John? She asked with alarm. "Is there really a fire?"

"Yes, somewhere in the building but no one can tell me where, only not to worry." He smiled. "I think the last man to say that was the Captain of the *Titanic.* We'll not be waiting around for the last lifeboat, dear." He leaned down and scooped her off the bed with his two strong arms, turned and walked out the door.

Ryan stopped at the nurses station and the staff looked up in shock at the big man carrying his wife and child.

"Why… you just can't up and leave, Mr. Ryan," the head nurse challenged him.

Authority didn't impress Ryan. It usually cost him something. There was no chance he was going to leave the precious packages in his arms in harms way.

"I'll be thanking you for your concern, Mrs. Nurse," he said as politely as he could, but his eyes told a different story. This was a man ready to take on an army of security guards who might try to stop him.

"You've been most kind to my family and you have my thanks. But we'll be leaving now and I would beg you not to try and stop me. I'm not in a debating frame of mind at the moment." He smiled at the nurse, then took a deep breath, blew it out and and sniffed the air.

"To tell you the truth, young lady, if I were you I'd be taking all the mothers and their wee ones outside. It wouldn't seem that the air is improving now, would it. And isn't it a bit strange that no one seems to want to talk about the hospital taking on the smell of a smokehouse? I've learned that the time to run is when things are too quiet.

"Now, good day to all you fine ladies," Ryan said. "Thank you for all your help, but Gen and I will be taking our leave with Liam now. God bless you and may you all be safe this day."

With that, his wife and baby safely in his arms, he carried his family down the south stairwell into the lobby and walked out the front door. John Ryan managed to carry his wife and newborn son the 18 blocks home to their tiny apartment, stopping only once to allow the new mother to sit beneath a tree and nurse her baby.

The smile on his face never wavered. There were two reasons for that. The first was his heart was full of joy. The second was so long as he managed to focus on smiling, he didn't have to think of the horror he was sure they had just managed to escape.

# Fifteen

~~~ ൭ ~~~

*"Trapped in a cauldron"*

Like a biblical swarm of locusts, so thick their flight appeared as a single great mass, the tongues of flame that gave the fire monster life on the ninth floor now merged into a hurricane of unfathomable heat.

Still the beast grew more ravenous with each passing second, devouring sources of fuel even before it could lick them with its incandescent fury. Combustible materials spontaneously burst into flame when their surface molecules reached a temperature of 500 F° – barely a third that of the cauldron of air now filling the corridor.

The ravenous monster knew its life was self-perpetuating only so long as it could find oxygen and sustenance. Both were now in plentiful supply and it gorged on them with the mindlessness of a crazed addict on a rampage.
~~~

A black, plastic telephone at a nurses station melted from the heat into an amorphous puddle whole minutes before fire actually swept the counter it rested upon. Mattresses and bedding, draperies and wallpaper, framed artwork on the corridor walls, ceiling tiles, linoleum flooring and wainscoting burst into flames from the crematorium-like temperature, fueling the gas and heat the beast needed to continue its insatiable repast along the entire length of the Ninth Floor – or at least as far as the closed north wing fire door. So long as the metal clad parapet held against the explosive pressures of superheated gasses behind it, the fire monster's flames could travel no farther. But even if it held back the flames, the smoke leaking around the door made survival in the north wing only temporary.

In the few rooms where patients and staff had huddled together in a frantic bid for survival in both the south and north wings, life hinged on whether the door to their sanctuaries remained closed, or could be held closed. If breached by fire, death was a certainty. If invaded by smoke, the same end was just as inevitable – it just came more slowly as one suffocated. But as of yet, no signs of help were visible and a patient's transistor radio blared the unwelcomed news from WTIC's reporter Dick Bertel that it was now evident the Hartford Fire Department did not have a ladder high enough to reach them on the ninth floor.

It was if the fire monster was listening.

As it consumed the entire central corridor, leaving it lifeless and nearly stripped of fuel, the beast, blocked from the feeding frenzy it craved in the north wing turned its awesome fury on the patient room doors.

A young intern who had stopped by the ninth floor to see a patient who was a personal friend, put his back to the door of a room occupied by more than a dozen trapped patients and staff. He dug his shoes into the floor, frantically seeking leverage against the hot gasses trying to blow him out of the way. He could feel the wave of pressure against his shoulder blades and fought to keep his knees from buckling under the enormous strain. Heat from the fire trying to eat its way through the door singed his back. But like many singular acts of heroism that day, the young intern held his ground, refusing to allow the monster into the room.

But how much longer could the dozens trapped at both ends of the ninth floor hold out without help? The fire had been raging now for nearly 45 minutes.

In rooms where survivors still held out hope, they could see the answer for themselves as more and more smoke found it's way into their temporary bunkers and the flames continued to eat through the doors and walls, which was their only protection from the conflagration.

The fire monster knew its time to kill was waning. It had only one course of action.

Turn up the heat.

# Sixteen

~~~ ~~~

*"We're out of reach"*

By now, it was evident to Chief Lee that the smoke billowing from the elevator penthouse on the Hospital roof had intensified. The small building contained the hoisting machines and controllers for the building's public vertical transportation system. He had yet to hear from Engine Company 2, whom he he'd assigned to hike up the south stairwell and inspect the rooftop structure. Lee had no way of knowing if there were passengers in any of the eight passenger elevators that travelled from the basement to the 13th floor, although he had a strong hunch there were – and that they were trapped.

The radio airwaves were too quiet and he wasn't getting any of the information he needed from his crews. Every second counted. Lee was about to explode into his radio at Walsh and Kelley for lack of information when it suddenly crackled to life. The elevators would have to wait.
~~~

"Car 1, Dispatch. Engine 3's Lieutenant Burnes just called in to report his company and Engine 4 are at the location at the far end of the south stairwell on number nine," Dan Kelley reported. Several firefighters had lugged hundred pound donut rolls of two and a half inch hose up the 18 flights of stairs and they were now hooked into the ninth floor standpipes.

Lee knew that Frankie Burnes was probably fighting the strong urge to swing open the stairwell door and hit the fire with water, but also that he was experienced enough to know it would be suicidal.

With a fire burning this hot, every gallon of water released on the flames would instantly create anywhere from 1,700 to 2,400 gallons of steam. If Burnes and his guys just charged into the corridor with open nozzles the explosion of steam would kill them all. Death by scalding was no more pleasant than death by burning. Their only hope was that the men on the fire floor had carried fog nozzles with them – a spray nozzle that broke its stream into small droplets that hit a greater surface area and dissipated heat faster, smothering the fire. Even then, they had to be extremely cautious in approaching a fire burning at this high a temperature.

"Burnes further reports that the door is super hot, Car 1," Kelley continued. "Engine 3 and Engine 4 are awaiting your orders, Chief. Over."

Just as he figured, Lee thought. Burnes was playing it smart.

"Dispatch, Car 1. Instruct Engine 3 and 4 to hold their positions. We need to get eyes on the situation before making our next move. Over."

"Roger that, Car 1."

As other Fire Company's in the building were beginning to report in to Poveromo and Lee, it seemed like hours since Engine 1 and Ladder 6, the first apparatus to arrive at the fire, had taken positions at the main entrance of the building. In fact, it had only been minutes. The crew of Ladder 6 was finally "raising the stick" – elevating and positioning their truck's 100-foot long ladder to the window of the last room of the north wing's east corridor that jutted out of the front of the building.

After expertly working with driver Joe Skidd to position the truck under the target window on the ninth floor, firefighter Richie Tajirian, the tillerman on the 40-foot long ladder truck had wasted no time in scrambling from his lone seat in the rear cab forward to the ladder turntable. For the moment, the ball was in his court.

The young firefighter played critical roles in the operation of the ladder truck, first as the man who steered the rear axle of the vehicle, a skill that few could master. The tillerman had to learn to steer the back end of the rig in the opposite direction as the driver. When the driver turned left onto a street, the tillerman had to steer right for just the right amount of distance to keep the rear of the trailer portion of the truck on the original street, then quickly steer left to swing the back end onto the second street.

He also had to be in constant communication with the driver when they were positioning the truck at the fire scene to raise the ladder into position. A 40-foot long truck was a challenge to jockey into exactly the right position to enable the ladder to be used efficiently – if at all. Once the truck was positioned, his assignment as tillerman also called for him to exit the single seat rear cab and scramble forwards to the ladder turntable to take over the control of raising, rotating and extending it into the proper position. He was always the first man up the ladder armed only with an axe. And the whole procedure had to be accomplished within minutes as lives hung in the balance.

The 25-year old Tajirian, with no more than three years of experience under his belt, was nevertheless extremely competent, fearless and highly trusted by his truck crew. Physically, one wondered how he managed to handle the steering job let alone climb aerial ladders wearing 40 pounds of turnout gear and carrying a 15-pound axe. At 150-pounds soaking wet, he hardly appeared built for the job. But not unlike many men who didn't fit the job description for being a hero, when the situation called for superhuman effort, Tajirian always answered the call.

"Raising the stick," he reported to his senior officer, Lieutenant Dan Nolan as he worked the turntable controls to lift the four-section ladder into a 70-degree position. Slowly, so agonizingly slowly, the ladder moved upwards from its bed on the ladder truck even as the young fireman could hear the screams for help from the windows above him. He tried to block out the sound. It was impossible.

Inside the Ladder truck, the radio blared with a message from Dick Walsh.

"Ladder 6, Dispatch," Walsh called for Nolan.

Exasperated, Nolan grabbed for the radio transmitter.

"Ladder 6 here, Dispatch. Over."

"Ladder 6, per the Chief, where are you guys with raising the stick? The situation is urgent. Over."

Nolan was ready to boil over himself and responded in frustration.

"Dispatch, inform the Chief we just finished pinning the jacks and chocking the wheels. We are elevating the ladder now. Will report when we are in position. Over." Walsh quickly responded to Car 1.

Lee was beside himself. "Jesus Christ," he swore in frustration. He looked up at the dozens of faces helplessly awaiting rescue. These were people who didn't have more than a few minutes unless they got some help. He was about to contact Nolan again but waited the obligatory 10 seconds to cool off. It was the wrong time to get into a pissing match with a subordinate under immense pressure.

There was a long pause while Danny Nolan was going through the same exercise. Then the Lieutenant couldn't contain himself anymore as he watched Ritchie Tajirian busting his hump trying to get the ladder in the air.

"Dispatch," Nolan began in response, then held his own breath for a moment before continuing. The situation required calm, and that's what he was going to demonstrate to his men even if it meant getting his ass chewed by the Chief of the Department a hundred yards from the action.

"Please inform Car 1 we are well aware of the situation. In fact, we can see and hear people screaming for help just like he can, only the screams are louder here," he said sarcastically. "With all due respect, Dispatch, we'll get this ladder raised the minute we stop wasting time on the radio. Over."

"Uh… roger that, Ladder 6," Walsh confirmed.

He waited as Walsh transmitted Nolan's message to the Chief and expected an angry retort. None was forthcoming. Lee knew the Lieutenant was right.

"The Chief says, 'Roger that,' Ladder 6. Carry on, and report when you've got the stick raised." Lee turned his attention back to getting information on the elevator situation.

Nolan wasted no time.

"Ritchie, rotate the stick to that last window on number nine and extend immediately,' the Lieutenant instructed his subordinate.

"About frigging time," Tajirian whispered under his breath, and again worked the turntable controls to turn the ladder towards the building. He watched impatiently as each of the four 25-foot extensions unfolded. The seconds went by. Tajirian was ready to race up the ladder the moment the ladder was in position. Then his heart stopped.

"Lieutenant," he yelled down to Nolan. "The ladder is raised to 80-percent at 70-degrees, but it's not enough. We're short. She's not even to the bottom of the windowsill on number eight. Hell, it's just clearing seven."

"Oh dear God..." the ladder truck's senior officer said under his breath. Per department policy, the 100-foot ladder was never to be raised more than 80-percent of its length because beyond that, its structural integrity was a question. Veterans who had been at the top beyond 80-feet used the analogy of being lashed to a kite in violently gusting winds, at least eight stories above the ground.

"We don't have a choice, I'm raising it to 90-percent at 80-degrees," Tajirian radioed. The Lieutenant was about to object, then glanced upwards and saw the fear on the dozens of faces waiting for help and wavered.

"God help you, Ritchie."

"No choice, boss," he responded.

The tillerman moved the controls and the ladders slowly extended to 90 feet and stopped.

"Shit..." Tajirian said to himself as he realized the additional 10-feet was only going to get the ladder to the top of the window on number eight. He didn't look down from the turntable, knowing the concern he would see on the faces of his fellow firefighters.

The young truck man glared upwards at the worthless ladder, filled with rage. He knew what was at stake. He called to his best buddy on the Ladder 6 crew, Ken O'Connell to join him on the turntable. O'Connell scrambled up on top of the truck. The two had a brief conversation. Tajirian pointed to Ladder 3 and Ladder 4, parked at the south and center wings where crews were raising their 100-foot ladders and would face the same problem. Not one of them was going to be able to reach number nine. Even as the thought came to him, he looked over at Engine 3 and saw Lieutenant Dave Meade barking into his radio transmitter, no doubt telling Dispatch that the ladder situation was hopeless. At the top of the hundred footer was Tajirian's friend, Sebby Lombardo with his arms outstretched, clearly asking "What the hell do I do now?"

Ritchie knew he had to do something. Hearing the screaming of the people above him was making his stomach churn.

The crowd below watched as O'Connell shook his head vehemently and argued with the younger man, but it was clear Tajirian's mind was made up. O'Connell finally shrugged his shoulders and shook his head, yes. He patted the tillerman on the shoulder.

Tajirian grabbed an axe and scampered up the steps with the agility of a monkey. Despite his heavy gear, he reached the top in record time, slowing only to deal with the dangerous swaying at the top of the last extension. Then he looked down and waved his free hand, giving O'Connell a signal.

While the crowd of firefighters who had gathered around Ladder 6 waiting to climb up behind Tajirian the minute he got inside watched, O'Connell abruptly grabbed two levers and raised the ladder to its full 100-foot extension and to a nearly completely vertical position. Ritchie Tajirian was now atop the fully extended ladder, raised in a near perpendicular position, precariously over its rated capacity.

There was a gasp from his comrades who couldn't believe what they were witnessing. Tajirian was holding on for dear life as he climbed the last couple of rungs practically straight up into the air holding on to the axe, the ladder dangerously swaying. The firefighter finally grasped the fly tips at the end of the ladder and realized that he was still short of the ninth floor window. Well short.

Eight feet, to be exact.

"Holy mother of Jesus," he said to himself, looking at the distance separating him from the bottom ledge of the window. Below, the firefighters who were mesmerized by the drama framed by the clouds and smoke above them, cringed at their mate's predicament.

"Dispatch, Ladder 6," Nolan reported, his voice quivering. "Please advise the Chief we've got our man in place and the ladder at absolute full extension. We're still at least several feet short of the windowsill on number nine, probably more." He paused.

"There's no way. We're out of reach," he reported, swallowing hard. "Over."

Walsh transmitted the news to Lee who closed his eyes in helplessness, trying to block out the vision of the potential victims waiting for rescue. Only God knew how many had already died because help couldn't reach them. Now it was all but certain there would be many more.

"Dispatch, Car 1," he began to respond, his mind racing with what to tell his officer. Ultimately, he didn't need to say anything.

As the crowd of firefighters, mostly hardened veterans who thought they had pretty much seen it all watched from below, Tajirian didn't wait for instructions.

"Aw shit," he said under his breath in complete frustration, but knowing exactly what he had to do.

"My mother's going to be pissed, but what the hell," the young firefighter said out loud to no one in particular, the roar of the wind wiping away his words. "This is what I get paid for." He clenched his eyes shut and whispered an Irish prayer one of his buddies had taught him the very first day on the job.

"Lord between us and all harm."

He thought one more second.

"That's all I got Lord," he pleaded. "Gimme a break here, huh?"

Carefully, Tajirian climbed up another rung, leaving only one remaining. The aluminum ladder teetered. With one hand holding onto a step, he yelled to a young nurse above to lean down as far as she could and take the axe out of his extended arm. She reached down and just barely managed to grasp it. He did the same with his helmet.

Then, with his hands free, the firefighter reached up and with the fingertips of both hands, grabbed hold of the mortar joints between the glazed white colored brick that was the signature of the hospital. Ever so cautiously, with only his feeble hold of the shallow spaces between the courses of brick keeping him balanced on the ladder, he managed to slowly pull himself up. Carefully, as if in slow motion, he raised each of his legs and stepped onto the very last rung of the ladder. Tajirian was now prone against the side of the building just under the ninth floor window, his face pressed against the bricks.

He forced himself to look up to see how far short he was of the windowsill, but saw instead a half dozen arms reaching out from the room above him, people frantically reaching to pull him inside.

"No," he screamed. "Not yet, you'll knock me over." The arms instantly disappeared back inside. He was still a couple of feet short. Jesus, Lord he thought. Weren't you listening? I just need a little help here. He cursed to himself at the near hopelessness of his situation.

Not that it was going to stop him.

"There's no choice," he hollered up. "I'm going to have to try and jump for the edge of the window sill." He heard someone above him say, "Oh, no," in panic, but ignored it. He stopped for a minute to think it through, looking for another option, then shook his head. There wasn't one.

It was time to focus.

Tajirian waited a moment, filling his lungs with air. He looked up again and hollered to the people above him.

"If I make it, then you'll have to grab me and pull me in. You guys up to it?" he said with the best fake grin he could muster. Inside, his heart was pounding, but there wasn't a shadow of fear in his eyes or on his face. He'd made up his mind.

"We're going to do this on the count of three, got it?" he said to the small army of people waiting to make a grab for the firefighter when he lunged for the window.

"Yah, yes, ok," came a chorus of half-hearted responses from a group of people who by now had just about given up hope. None of them thought he could make it.

Chief Lee watched in horror, suddenly realizing what his junior man was about to do.

"Dispatch, Car 1," he radioed frantically.

"One," the young firefighter called out even as Lee was calling to stop him.

"Dispatch here, Car 1," Dick Walsh responded.

"Dispatch, inform Ladder 6 there's got to be a better way," Lee said. "Order that man to stand down, immediately, he is not to jump," he said. "Over."

"Two," Tajirian hollered, readying for the leap. Above him, hands reached as far out from the window as possible in anticipation of grabbing the man who was about to do something insane.

"Roger that, Car 1," Walsh responded and transmitted the instructions to Dan Nolan in the cab of the Ladder truck.

Nolan keyed his transmitter to respond.

"Rog.." he began.

Before Nolan could finish his response, Ritchie Tajirian, who became a firefighter because he wanted to help people who needed help the most, threw caution to the wind

"Three!" he screamed.

To the crowd below, it was as if time stood still and the world became absolutely silent.

Maybe it was his small stature.

Maybe it was the strength of the spring in his legs.

Maybe it was the determination in his heart.

Maybe it was God telling him, "Today is not your day to die, son."

Whatever it was, however it happened, Tajirian leapt off the very top rung of a 100-foot long aluminum ladder and with the fingers of one hand barely managed to grab hold of a thin metal window ledge on number nine.

He hung there for just seconds, but it was a lifetime for him and the hundreds of eyes watching him from below in awe and amazement at his bravery. In those few seconds he was virtually suspended in space until the frantic hands of the patients and staff inside the room on floor nine could secure their hold on him and drag him up the side of the building and over the windowsill, where he fell to the floor in a heap.

Slightly dazed, he looked up at the shocked looks of the people who had pulled him in and slowly grinned at their smoke covered faces.

No one said a word. There weren't words to describe what they had just witnessed.

Of all people, it was Trajirian who broke the ice.

"Christ, it's been a shitty day, huh?" he said in greetings and incredibly, the dozen or so people in the room, trapped in a seemingly hopeless situation and just minutes from death, broke into gales of laughter.

Below, a roar of astonishment rose from the crowd as deafening as the voice of approval heard at a tickertape parade on New York City's Broadway for the country's newest hero. In the south end of the small city of Hartford on this afternoon, there was no question about who was the hero of the hour. He wasn't Irish, but the name Tajirian would be the toast of every Pub in the city on this night.

Lee shook his head in amazement.

"Well I'll be damned," he said into his radio, shaking his head. He looked skyward, thanking his maker for saving one of his men, and for giving him guys like Ritchie Tajirian to command.

Realizing other Ladder men might try the same stunt, Lee didn't hesitate to give new instructions.

"Dispatch, Car 1," he bellowed into the microphone. "Instruct Ladders 1, 3 and 4 that we have a man inside. Repeat, we have a man inside number nine. Under no circumstances should they attempt to make access from the ladders. We are out of reach. Instruct the man at the top of their aerials to hold their positions, but to get close enough to communicate to the entrapped occupants ways of keeping smoke and fire out of their rooms. "

Lee paused while Walsh forwarded his directive to the men working the radio in each apparatus.

"Dispatch, Car 1, with further instructions. Have the remaining crews of Ladder 3 and 4 go to number eight. Begin evacuating the floor as advised by the head nurse and the hospital fire marshall. Instruct Deputy Chief Mullins to assume command of the rescue effort on number eight.

"Have Ladder 1 take its remaining crew and go to the landing on number 10 by the north stairwell." Lee was using every bit of manpower he could muster.

"Roger that, Car 1," Walsh responded and relayed the instructions.

"Dispatch, Car 1," Lee called again. "Instruct all units in the stairwells to standby for further instructions. Awaiting a report from our man inside as to the situation. He'll make the call when we're ready to attack. Over."

"Roger that, Car 1."

Walsh transmitted immediately.

"Per order of Car 1, all units on standby in the stairwells hold your positions and await further instructions from the man inside," he said firmly, knowing that the crews waiting outside the fire floors were itching to blow through the doors and go to work. But that could be fatal without knowing what was waiting for them.

Inside the north wing of number nine, without thinking about the insanity of what he had just done, Tajirian looked out the window and beckoned to O'Connell, Nolan, Booth and Kelley to follow him in. As they arrived at the last rung, he reached down and pulled them inside.

Nolan smirked at the young man and shook his head in wonder as he stepped over the window transom. "Tough act to follow, Ritchie. Good work. What's the situation?"

"Heavy smoke, boss, but we can cure that. The door is hot as a bitch but the pressure isn't what I expected. This mother may have burned itself out or it hasn't gotten this far. I'm going into the corridor after I button up this room."

"Yell down and find out if we have a crew on the stairwell landing," Nolan yelled to O'Connell. "We need water in here."

Ken O'Connell hollered out the question, which was passed down the ladder by men coming up. Driver

Joe Skidd radioed Dispatch. Dan Kelley relayed the question to Chief Lee.

"Ladder 6, Dispatch," Dan Kelley called back a moment later with the answer. "Car 1 indicates Engine 6 should be on the landing, hooked into the standpipe and awaiting instructions. Also, Ladder 1 is currently making its way up the north stairwell to number ten, which appears to be clear of fire. Per orders of Car 1, instruct the crew of Ladder 1 to hold at number nine and join up with Engine 6. You will have 10 men ready to hit the north wing in five minutes, Ladder 6. When you are ready to hit the corridor, open the stairwell door if the situation is clear. Your backup will be ready."

Skidd yelled out to a man on the ladder to pass the word to Nolan, still in the patient room on the ninth floor.

Lee was pleased. He would have more than a full 10-man compliment to hit the north corridor within minutes with two and half inch lines, plaster hooks and irons. If they could hose down the corridor, evacuate all patients and staff, then they could open the north wing fire doors and attack the center and south wings. Lee still had no idea of the conditions that lay behind the one-piece north wing fire door but the heavy smoke that continued to squeeze around it and above the plenum told him it was still plenty hot.

Inside, Tajirian was barking orders to the survivors in the room he had gained access to with his amazing leap. Men on the other Ladder trucks surrounding the Hospital were doing the same.

"Run the water, wet towels, sheets, blankets and run them around the door and the floor. I'm going out into the hall," he told a horrified nurse. "Pull the door tight behind me when I leave."

Tajirian motioned to Nolan that he was about to take the step out. Nolan stopped him.

"Ritchie, you're only a few feet from the stairwell door. We got two Companies there – Engine 6 with John Larkin and Ladder 1 with Dwight Schaeffer and Frank Droney... at least seven more behind them. If the hall is clear of fire, go to the door and have the boys soak the hall. If there's fire, come back in. Understand?"

Tajirian nodded his head, but there was no way he was coming back inside no matter how hot it was in the north wing corridor. He knew there were dozens of people trapped in the north wing alone and there was no telling what the situation was farther down the hallway and crossing wings.

Just then, Joe Skidd sent word up the ladder that the crew of Ladder 1 had arrived and was in place on the ninth floor landing with Engine 6. They were ready to attack.

"Roger that boss," Tajirian said, then put his helmet back on and buttoned his collar. He opened the door and stepped into the east extension of north wing corridor with nothing but an axe in his hand. The young firefighter stepped into smoke as black as night and could feel intense heat on his face. No doubt about it, the fire monster was lurking close by. He turned left and slowly advanced to the main corridor, feeling his way along the wall. He knew he was in the main corridor when he ran out of wall. The smoke was so heavy he had to drop to his knees and suck what little air there was off the floor.

He looked left again and peered down the long hallway searching for signs of the north wing fire door. Although it was less than a dozen yards ahead from where he stood, it was completely hidden by the impenetrable smoke. There was no visible fire, but he could see an orange glow growing ahead and assumed it was in the area of the fire door. Tajirian could feel the pressure building up and knew it was only a matter of minutes before the door blew.

He turned around and ran the 20 paces back to reach the stairwell at the other side of the corridor, found the door and threw it open, startling the waiting crews on the landing.

"Larkin, Droney, hit it hard now," he yelled. "We need to get water on that fire door. I can't see it but it's glowing and I don't know how long it will hold!"

"Then get out of the way, son, we've been waiting for ya!" Tajirian heard Frank Droney's gravely, Irish brogue call out from the stairwell.

No sooner did he get the words out of his mouth than John Larkin and Frank Droney burst through the open door, backed up by two men on each hose, leading the stampede of firefighters with blood in their eyes. The two veterans were holding the fog nozzles of charged two and a half inch lines. They aimed at the ceiling first and worked their way down, soaking and cooling the combustibles of the north wing ahead of the fire door and kept moving. Nolan and O'Connell joined them as they heard the commotion.

Behind them, Mike McNamara, Billy Powers, Joe DelCiampo and Eddie Stroniawski provided back up and carried the lines that they slowly advanced into the corridor. Tajirian, O'Connell, Nolan, Dwight Schaeffer, Ed Grady, Joe Edmunds, George Murphy, Vernon Tyson, Joe Curtain and Frankie Zazzaro moved from room to room, seeking survivors and all issuing the same instructions.

"Wet towels, sheets, everything. Line the doors. And keep them shut," they ordered survivors who had managed to find safe refuge. Tajirian stepped into a room where the door had never been closed. He took one look and closed the door behind him. It was too late to help anyone inside. The smoke had simply overwhelmed the occupants.

Only a few of the first men to confront the fire had the advantage of Scott Air Packs. Droney had made sure the new guys were wearing them. The rest of the crew ate smoke without complaint. But even the hard noses like Larkin and Droney knew that a man without a mask could last maybe two minutes in the heavy smoke, then have to race to an open window and get air.

Droney called for help.

"Billy," he called out to Billy Powers. We need Scott Packs up here," he said, despite the veteran's personal feelings they were for sissies. "Get downstairs and find a phone and call Dispatch. Let em' know we're gonna lose some people without bottles." Powers hesitated, unwilling to leave his crew. Droney stared him down. "Get a move on, son." Powers nodded and ran.

A few minutes later, Chief Lee's radio crackled to life and Dick Walsh relayed the message. Lee immediately called Bob Martin who was inside at the Fire Control Station.

"Have Dispatch get Bob King's crew to charge every Scott tank he can and go get 'em," he ordered his driver. "Bring the spares with you and have them recharged as well. And Bob, see if you can get a report from King on how many men we'll have coming in for the night shift. Instruct him to order every available man to report to his company at this location. Got it?"

"Roger that, Car 1, effort is already underway." Martin responded.

At 275 Pearl Street, Lieutenant Bob King was working his crew as fast as they could move in recharging the depleted Scott Air Packs. He and Dispatchers Dan Kelley and Dick Walsh were also hitting the phones hard ordering in every man scheduled to work the coming night shift and "on call" status men. Many had already reported in after seeing the news on television.

Inside number nine, John Larkin and Frank Droney were advancing their lines slowly down the corridor. Finally they came to the north wing fire door, barely visible as the water cleared some of the smoke. Dwight Schaeffer and Dan Nolan came up behind them.

"Well, there's only one way to find out what's happening back there, hey boys?" the cool Droney yelled out to the three of them.

"Yah, I don't think this bastard has any intentions of putting itself out," Larkin said.

"Hey, Vern," he yelled out to Vernon Tyson, the first man from his company he saw. "Yell down and tell the driver of Ladder 6 to inform Dispatch that we're about to open the north wing fire door." Larkin wasn't about to wait for permission and quickly thought through the consequences of what they were about to do.

"Aim those nozzles high when we open this door," he yelled to Ed Grady and George McGann who had taken over the brutal job of wrestling the heavy, pressurized water lines and brass fog nozzles. "Here we go!"

Droney unlatched the fire door and immediately felt tremendous pressure. "Oh shit," he thought, but wasn't surprised. He tried to push the heavy door back into place to secure it, but it was too late. The fire monster knew an opportunity and wasn't about to let it pass.

"She's going to blow back!" he screamed out to the dozen men behind him. Suddenly, the deafening sound of a roaring jet engine at thrust burst over the top of the door and a massive wave of fire rolled along the ceiling above the firefighters who were now trapped in the north wing corridor in a huge backdraft. Unknown to them, an oxygen line had burned through in a room somewhere ahead, which was supplying the fire monster with a steady supply of one of its most critical needs.

"Get down!" Larkin screamed. "Back out!"

"Hug the floor," Droney yelled almost simultaneously, throwing himself down. He screamed to Grady and McGann on the nozzles of the two hoses, the only weapons they had to defend themselves.

"Hit the ceiling. Aim high! She's gonna roll right over us... god damn it..." Droney had his face to the floor, trying to find air to breath. The linoleum was hot on his skin. Above him, the raging fire monster raced along the ceiling, waves of flame dancing and undulating like a rushing tide in the shallows of a shoreline.

For an instant, he thought how beautiful the fiery scene was. But the heat that seared down upon him quickly reminded him that the beast would not be satisfied until it ate them all.

Flames blew out the window at the end of the north wing, scaring the hell out of Joe Skidd, who had reluctantly stayed behind the wheel of Ladder six to man the radio and coordinate with Dispatch, Chief Lee and Deputy Chief Poveromo. Shards of glass rained down on the truck.

"Dispatch, Ladder 6, " Skidd spoke into the radio transmitter gripped in his huge hand. "I believe we've just had a tremendous backdraft in the north wing. We have fire visible in the corridor."

Walsh transmitted the news to Lee who had seen the burst of flame out of the north wing window. His grasp on the transmitter in his hand tightened. There were at least a dozen men in that corridor, he knew. And once again, he had no way of getting them help.

Firefighter Joe DelCiampo crawled on his hands and knees and raised his head above the window, flames rolling across the ceiling just above his helmet.

"Joe," he screamed down to Skidd in Ladder 6, "she just blew back on us, think we have an oxygen feed. Gotta get it shut down. Do we have water on the south or center wings yet? Hurry up man, we're in trouble here." Skidd radioed Dispatch to pass the message to the Chief. He was boiling in frustration being stuck in the truck while his buddies were in a world of shit.

Droney, still on the floor, stayed calm, but worried for the couple of guys on his truck without much experience. The smoke that was billowing in to the north corridor was so thick now that he couldn't see more than a few other guys directly in front of him. Who the hell ever had the bright idea of making turn-out coats black, he asked himself. It couldn't have been a fireman. Where the hell was everyone?

Ritchie Tajirian, Dan Nolan and Frankie Zazzaro had heard the roar of the backdraft just in time and dove into what appeared to be a linen closet. One of them kicked the door shut as a wall of flame shot right through the area where they had been searching rooms.

"Dispatch, Car 1," Lee called. "Patch me through to Deputy Chief Poveromo, quickly."

A couple of minutes later, Jim Poveromo was on the radio with his boss.

"Jim, get to Tim Kelliher. He's got Engine 12 snaking a water line up through the center wing to the fire floor. They broke the windows out and he's got a hose roller hooked up but it's taking them forever – tough job. He just sent a man to report that it's going to take them at least another 15, 20 minutes. They're only to number four.

"You know what a bitch of a job that is, Tom," Poveromo replied. Timmy will get it done…"

"I've no question about Kelliher, Jim… but we need that line now. I've got guys trapped in the north wing and still can't hit the south side. God only know what's happening there."

"Get over to Tim and get his Irish up, will ya? To be honest, I also need him for another job, quickly. Understood?"

"Roger that, Chief. Over."

A few minutes later, Lee watch as Poveromo met up with Tim Kelliher in the all-glass center section of the High Building. He watched as he saw the Deputy Chief put an arm on the Captain's shoulder and talk to him face to face. Kelliher pointed upwards and shook his head as if he was arguing. Lee knew the man. Without even being able to hear the conversation he knew

Kelliher wasn't making excuses. He was voicing his raging frustration at the impossibility of the job.

Inside, Kelliher had heard enough from Poveromo. He turned to his crew pulling the hose.

"God damn it, get that hose moving you frigging probies," he chided the crew of Engine 12 and Engine 1 and the handful of volunteer male aides who had pitched in. "I've just learned we've got a whole shitload of guys trapped in north nine. We're their only hope. We've got five minutes to get water on nine. Understood?" There was no response. Only the sound of men grunting louder as they stepped up the pace of the back-breaking work.

In the center glass stairwell, the smoke was heavy even as low as number four. Thank God the windows had been smashed open, Kelliher thought. Every few minutes he had to lean out and gasp for a quick breath of fresh air. He could only imagine the smoke situation upstairs and knew the guys trapped up there had nowhere near enough Scott Air Packs for the job. They were all used to eating smoke, but this was thick, like soot soup. No man could handle smoke this heavy.

He glanced out to the turnabout in front of the main entrance 50-feet down for a moment, studying the miles of hose now covering the Hospital grounds and the hundreds of people scurrying over them as they evacuated the building. Then, in the midst of all the chaos, he saw something that took a minute to register in his smoke addled brain.

It was a dog. He blinked twice. It was still there. A great big German Shepherd lying in the middle of the horseshoe green staring motionless at the front door.

"A dog?" he thought out loud. What the hell was a dog doing in the middle of this bedlam?

# Seventeen

~~~ ~~~

*"We're too late…"*

"Car 1, Dispatch. We just got a call that a runner from Engine 2 is on his way to you to report on the penthouse situation. Over," Dan Kelley reported.

"Well it's about frigging…" Lee was cut off in mid sentence by the sudden appearance of a breathless firefighter, his face covered with sweat and blackened by soot. He was exhausted and trying to speak.

"Chief… Company 2…" the young man spit out, unable to continue from lack of air. He bent over at the knees, trying to catch his breath. The firefighter had run from the rooftop, down 26 flights of stairs and across the turnabout to report to the chief at his car. It was an effort analogous to the Greek runner Pheidippides epic run from the battlefield to inform his generals of the Army's victory over the Persians at Marathon in 490 BC. The young man had died after following orders. Lee thought in horror that he might see history repeat itself.
~~~

The Chief put his hand on the man's shoulder to steady him and yelled for Bob Martin to bring him some oxygen.

"Bob, get a mask on this man, quickly," he said. Martin placed a Scott Air mask over the firefighters face and air flowed into his lungs. After a few minutes of taking in giant gulps from the mask, he was able to stand up and report what Company 2 had found.

"Firefighter Marshall Slavkin, Engine Company 2, reporting sir," he said, still breathing heavy. "Captain Joe Boucher sent me to let you know the situation in the elevator penthouse sir." He put the mask to his face and took another deep breath.

"We had a couple of Scott Packs with us, sir, so the Captain sent Sonny Lewis and Jim Walsh inside to further ventilate the structure. The smoke was thick as friggin' sewage but worse was the heat coming up that shaft fried all the relays in the controllers.

"The Captain had Maxie McCullogh and George Wolk shut down the motors. If we get flame in the hoistway the grease on the ropes could burn 'em through and then the elevators would just be sitting on the brakes. And they ain't fireproof neither, Chief. If the motors catch, the ropes will definitely bur..." Slavkin stopped with an embarrassed look darkening his already soot-covered face, suddenly aware that he was telling the Chief of the Hartford Fire Department a lot of stuff he probably knew more about than he did.

"Sorry, sir," the firefighter offered.

"For what?" Lee said, looking the exhausted man in the eye. "Good report. Tell Captain Boucher that was good work."

"Thank you sir, will do..." Slavkin said, relieved. "We got Leo Delaney on a hose up there now, just in case we see any fire in the hoistway."

"What's the status of the cars?" Lee asked.

"Chief, five out of eight cars are non functional. The Machine Room is cooked. Most of that stuff up there isn't going to run again."

"Do we have entrapments?" Lee inquired of the still gasping Slavkin.

"Multiple, Chief," the firefighter reported.

"It appears that we have entrapments on elevators number three and six," the firefighter said and Lee just shook his head. The list of impossible situations he was facing was growing by the minute.

"Three is shut down on number nine – at the fire floor – and has three occupants who are in contact with the Lobby desk using the elevator telephone that is somehow still working. Six has five passengers, including a patient on a gurney and an elderly couple. The car is stuck at number eight. We've instructed all passengers to lie down or get as close to the floor as possible. The patient on the gurney is using a portable oxygen supply. That's all I got, Chief. We need to move fast because if the smoke doesn't kill those people, the heat will."

"Good job, Marshall," Lee said. "Report back to your company and tell Captain Boucher to stand by on the roof until I relieve him. You're right. Fire in the hoistway would be another disaster to deal with. Be ready."

"Roger that, sir," Slavkin said and turned to face the long climb back to his crew.

"Move fast?" Lee thought back to Slavkin's comment. Now there was an understatement. It was a miracle any of the poor trapped bastards were still alive with the density of the smoke and heat, particularly those passengers in elevator three stuck at the ninth floor. There was no way to reach any of them through the elevator doors on nine, and the situation on number eight was still unclear but it was a good bet there was at least heavy smoke in the hoistway even below the fire floor. The only way out on nine was through the escape hatch in the ceiling. Those people could ladder up to the 10th floor and then walk down the stairwell to safety. On eight, they could pry open or smash the doors if necessary to get access to the five people trapped inside. That is, of course, if there was no fire showing on eight. As of yet, there were no reports of fire any higher than nine. His bigger concern was evacuating patients up a ladder in a dark hoistway. He'd been there himself. People tended to panic when they got outside the elevator and found themselves in the huge, pitch-black open space of a multiple car hoistway.

Just then, the radio interrupted his thinking. It was Dispatch with more good news.

Dick Walsh didn't sugar coat it.

"Chief, just spoke to Joe Skidd in Ladder 6 at the north wing. Somebody from Droney's crew was able to holler down to him that most of Ladder 1 and Engine 6 are pinned to the floor and they've got four men from Ladder 6 trapped in a closet ahead of them with no way to reach 'em. They urgently need water from the center or south wings and Scott Packs. Over."

Lee shook his head, spinning with the calls for action and relief that were mounting up faster than he could sort through them and move assets into place. But hesitation was not an option.

"Dispatch, confirm the location of Engine 3 and Engine 4. Over."

A minute passed, then two. Walsh came back on.

"Lieutenant Burnes reports via landline on number eight that Engines 3 and 4 are located on the south wing landing on number nine, Car 1. Awaiting orders. Over."

"Inform Burnes that we have men trapped in the north wing," Lee barked. "The south wing may have burnt out enough to enter. Tell him to hit the corridor with everything he's got and advance as fast as possible. They may get relief from a hose pull ongoing in the center wing. Tell him to go now! Over."

"Roger that, Car 1," Walsh responded calmly, masking his anxiety over the orders he was about to pass on to the two Engine companies.

Walsh passed the instructions to firefighter Art Kieselback, manning the telephone for Engine 3's Lieutenant Frankie Burnes who had raced back up the stairs to nine to prep his crew and the guys from Engine 4. Burnes hadn't waited for the Chief's orders. He instinctively knew what Car 1 was going to order. He was followed up the stairs by another man wearing a big number "3" on the faceplate of his helmet. It was Lieutenant John Kelliher, older brother of Tim Kelliher, who had had been scheduled to come in for the night shift beginning at 6 p.m that afternoon.

John Kelliher hadn't waited for the phone call summoning him in for duty. He was in his car headed for the scene less than five minutes after hearing the news reports on the radio and hunted out the location of Engine 3, immediately reporting for duty. Although they were of equal rank, Burnes remained the man in charged. But the appearance of the older, experienced

Kelliher provided a big psychological boost to the men on the landing waiting to face the hell they knew was behind the stairwell door.

"Good to see ya, Lieutenant," Eddie Walsh yelled out, speaking for the group. "A lousy way to spend your day off though."

"There's no place I'd rather be, Eddie," Kelliher grinned. But every man there knew he wasn't joking. You couldn't keep a Kelliher away from a fire like this, when so many of his brothers were in harms way. It was in his blood, as it was for his younger brother Tim, and his father before him, all Hartford firefighters. There would be more Kellihers who would serve in the years ahead.

Burnes turned to the eight other men grouped around him from the two engine companies. Two of them were probies and their eyes were wide. He remembered that mix of fear and adrenalin. It could make you do things you'd regret – hesitate or move ahead blindly. Either bad decision could get you killed fast.

"Ok, boys," he called to them. "Just heard from the chief. Glad to have John with us. We're going to open this door and hit the floor with everything we've got. We have at least 10 guys trapped at the other end of the building and there is no way to reach them – except us."

He listened to the low rumble of concern that rose up from the group. Nothing invigorated a firefighter more than knowing a brother was in deep shit.

"We also have no idea what's inside there, guys. It's probably burned itself out some, but to what degree is unknown. We still have heavy smoke and there are a lot of trapped people. God only knows what else..." He hesitated and let his words sink in, prepping them for the worst.

"Danny Abbate and Billy Murphy take the nozzles. Joe Attardo and Billy Walsh from 3's and Joe Biancamano and Frank Stoto from 4's, back 'em up. You guys on the hose end, stay low but aim high. There's no telling what we're going to find inside, especially in the patient's rooms so think before you act. Let's not make the situation worse. Got it?"

Every man nodded his head.

Engine 4's Lieutenant Joe McSweegan piled on.

"This ain't going to be fun, guys," he said. "You probies stay close to the old folks," he added looking right into the eyes of the two boys newest to the crews. "This is one time it will be worth listening to their bullshit."

"Collars up, coats tight, hats strapped, probies," a gravely voice, scarred from years of eating smoke hollered from somewhere on the landing.

"Lines charged?" McSweegan hollered to the engineer on the standpipe.

"Roger that, boss," replied Tom McInerney, checking again as he said it.

Burnes and McSweegan looked around the landing, both wondering how many of them would make it through this. They probed their eyes, looking for signs of panic. They were good to go.

"What are we waiting for?" Engine 3's John Officer said, determination in his voice.

"Hit the door, now!" Frankie Burnes yelled and kicked open the stairwell door. The two hose men and their backups opened their nozzles even before advancing into the corridor, aiming high at the ceilings.

"We've still got fire!" Engine 4's Frank Stoto yelled, assaulted by the intense heat still coursing through the corridor as the fire monster was still feeding on the combustibles all around them.

"Hit the patient room doors, Danny," Engine 3's Eddie Walsh screamed. "They're burning through…"

"Keep us wet guys," Johnny Baine from Engine 4 yelled. He and Eddie Walsh, John Slattery and Bill Walsh moved ahead of the hosemen, kicking in doors that weren't burning to check for survivors.

"Close the door, you're letting in smoke!" A nurse screamed as the door to the patient room in which she and a half a dozen other survivors were hiding suddenly burst open. John Slattery was only too happy to oblige.

In other rooms, there was no reception. The firefighters lost count of the number of bodies they found. Still they pressed on.

As the 10 men of the two engine companies blew into the south wing of the still raging fire on the ninth floor and Lee waited for their report, the chief turned his attention back to the elevator situation. And he desperately needed more guys with serious experience. Lee knew where to look.

"Car 1 to Dispatch. Over."

"Dispatch, Car 1. Dan Kelley, sir. Over."

"What's the status on Box 417? Can any of the apparatus assigned be relieved for new assignment? Over."

"Standby, Car 1," Walsh responded and contacted District Chief Shortell, still off line at Zion and Ward.

"Car 1, Dispatch."

"Dispatch, Car 1," Lee responded, crossing his fingers.

"Car 1, per District Chief Shortell, Box 417 is still active as we speak, although the fire is under control. But all units remain committed."

Damn it, Lee thought. Another idea hit him.

"Dispatch, where is Ladder 5 and who is the senior officer? Over."

"Ladder 5 has been moved from Sisson Avenue to 275 Pearl and is on standby. The senior officer is Lieutenant King. He's overseeing the Scott Air Pack replenishment and calling in the night guys, chief, per your orders. Over."

"I'm losing it," Lee thought to himself. He was moving so many men so fast he was forgetting who was where. And what the hell was happening on the south wing, he suddenly thought. He'd had no report from Engines 3 and 4.

"Bob King?" Lee focused again. One thing at a time. "Dispatch, per my orders move Ladder 5 to Box 5141 immediately.

"Transmitting. Over," Dan Kelley responded.

"Have Lieutenant King and his crew relieve Captain Kelliher and add the crew of Ladder 5 to the hose pull to the center wing on number nine. Instruct King to get to a landline and contact me immediately. Over."

"Roger that, Car 1. Transmitting. Also, Car 1, be advised we just had a call from Deputy Chief Clinton Hughes in Wethersfield. Over."

"Jiggs Hughes?" Lee said in surprise.

"Roger that, Car 1," Kelley responded. "He's been monitoring our 3-3 situation and has offered mutual aid. Said he could have a piece and a crew anywhere in the city you need within 20 minutes. Over."

Lee finally had fleeting reason to smile. It was not unlike the Wethersfield Deputy Chief to respond as he had. It was only five years before when Hartford had come to the aid of the small neighboring town, bordering the city's south end, when a massive, four alarm fire struck the Wethersfield Lumber Yard. Hartford had sent apparatus and manpower along with several other local volunteer fire departments when virtually all of Wethersfield's resources were locked in a four-hour battle to knock out the biggest fire in its history. Lee and Hughes had become good friends as a result. The Hartford Chief even drove across the City line occasionally to gas up his family car at Hughes Brother's Garage on the Silas Deane Highway. It was an excuse to look up Jiggs and his brother Speck, an engineer and rising leader in the Volunteer Department's Company 2, whom he also gotten to know well.

"Car 1, Dispatch. Let Chief Hughes know that his help would be greatly appreciated. Our shorts are showing in the south end right now. A pumper and crew stationed at the new Franklin Avenue barn would give me some piece of mind if a Box comes in anywhere in the neighborhood."

Less than 20-minutes later, Chief Hughes and his brother Spec and five other firefighters arrived at the Franklin Avenue Station. Spec, an Engineer in the Department, expertly backed Wethersfield's gleaming Engine 2, a Ward LaFrance pumper into the driveway outside the new firehouse.

"It wouldn't be right for us to be the first piece in their new barn, Jiggs," Spec had commented when he refused to back the truck into the engine bay, following an unwritten code of etiquette that only the brotherhood of firemen would understand. Jiggs had nodded in full agreement.

At the Hospital, Lee managed to get Deputy Chief Jim Poveromo on the line.

"Jimmy, get Tim Kelliher on a line for me so I can talk with him."

"Roger that, Chief."

Kelliher, who was moving heaven and earth to get a hose to the center section of number Nine, spoke with Poveromo and quickly located a telephone. Dispatch put him through to Lee.

"Engine 12 reporting, Chief," Kelliher responded breathlessly. He had a fleeting thought that he was getting to old for this shit.

"Tim, we have multiple elevator entrapments in two cars, one stuck on number nine with three passengers, another on number eight with five," he said. "Make your way to number 10 and take command of the crew of Engine 10. You have five men there on standby awaiting my orders. There is no fire showing on number 10, only smoke. Organize a rescue operation, ASAP. We're running out of time, Captain. No telling how long those people can handle the smoke and heat, especially on nine. Any questions?"

"Clear as a bell, Chief," Kelliher responded calmly, hiding well the churning in his stomach. He was not a fan of having civilians climb 12-foot ladders in pitch-black elevator hoistways.

"Will the District Chief relieve me, sir?" Kelliher asked in genuine concern. "We're making progress here but someone needs to punch the buttons to make it happen. Over."

"Engine 12, you will be relieved by Ladder 5's Lieutenant King, hopefully within the next few minutes. Over," Lee responded.

Kelliher breathed easier.

"Good call, Chief," the Captain responded. "I'm making my way to 10 now using the south stairwell."

At 275 Pearl, Lieutenant Bob King, already a 10-year veteran of the department, had driver Eddie Sullivan pulling Ladder 5 out of it's temporary quarters even before Dan Kelley completed the transmission of the chief's orders. With horns and sirens blaring, the pumper shot up Main Street like it was on rails.

Ladder 5 was 10-2 on Seymour Street within minutes with firefighters Harry Keating, Andy Ouellette, Jimmy Steele, and "Melody" Mike Scherban completing the crew. Scherban was nicknamed "Melody" because he was always singing to himself. Today, as the 85-foot Ladder 5 truck pulled up on Seymour Street, with black smoke still pouring from the building and a hundred or more trapped survivors looking down on their arrival, Scherban was atypically quiet. There wasn't much to sing about.

King wasted no time in taking command of the demanding hose pull, which had now reached number six as he relieved his good friend Tim Kelliher. As instructed, he contacted Chief Lee on arrival.

"Bob, I got more shit situations than I can handle," he said. "That line up the center section is critical. We got at least 10 men stuck at the north end of that corridor. We must get a line to them. The boys from Engine 3 and 4 just hit the south wing but I think it's going to be quite a while before they're able to advance to the north. I got a bad feeling about this, Bob. Make it go away. Get a line to those guys. Got it?"

"Give me 10 minutes," King said.

"You got five," Lee responded.

"Roger that, Chief," the Lieutenant said and was off the phone without another word. From his location at Car 1, Lee watched King enter the center section and personally help haul up the hose.

"Bet the son of a bitch has it done in four minutes," Lee thought to himself.

Meanwhile, Captain Tim Kelliher had raced up the south stairwell to number 10 and immediately met with Lieutenant Joe Guthrie, the senior officer of Engine 10.

"For Christ's sake, Tim," Guthrie complained, "we've been sitting on our asses up here while the frigging world is going up in flames. My guys are antsy. What's the plan?"

"Couldn't be helped, Joe, chief's got his hands full. We got a couple of elevators full of people to get out, one parked on nine, the other one on eight. How many guys you got?" Kelliher asked.

"Tommy Burke, Vinne Dicioccio, Bobby Read and Billy DeMar. All raring to go, Captain.

"You got any more details on the situation?" Kelliher asked. "I was told that the passengers have been talking with the security guys in the lobby by telephone." He coughed. The smoke was heavy up here.

"I've confirmed what you know. We've got three people still breathing in elevator three stuck on number nine. There's another five in car six that is parked at number eight. We can get the people on eight out by just leveraging the doors, but they are relatively safe for the moment. The car stuck on nine is a more urgent situation, Captain. But it is imperative that we get water into both of those hoistways ASAP to cool down tthe cars. If those people don't die from smoke, the heat is going to fry them."

"We got a ladder up here yet?"

"That's why I'm alone," he responded. "My guys hightailed it down the stairwell to retrieve a 12-footer. It's going to take some time to maneuver it back up the stairs. It's the only way to get it here. The Ladder trucks can't reach us."

"Shit..." Kelliher thought. There was no telling what kind of shape the three passengers stuck on nine were in, although it was encouraging they were communicating by the car telephone. The smoke and heat inside must be god-awful.

"We need to open the doors on number 10, but that's going to open up the floor to even heavier smoke if nine hasn't been ventilated yet. To my knowledge, they're still trying to knock it down," Kelliher said.

"Don't think we have a choice, Captain."

The senior firefighter didn't hesitate. "Right. Let's go."

The two men ran the hundred yards to the elevator lobby, dodging doctors, nurses and other firefighters who had joined in the effort to evacuate the 135 patients occupying the smoke filled floor. They were pushing patients in hospital beds, in wheelchairs and some were even being carried. Both Kelliher and Guthrie were badly winded by the time they reached the lobby, neither man equipped with a Scott Air Pack.

Guthrie turned right into the central elevator lobby and went to the first elevator. "It's this car here, Cap," the lieutenant said as he used his fingers to try and pry the doors open. No luck.

"Hell, we need a Halligan tool or a pry bar, even an axe," Kelliher said. "No time to fetch a door key from one of the maintenance guys. "Go see what you can find out in the corridor. I'll try to establish contact."

As Kelliher began yelling to the stranded elevator passengers, a war was being fought one floor below.

The crews from Engine 3 and 4 had blown through the south wing stairwell landing to find the corridor still in flames and heavy smoke, but were able to advance slowly with two pipemen spraying the ceilings, walls and floors with wide open fog nozzles.

Frankie Burnes opened a door to an empty patient's room on the east side of the south wing and smashed open one of the windows. He yelled down to an engineer manning a pumper. He couldn't make out who it was but got his attention.

"Hey pal, Frankie Burnes, Engine 3. Do me a favor and call Dispatch... tell them to report that Engine 3 and 4 are located in the south wing. We still have heavy fire and smoke, intense heat..." The Lieutenant suddenly coughed and gagged as he tried to report, still overcome by just a few minutes exposure to the oven-like corridor. "Gimme a minute, bud." Burnes dropped to one knee as he struggled to suck in fresh air and keep from puking. With sheer willpower he pushed himself back to his feet.

"Tell him we're making some progress towards the north," he contined. "But we need Scott Packs, man, tell him we need masks. OK?"

"You got it, Lieutenant," the firefighter hollered up to Burnes and was off and running toward the Chief's black car.

Lee saw the big firefighter coming at him.

"Joe Carey, driver, Ladder 3 reporting for Lieutenant Burnes, Engine 3, sir," said Carey with some difficulty. He had just helped hoist a patient in a hospital bed down 16 flights of stairs and was already winded when Burnes yelled to him. He bent at the waist for a few seconds, taking deep breaths, then addressed the Chief. He repeated Burn's message to Lee almost verbatim.

There were times the chief hated his job. Especially like now when it demanded that he facelessly bark orders through a radio that forced men to put their lives on the line. Sometimes he hated the security "Car 1" gave him. Right now, he'd give anything to be up on number nine doing the real work and eating smoke.

"Lieutenant Martin, Car 1. Over."

"Martin here, Car 1." The Chief's driver was weaving in and out of traffic with a carload of Scott Air Packs that had just been replenished at 275 Pearl Street.

"Where the hell are those bottles and masks for the guys on nine, for Christ's sake?" Lee demanded, losing his patience.

"Working the problem as fast as we can, Car 1. District Chief Pomovera had Dispatch put a call into the State Police to lend a hand. We've got troopers ferrying Scott Packs now and I'm two blocks away with a car load, Chief."

"Good work, Bob. Getting the 'Staties' involved was a good idea. But get whatever masks you can to the south and north stairwells on nine on the double. I don't care if the friggin' Governor delivers them. Over."

"Roger that, Car 1," Martin responded, allowing himself a grin.

"And order the Maintenance Shop Division to get their trucks in here to take over the air replenishment problem, on the double," Lee said, moving the equipment to replenish Scott Air Packs on site. We can't keep waiting on these or we're gonna lose a guy."

"Roger that as well, Car 1. Transmitting now."

Suddenly, Big Joe Carey was back in Lee's face.

"Sorry to interrupt, sir, but I've got a new message from Lieutenant Burnes, Engine 3," Carey said, breathing heavy.

"You ok, son?" Lee inquired of the Lieutenant.

"Fresh as a daisy but could use a good blow, Chief... we all could. Burnes said to tell you the good news is they're still advancing on this mother. Slow going, but moving."

'That's the good news?" Lee said, hoping for more." Afraid so, Chief," Carey said and hesitated. "Tell me," Lee said, bracing himself.

"The bad news is the guys from 3 and 4 have found multiple fatalities. They're going room to room. Burnes said it's going to be a big number."

Carey hesitated again. There was a long pause and for the chief, silence as he tuned out the chaotic world of sirens, horns and screaming people all around him, thinking only of Carey's final words.

"Lieutenant Burnes told me to tell you..." The big man had trouble finishing his sentence.

"What, Joe?" Lee demanded. Carey looked up at the Chief, shaking his head.

"He told me to tell you that we were too late."

# Eighteen

~~~ ೨ ~~~

*"Nothing needed to be said..."*

By now, a steady stream of patients, those whose medical conditions made it possible for them to be discharged without endangering their well being were being led or wheeled into the lobby from various floors throughout the hospital. Most were walking but there were some being assisted by nurses, aides, doctors, firemen, state or local policemen who joined in the massive evacuation operation. Some walked down the stairs holding the hand of a nurse, others were carried down multiple flights of stairs in the arms of an oversized fireman or cop, still others were carefully maneuvered down the narrow, smoky stairwell still in their beds or in wheelchairs by teams of men and women. Every available pair of hands was pressed into service. Perhaps the scale was less impressive, but for those saved it was an effort no less admirable than the evacuation of Dunkirk in the spring of 1940, when ordinary civilians came to the rescue of trapped Allied
~~~

forces and probably saved Britain from Hitler's grasp. People did extraordinary things spontaneously. Nothing needed to be said.

Nearly 800 people were patients in the Hospital that day, not including those in temporary rooms in the Emergency Room. T. Stewart Hamilton made the decision to evacuate everyone possible from his hospital. But that was going to take some doing.

There were those who could be moved, and those who couldn't. The critically ill, those in surgery or post op, in the intensive care unit, and women in labor would only be evacuated if absolutely required, Hamilton decided, only if they were in danger. Anyone else, those who could be treated at other hospitals or continue their recovery at home would be evacuated as soon as possible.

With a series of telephone calls, he put the operation into motion. Neighboring hospitals St. Francis and Mount Sinai opened their doors to take patients who could be evacuated but needed continuing care. Family members were called to help transport those who could be released. Hospital staff, including doctors, began driving patients to their homes. That night and into the next day, hospital staff doctors would visit every patient released to home care to check on their well being and to see if admission to another hospital might be necessary.

Bizarrely, as patients still trapped on the burning ninth floor watched helplessly, a long line of ambulances and hearses began queuing up on Seymour Street.

In the Emergency Room, Stewart issued the same instructions. Treat patients as quickly as possible and release them, or if necessary, arrange for admission to

St. Francis or Mount Sinai Hospital's. That included Charles Whitemore, who had been brought in earlier that morning after being run down by a speeding car off Franklin Avenue.

Whitemore had regained consciousness shortly after arriving at the ER and miraculously had no serious injuries other than a concussion, a gash in the back of his head, facial lacerations and bumps and bruises. He was one lucky man. But you wouldn't know it from the way he was carrying on.

At the moment, he was being held by the Hospital for observation because of the concussion. A surgeon had stitched up his scalp and the Korean War veteran was fully conscious and aware of his surroundings.

Unfortunately, with no way of knowing, the Hospital staff was unaware that Whitemore suffered from severe emotional issues from his war experience and just thought his odd behavior was the man's nature. They were also unaware of the existence of his best pal, his German Shepherd, "Sarge," whom he called for incessantly. He was so agitated and worried at the unknown whereabouts and safety of his dog that a doctor ordered him to be sedated.

Whitemore finally succumbed to the mild tranquilizer that he had been given, despite his best efforts to fight it off and go searching for the only being in his life that meant anything to him. The drug eventually took hold and he slept, completely oblivious to the fact that the room in which he was being held carried the strong smell of smoke, which was stirring up the staff with worry. Instead, the Veteran dozed, dreaming only of his beloved companion. If he'd been able to look outside, he would have seen Sarge still waiting for him, hours after his master had been admitted to the ER, lying on the green in the center of the turnabout in front of the hospital. Despite the chaos around him, with hundreds of patients, staff, fire and policemen milling about, Sarge never flinched. His eyes remained glued to the door where he saw people coming and going.

Young Tim Kelliher Jr., breathless after hopping off a bus on Main Street and racing through Bushnell Park, had arrived just moments before his father, Tim Sr. was relieved of commanding the hose pull through the center wing windows to number nine. The boy blew through a police line set up on Seymour Street despite the protestations of a number of cops who had no time to chase the kid. Suddenly he found himself in the turnabout green, standing amidst the miles of hose crisscrossing the entire front of the hospital building.

It was fate that amidst all the commotion and urgency surrounding him, that as he intensely scanned the building for signs of his father, he happened to look up to the fourth floor. There was his dad, safe and barking orders. The young boy was relieved to the point of tears to see his father and watched as he shook the hand of Lieutenant King, a great family friend whom he knew well and admired immensely. Tim Jr. had no idea what was transpiring, only that the father he adored was safe and obviously had just received a new assignment. If he'd known what it was, he wouldn't have felt so good.

Unconsciously, the boy walked slowly towards the hospital, mesmerized by the sight of his father and oblivious to the bedlam surrounding him. He suddenly tripped over something large and soft at his feet and tumbled to the ground, looking up to stare into the face of a very large, very hairy dog, growling with his teeth bared. It was Sarge, and he was in no mood to play.

Kelliher slowly backed away from the Shepherd and rose to his knees, never taking his eyes off the anxious dog.

"Whoa, boy, what are you doing here?" he said to Sarge, who only growled in response.

"It's OK, buddy, I'm not going to hurt you, I promise," the boy said and reached out his hand to pet the frightened animal. Sarge snapped half-heartedly at the attempt. He was frightened and anxious for his owner.

"Betcha you're waiting for someone," the young Kelliher said to the dog. "Someone inside."

He knew there was no way he was going to get by the cops at the front door and he wouldn't know where to begin to look for his owner anyway. Tim had another thought.

"You know what, buddy, I'm waiting for someone myself. My father. He's one of the guys inside fighting the fire. He's a Captain," he said with pride.

"Why don't we wait together?"

With that, Kelliher sat down next to the unsettled dog and reached out to pet him again. This time Sarge didn't react, other than to lay his nose down on top of his two front paws again and resume his rigid stare at the front door. His master would come for him. He knew it.

Tim was thinking the same thing about his dad.

# Nineteen

~~~ ~~~

*"Go, save those people…"*

On number 10, Kelliher and Guthrie had managed to pry open the doors of elevator car three with the blade end of a borrowed axe and were staring down the seemingly bottomless hoistway on either side of the stuck elevator, one floor down. Thick, black smoke was billowing out of the opening making the visibility almost impossible and adding to the urgency of evacuating the entire floor. Intense heat was also coming out of the shaft and Kelliher wondered if they could move fast enough to save the entrapped passengers. Soaking the two trapped cars with water was the first priority.

All around them was a desperate effort to move every patient off the 10th floor and similar operations were beginning on the 11th and 12th. Despite the chaos, Kelliher ordered Guthrie to grab the first two hospital aides he could find to help him drag the inch and a half hose attached to the standpipe in the north stairwell to
~~~

the elevator lobby on number 10. They had to get water, fast.

While Guthrie was hustling to get to the hose, Kelliher called down to the elevator stuck at the fire floor but got no response. Helplessly, he waited for the water line and the ladder they would need if the elevator occupants had any chance of survival.

Minutes passed. Kelliher's repeated calls into the hoistway went unanswered in both stuck cars. He feared the worst. While waiting, Guthrie used the landline established on the floor to talk with hospital maintenance to ensure that power to all the building's elevators had been killed and locked out. The last thing they need to happen was an unanticipated startup of the car they were working on.

Five minutes later, the four firefighters of Engine 10 jogged up with the 12-foot ladder that they had managed to snake up 20 flights of stairs through a mob of people being evacuated from the upper floors of the Hospital. Their faces were blackened by soot and each of them was sucking for air. Not one of them had the luxury of an oxygen mask. As they reached Kelliher, standing by the open elevator shaft, the four firefighters dropped to their knees. Two of them wretched.

"God damn it, we got any Scott Packs up here?" Kelliher hollered in frustration to no one in particular.

"Hell, no, Captain. You know we don't have near enough for the department," one of the men said.

"Son of a bitch," Kelliher mumbled, unable to do anything.

"Get over to a window and take a quick blow guys," he said. "Make it quick. I'm not always this generous." The exhausted firefighters managed a grin or muffled laugh but each took him up on his offer, struggling to their feet.

They were all back within five minutes, coughing badly, but able to perform.

"Guthrie's gone to get an inch and a half line from the stairwell. We need to get some water on those cars before we attempt to get on that elevator. It's probably hot enough to fry an egg on the cartop on nine," Kelliher explained. He pointed to two of the firefighters.

"You two guys help me get this ladder positioned in the doorway to the nine car. Let's be ready to climb down when the water arrives." He motioned to the other two. "You guys go see what's holding Guthrie up with that hose. Hurry up," he barked.

"C'mon, let's get this thing in the hole," Kelliher said with a scowl to the two men who had already picked it up at either end.

Slowly, the three men tipped the edge of the wooden ladder over the edge of the hoistway landing until it was firmly positioned atop the elevator car. The smoke was fierce and Kelliher was loath to send any man into the hole without an air mask and lights. But there was no time to get the equipment they'd need, 10 floors below. He knew that time was running out for the three people in that elevator – if it hadn't already.

More minutes passed while they waited for the hose. Finally, Guthrie, Burke and Dicioccio arrived dragging the line and Kelliher ordered them to put a constant spray of water over the two stuck elevator cars immediately. Vinnie Dicioccio grabbed the nozzle and opened it up. It was a struggle, but he was able to handle the inch and a half line himself.

Even through the noxious smoke coming up the hoistway, Kelliher and the Engine 10 crew could see steam come off the elevator cars as the water hit the overheated metal. They could only imagine what it was like inside.

Tommy Burke volunteered to be the first man down the ladder, dangerously slick from the constant spray of water falling on the rungs. Guthrie handed him the borrowed axe and down he went, one rung at a time. Billy DeMar held the top of the ladder to steady it while Bobby Read climbed onto the top rung, ready to follow Burke down.

It took a long ten minutes for Burke to reach the elevator on nine. Climbing down through the torrent of water in almost complete darkness because of the smoke made the going treacherously slow. When he stepped off the bottom rung, he immediately pushed the emergency stop switch on the run box on the top of the car and then hollered up for Read to start down. Neither man had any gear with them to tie off to the cartop to avoid falling off the slick platform. Their situation was extremely precarious.

Burke banged on the escape hatch with the butt end of his axe to get the attention of the occupants. From inside, he heard weak responses from at least two people. He pried open the escape hatch and peered inside the darkened car with a flashlight. Two soot blackened faces stared up at them, one standing and grinning, the other sitting in the corner looking very ill. Lying on the floor was a third person, a woman who looked to be far along in pregnancy. The man was caressing the woman's hair, softly, whispering that everything would be all right, but he was coughing badly. Read stepped onto the car top and shone his flashlight inside. He saw that water was pouring into the car but it was rapidly dissipating from the intense heat that was still evident inside.

"Oh, shit," he said, when he spied the young woman. Their situation had just gone from bad to extremely bad.

The occupant who was smiling was a young man who appeared to have it together despite what he had been through for nearly the last hour.

"How you all doing?" Burke asked the passengers. The young man, probably in his early twenties, responded that he was fine, just a little sick to his stomach from the smoke and heat but he thought the guy with him, who appeared to be somewhere in his seventies was struggling to breath and the pregnant woman had passed out twenty minutes earlier.

"She's still breathing, I keep checking, and she has a pulse," the young man said.

"What's your name, son?" Read asked.

"Donello. Donello Delorenzo, but they call me Danny," he replied, coughing. "I was here visiting my sister, she's having a baby. Did the fire get to the maternity…"

"No, Danny, no fire on number three or four. I'm sure she's all right," Read said to calm him. "Listen, we gotta concentrate on getting these two other people out of here quickly. You think you can give us a hand?"

"Sure," Danny said, breaking into a grin again. He was just happy to be alive.

"Sir," Burke addressed the older man who was still sitting on the floor. "How are you feeling?"

"Not so good," the man replied weakly. "Can't breath."

"We're going to get you out of here," Burke said. "Just hang on." He looked upward at Kelliher and Burke whose figures he could just make out through the smoke. They were backlit against the afternoon sun that provided some light through the windows across from the elevator lobby. The combination of the smoke and sunlight made the two officers appear ghostlike. It gave Burke the creeps.

"Cap, we need oxygen down here on the double. I've got an older man here who's in distress and a young woman, late twenties who's passed out and very pregnant."

Guthrie didn't wait for an order from Kelliher and ran into the corridor looking for any firefighter with an air mask. The smoke made it hard to distinguish anything but he finally spied a nurse who was helping to push a patient in a bed toward the south stairwell.

"Miss, we badly need oxygen for a couple of people trapped in one of the elevators. Do you have any kind of emergency oxygen bottles and masks anywhere on the floor?"

The woman, whose face and white uniform were covered with black soot, stared up at him and didn't respond immediately. She seemed dazed.

"It's really important ma'am," Guthrie said.

She shook her head, almost as if to clear her head.

" No...I mean, I'm sorry. I'm just trying to think where the oxygen tanks are," she said. "I'm so confused... wait a minute, follow me."

The nurse ran back toward the north wing and into what appeared to be a storage closet. Guthrie followed her inside. She threw open the doors of several metal cabinets, frantically looking for what he needed then suddenly said, "Ha... I knew they'd be here." She reached into a cabinet and pulled out two metal cylinders, each about eighteen inches long and a couple of masks and lengths of tubing.

"Here," she said, smiling at the firefighter. "These ought to help. If they don't… I can't…"

"These will do fine, ma'am, in fact they'll probably save a couple of lives. Thank you." He turned to head back.

"Mr. Fireman," she stopped him with a hand on his coat, her voice shaking. "Are there any… I mean has anyone been hurt or…" She couldn't finish the sentence. It was all so surreal.

Guthrie didn't answer, but dropped his eyes. She read his face.

"Oh, dear God, how could this happen?" she said, almost whispering the words to herself. Tears came immediately to her eyes.

"I'm sorry," the firefighter responded, turning away from her. He wasn't sure there was anything else to be said. But he tried.

"We couldn't reach them… I don't know how many…"

"Shh…" She held up a finger and pressed it against his lips. "Go, save those people." Guthrie turned and ran from the room, suddenly finding himself weeping as he ran back to the 10th floor elevator lobby with the precious bottles. The conversation with the nurse had brought him to a place all firefighter's desperately tried to avoid in the middle of a job: where the flames turned into faces and charred bodies.

He wiped his eyes before reaching Kelliher and handed the bottles to Billy DeMar. "Get these down there man, please, I need a blow," Guthrie said.

"On my way sir," DeMar said, stepping onto the ladder and beginning the descent.

"You ok, Joe?" Kelliher asked the Lieutenant.

"Yah, just need some air, Cap," and walked away, his shoulders hunched over.

It occurred to Kelliher that it would be a rough night for a lot of the guys here who would relive everything they had seen and done today… and the fact that they had not been able to reach the victims.

"Let's make sure we don't have more names to add to the list," he said to himself, turning his focus back to the three victims one story below him, trapped in a metal box in a burning building.

DeMar handed off the oxygen bottles to Bobby Read who dropped through the escape hatch and on to the floor of the elevator car, careful to avoid the woman. He leaned down and checked her pulse. It was weak but she was still alive. He strapped a mask over the prone woman, then passed the other bottle to Tommy Burke who did the same for the old man.

Read yelled up to DeMar.

"We gotta get this lady out of here," he said. "She's in real trouble. Way too weak to climb up that ladder and I don't think we have time to rig a sling to haul her up to the landing."

There was no response from his partners.

"Any ideas, guys? We're wasting time."

Nothing. Burke took over.

"Billy, we're going to hoist up the gentleman first." He glanced at Read who shook his head in agreement. Then he looked at Danny, wondering if the kid was going to lose it on him.

" You can wait a minute, can't you Danny?"

"No problem, sir," the young Italian boy responded without a sign of anxiety.

"Good. Maybe you can give us a hand, too."

"Yes sir," he said, coughing. "Just wish I could catch my breath."

"Borrow the mask from your friend there and take a few deep breaths. That will help," Burke told him.

The old man took off the mask and handed it to the boy. Delorenzo quickly did as Burke instructed and handed it back to the elderly man. It seemed to help.

"Ok," Burke said. "Bobby and I are going to reach down and grab your hands, sir and we're going to hoist you up while Danny gives you a boost. We'll have you out of here in no time."

But first he called up to Kelliher and Guthrie.

"Captain, Lieutenant... we're going to send the older fella up first. I suggest you send Vinnie half way down the ladder to intercept. That will give us a man for him to hold on to and one to back him up.

"Roger that, Tommy," Guthrie called back.

"But we also better get a doctor and a gurney ready for when we get this lady up to the landing. I think their gonna want to move her to Maternity or something," Burke guessed.

"I'm moving on that now," Kelliher called back into the blackness, unable to see exactly what was happening on top of the elevator car.

"Ok, Pop," Burke said lightheartedly to the old man, trying to put him at ease. We're going to hoist you up now on the count of three. Ready guys?"

"Ready," Delorenzo and Read responded.

"Ready Pop?" The old man shook his head.

"Then let's go... one, two, three!" Burke and Read picked the old man up and raised him shoulder high. From the cartop, Billy DeMar reached down and grabbed his arms while Danny got underneath the man and pushed up under his butt. DeMar helped him through the small escape opening then slowly helped him to stand. The old man held up his arms in front of his face to ward off the spray from the nozzle that Joe Guthrie was now aiming at the two stalled cars.

"Sorry, Pop, but we gotta keep things cool down here until we get you out."

The old man shook his head in understanding.

"Ok, good start, Pop. Now let's get you up the ladder. Firefighter Read is going to be right behind you when you start to climb and another one of our guys, Vinnie Dicioccio will meet you half way up. That way you'll be sandwiched in between the two of us. We do this all the time," he lied, grinning. "Piece 'a cake, right?" A slight smile came to the old man's face. He was anxious and weak.

With Bobby Read staying close behind, the old man began making slow progress up the ladder while Dicioccio moved down towards him.

When he got to the firefighter, he waved him off, pulling the oxygen mask off his face for a moment.

"Wait a minute fellas, I gotta take a rest, please," he said.

"We can't wait long, Pop, we gotta get that poor lady out of that car," said from behind him.

"You're right I'm sorry. Let's keep going." He put the mask over his face again. The old man thought about his own grandchildren for a minute and wondered if he'd ever see them again.

Slowly they climbed the last ten feet and after Dicioccio scrambled over the landing, he and Guthrie took the elderly man's hand and hoisted him on to the 10th floor landing. He was pale and was clutching his chest. Even with the oxygen mask he gasped for breath.

"Think this poor guy one is going into shock, at a minimum, probably worse," Guthrie said in alarm, holding the man up. "Hope the Captain has found us a doctor." Just as he said it, Kelliher appeared with a doctor, two nurses and a gurney.

"I think you're going to need some help, Doc, Guthrie said. "This man appears to be in some sort of cardiac or pulmonary distress."

They placed the old man on the stretcher and quickly wheeled him away towards the north wing where the smoke seemed to have abated some.

"Good luck, Pop," Read called from several feet down on the ladder. "C'mon Vinnie, we're going to need some help down there with this woman. I'll go back down with Bobby and Tom, you go and find a length of two and a half inch hose that we can use to make a sling, ok? Meet you down there."

Read just about slid down the ladder to the elevator and found Burke and DeMar already trying to hoist the young woman on to the cartop with the assistance of the young Danny Delorenzo. She was leaning against the wall of the car, propped up by Burke and DeMar. DeLorenzo looked on, badly in need of oxygen but refusing to complain.

"She can't stand, Bobby, no legs. We're gonna have to do this the old fashioned way," Tommy Burke yelled up.

"Let's get her up here first then. Same drill," Read instructed them. "Ready on my count… one, two, three!"

Despite her pregnancy, the woman was much lighter than the older man and the four men got her on top of the elevator car fairly easily. Read helped her sit down on the car top. But now came the hard part.

"Honey," Read said to her, "what's your name? I'm Bobby."

She looked up at him, her face blackened, breathing heavily into the oxygen mask. There was no response.

"She's out of it, guys. We gotta move fast here. Where the hell is Vinne with that hose?"

"What are you, blind?" Dicioccio laughed from halfway down the ladder, a hundred pound donut roll slung over his shoulder. The smoke was so bad, Read hadn't seen him.

"Way to go Vinnie," Read said and a small cheer rose up from inside the car. Burke and DeMar hoisted themselves through the escape hatch and then reached down and helped Danny Delorenzo up through the hole.

"Boy, am I glad to be out of there," the young man sighed.

"Think you can make it up that ladder, Danny? We need to get to work here," Burke said.

"No sweat," he said.

"Cap?" he yelled up to the landing. "We got a passenger on the way up. A brave kid. He was a big help to us."

"Glad to hear it," Kelliher said. "C'mon up kid. We can always use another good man." Delorenzo broke into a grin again and took to the ladder with a sure grip. He was topside within minutes and a nurse took him to a window to get air back into his lungs.

Burke turned back to the girl.

"She still breathing?"

"Yah," Read said, "but shallow. We gotta get her out, quickly."

"Vinnie," he said, "take the end of the two and a half and wrap it around her ankles, then around her waist. I'll get it around her chest and under her arms and make a sling. The only way to do this is to drag her up that ladder."

"I'm the biggest of us, I'll take the lead," Billy DeMar said, for once glad to be the big, burly lug his buddies kidded him about.

"We're going to have to wrap the sling around your neck and shoulders, Billy, and rest her on your back," Burke said. "Bobbie, you bring the bring the rest of the hose up to the landing and you, Guthrie and Kelliher can pull. I'll take her weight from the bottom. Vinnie, you get behind me. Everybody agree?"

They all nodded. There weren't many options they knew if they had any chance of saving her. Quickly they trussed the young woman with the hose then Bobby Read scampered up the ladder and shared the plan with the Captain and the Lieutenant. Another crew of medical personnel was waiting with a gurney. Billy DeMar wrapped a length of hose around his neck and under his shoulders and leaned against the bottom of the ladder as Tommy Burke positioned the nearly unconscious woman against his back.

"Let's go, Tom," DeMar said and took the first step up the rung, feeling the weight of the girl tighten around his neck. Burke pushed from beneath.

"All right, you guys at the landing. We're coming up. Start pulling," DeMar hollered up.

Slowly, cautiously but with fierce determination, the group began hoisting the woman up the ladder. DeMar had to stop once, just to catch his breath. The smoke was so heavy and he felt lightheaded. But he was going on, one way or another. The only thing that kept him from passing out was the spray of cold water that Guthrie still had trained on them.

With a mere five-feet to go, DeMar took a tentative step upwards with his right foot but the rubber sole of his boot slipped on the wet rung. He began to fall backwards before catching himself, but knocked Tommy Burke's grasp of the ladder loose. Burke slipped over the side and was dangling in mid air, both hands desperately clutching a rung. Vinnie Dicioccio reached down and grabbed Burke's arm.

"I gotcha, Tommy," Dicioccio yelled, but at best he had a precarious hold of his buddy.

DeMar was in worse trouble. All of the girl's weight was suddenly transferred to the lead man in the procession who was in danger of being pulled backwards off the ladder. Just when he thought all the weight was going to pull him over, he suddenly felt a strong hold on his upturned coat collar. It was Bobbie Read, who had launched himself from the platform headfirst to grab his buddy, while Joe Guthrie leaped to grab his legs. Kelliher sat on the floor and held Guthrie by the boots. It was a human chain, the links of which were precariously loose. A nurse spontaneously grabbed the hose that Guthrie had dropped in the chaos and aimed it back down into the hoistway.

"Tommy, swing your legs over and get back on the ladder," Read screamed to his crewmate. "I've got

Billy and the girl. I don't know who the hell has me, but don't let go, whatever you do!"

"Hurry up, Tommy," Dicioccio yelled. "I don't know how much longer I can hold you."

Burke managed to swing himself back on to the ladder and grabbed the girl's legs. Dicioccio pushed back up against him. For the moment, they were safe.

"Everyone take 30-seconds and regroup," Kelliher yelled down. The seconds passed. Then DeMar found his footing and managed the next step. Slowly, Tim Kelliher got to his feet, still holding Read's boots and pulled with all his might until the firefighter could finally stand again at the landing and grab DeMar's arms for the final few feet to safety. Once he was prone on the landing, Kelliher and Guthrie grabbed the girl and pulled her over DeMar's back and on to the floor. Burke and Dicioccio collapsed face first against the ladder frame, and DeMar sucked in great grasps of smoky air trying to breath. A nurse slapped a facemask over his mouth to get some oxygen back into his lungs.

A doctor quickly examined the girl, then motioned to the nurses to help her on to the waiting stretcher.

"We need to need to get her downstairs to Maternity ASAP," he said. "We're going to lose her and the baby if we don't stabilize her in the next few minutes."

A nurse shouted to him.

"Doctor, I think her water broke. Let's go."

"How the hell are we going to get her downstairs?" the doctor said, as he was giving the girl chest compressions. "Here," he said to another nurse, take over. I've got to get some fluids in her." He grabbed an intravenous catheter from a nurse and quickly found a vein, inserted the needle and opened the IV bag. She was badly dehydrated and in danger of going into pulmonary shock.

Without a word being said, Burke and Dicioccio scrambled up the ladder and joined DeMar and Read in taking a corner of the stretcher. They raced through the parade of people abandoning the floor and pushed their way into the south stairwell carrying the stretcher. It was less congested than the north and closer to the Maternity Ward. Despite their exhaustion, the four men literally lifted the woman and the stretcher over their heads to maneuver it down the staircase to the fourth floor. Nurses scrambled in front of them to ready a room and a team to treat her.

Within minutes, the young girl was in a prenatal intensive care unit, safe from the flames and smoke but nowhere near out of danger, surrounded by a team of doctors and nurses who were doing everything humanely possible to save her and her baby. The four firemen watched in silence for a few seconds, gasping for breath.

"Well, that's something we don't do every day," Tommy Burke finally said, grinning.

"Yah," Read laughed. But then Vinnie Dicioccio brought them back to earth.

"Hey guys, remember we got another problem on eight?"

"Oh, shit," said Billy DeMar and the four firefighters were once again running up the south stairwell where they found Kelliher and Burke already working to pry the elevator doors open on the eighth floor.

"You guys take a nap, or something?" Kelliher asked, looking to all the world like he was completely pissed off.

"Cap…" Read began.

"Get over here, you numbskull," Kelliher laughed. "Good work you guys, but let's get this one done before we take a blow."

Minutes later, the five people entrapped in elevator number six had been freed. They simply stepped out on to the landing, thankfully no worse for wear other than minor smoke inhalation and heat exhaustion and were escorted to the north stairwell by Guthrie. Mission accomplished.

"You guys all take a blow," Kelliher said. "Find an open window and get some air into those lungs. I'm going to find a phone and let 'Car 1' know the elevators are clear." He took a few steps away, then stopped.

"Hey," Kelliher said, turning back to the men. "Lieutenant Guthrie, you got a hell of a crew here. You'd almost think I trained them myself." His face was drawn into a deadly serious glare as he said the words, stopping Guthrie and his Engine 10 crew by surprise. Then Kelliher's face broke into a huge grin, not something the Captain did very often.

"My mother wanted me to be a priest," he said. "It would have made her happy."

Kelliher reached up and tipped the brim of his helmet to the crew in respect.

"But then I never would have had the privilege of working with bums like you."

He hurried off to find that phone. Lee would be pleased.

# Twenty

~~~ ❧ ~~~

*"First in, last out ..."*

On the north wing of number nine, the men of Engine 6 and Ladder 1 were making progress against the fire monster that only minutes before had them pinned to the floor and hiding in closets. Somewhere deep in the bowels of the building, maintenance had shut down the oxygen supply that was piped throughout the building into patient rooms. The oxygen had been feeding the beast when the firefighters opened the north wing fire door.

Robbed of new combustibles, its precious air supply gone and pummeled by thousands of gallons of water and dozens of men determined to kill it, the beast was dying. But it would do so begrudgingly, inflicting as much pain and destruction as it could before its last tongue of flame had been extinguished.

"Aim high," Frank Droney yelled to Ed Grady and George McGann who were still on the nozzles of the two and a half inch lines that were the only thing
~~~

between the dozen men in the north wing becoming new victims of the monster that effectively had eaten the Hospital's ninth floor. "We're getting there boys," he yelled in encouragement.

Most importantly, the pressure of the murderously hot gasses had abated. As they moved forward, spraying the ceiling, walls and floor, behind them nurses were emerging from patient rooms and leading those who could walk in a human chain down the north stairwell to safety.

In the center wing, Bob King's team had just reached the windows of the eighth floor with the hose pull.

"Ok, you guys, lets drag her up these last two flights of stairs to number nine and break through," he yelled to the crews from Engine 1, Engine 12 and Ladder 5 who had accomplished the brutal task of hauling thousands of pounds of hose up to the fire floor.

"I don't know what we're going to find when we get inside," King warned. "But I know we've got fire in both directions. You guys from Engine 1, head north until you find the crews from Engine 6, Ladder 6 and Ladder 1. Engine 12, head south. We've got Company's 3 and 4 on the floor down there, but I've got no idea of their status. Engine 5, use your plaster hooks and irons to rip out the shit in the ceilings. Me, Eddie and Mike will head south. Harry, Andy and Jimmy you go north with Engine 1. Check every room for entrapments. Ok?" He looked at their faces, searching for questions or doubt. King saw nothing but determination.

"Let's give those guys some relief," he finished.

With the line now charged from the standpipe at the front entrance nine floors below, King kicked in the stairwell door. Engine 1's Lieutenant Robert Lee, who'd come in after the Second Alarm was called, was on the nozzle and backed up by his Captain, Bill Kenney and Marty Conroy. They stepped into the center wing corridor hitting the ceiling with a blast of water that drowned the fire still burning above.

King's jaw dropped at the scene before him. What had been a pristine, antiseptic environment, with its light green walls and glistening, polished brown floors, had been turned into a nightmare of charcoal covered ruin. There wasn't a man in the group who hadn't seen the worst of what fire could do, but the burned out hallway of the hospital was a shock for them all. This was a hospital. It was surreal.

As ordered, Engine 12's Sal Tedone took the nozzle and moved south, Bobby Parent and Tommy O'Neill backing him up. Firefighter Clinton Rowland stayed behind, managing the group of hospital volunteers that were dragging the heavy canvas hose up the stairs behind them.

As King's crew from Ladder 5 and Engine 12 turned toward the south wing and attacked the ceiling with plaster hooks to drag down the last remnants of the burning, sugar cane-based tiles, everywhere they looked were signs of the fire monster's rampage.

Not far from where they entered the hallway they turned into the south wing kitchen to look for survivors and knock down flames that were still raging in the ceiling. The door to the room was broken off at one hinge, like it had been kicked opened with tremendous force, and hung cockeyed, leaning against the wall. A huge section had almost burnt through. Unknowingly, the very first room the firefighters had entered was the blackened remains of the dead end chamber where a helpless nurse dietician had run for shelter when the fireball had first hurled down the corridor.

Terrified, she had slammed the door closed behind her and grabbed a fire extinguisher. But the pressure from the super-hot gasses was so great they blew open the door and a wave of fire overwhelmed her where she stood. The remains of her body were still burning as Lieutenant King entered the room, the useless extinguisher still clutched in her hands. Only the stainless steel fixtures and counters endured as evidence that the room had once been a kitchen.

"Sal," he called to the nozzle man from Engine 1, "soak this room down, will ya?" he ordered without referencing the body. Sal Tedone got the message and silently used his fog nozzle to drown the flames still cruelly licking at the woman's body. He tried to be gentle as he hosed her down, the sorrowful thought crossing his mind that someone from her family would have to identify the pile of smoldering flesh and bones as one of their own. Tedone shook off the emotion as he and the rest of the crew backed out slowly and closed the door behind them. But he wasn't the only one of them who would carry the image of her agonizing death for a very long time.

The medical examiner would have to visit here before anything else could be touched, King knew. But all he could think of as they advanced towards the south wing was what other horrors they might find.

To the north, Engine 1 cooled down the remaining flames they encountered, mostly sections of ceiling that were still burning, kicking open treatment and patient room doors as they went. They moved fast through the still heavy black smoke, staying low where there was a little bit of air to breath. Unexpectedly, out of the noxious charcoal fog, they saw the outlined figures of the men they had worked so hard to come and rescue, framed against the afternoon sun that was streaming in from the west side windows. It was the team of guys from Ladder 6, Ladder 1 and Engine 6 who had been trapped in a fiery backdraft since they had opened the north wing fire door.

"Nice to see you guys," Frank Droney called out in jest. "You guys have a nice afternoon?" He coughed deeply. Black rivulets of sweat were running down his soot-covered face. The whites of his eyes, shaded by his heavy helmet, leapt from his blackened face in contrast. They were the eyes of a very tired man who had seen a lot today.

"Shit, must have been hot in here, Frank," Bill Kenney said, not finding Droney's attempt at humor funny at all, but immensely relieved to hear the Irishman's voice.

Kenney had seen the back of the north wing fire door and couldn't believe the intensity of heat it had held up to. If it had given way, a dozen firefighters and probably 50 more patients and staff would be dead now. Instead, everyone in the north wing had survived.

"All men accounted for?" Kenney asked.

"T'would be a lie to tell you we haven't lost a few gallons of sweat, Captain, but thank the Almighty that's all we've lost," Lieutenant John Larkin responded.

"Good stop, guys," Kenney complimented the exhausted firefighters. "You got Scott Air Packs, right?"

Larkin laughed then coughed again, fighting to keep the bile down in his gullet. He shook his head, no. That's all Kenney had to see. Jesus, he swore, he was going to raise some kind of hell about the Scott Air Pack situation when this was done. He wouldn't be the only senior officer to protest the unforgiveable shortage of a most critical piece of equipment for men risking everything to save a life.

"Hell, this ugly bastard had its way with us, Captain," Droney responded, not willing to be called a hero when he didn't feel like one. "We were lucky. There just wasn't much left to burn and we had good men on those nozzles," he added, giving a nod to Ed Grady and George McGann who'd been on the end of those lines.

Kenney waved off Droney's humility.

"We didn't lose anyone, Frank. That's a good stop in my book, any day. There wasn't a God-damned thing we could have done to help these poor…" he stopped, unable to go on. "We never had a fighting chance, any more than they did. We'll let the engineers and code geniuses figure out what went wrong here. But don't you hang your head, firefighter. We did all we could. None of us has anything to be ashamed of."

Quiet descended over the group. It was hard to call this one a win.

"C'mon," the Captain said, refocusing. "We still got work to do.

"Ladder 6 and Engine 6, remain here and help with the evacuation of everyone left in these rooms. Search the entire wing thoroughly. Get everyone down to number eight at a minimum. Lieutenant Larkin, get to a phone and call Dispatch. Have them alert Car 1 that the north wing is clear and we are assisting with evac." Larkin hit the stairwell.

Kenney looked around at the crews from five companies. They were all dead tired, barely able to breath in the smoke that still choked the corridor. It didn't matter. There were miles to go before their work was done.

"First in, last out," the Captain said to them, not having to explain any further. To a man, they nodded.

"Ladder 1 and Engine 1, let's head down to the south wing and help those guys kill this thing once and for all. Recheck rooms on the way."

King's team wasn't finding the going so easy. The hallway was still unbearably hot and fire, especially in the ceiling hanging above he and his crew was still very much in evidence. Sweat mixed with water as the Engine 5 guys tore what was left of the flaming tiles down to hose them. Smoke was still heavy and blinding, and they almost had to feel for patient room doors. They were charred badly; some had nearly burned through.

Where doors were open, they knew chances were they would find one of two things inside: the room would be empty – or it would be the final resting place for victims who had died a most hideous death.

There were no injured to be rescued. Trapped patients and staff were either dead or alive. There were far too many of the former. Even the battle hardened King, who had seen about the worst the fire monster could do in his ten years in the Department, was shocked by the number of dead.

Hitting hot spots as they backtracked through the north wing and as far as the main elevator lobby, Ladder 1 and Engine 1 had reached the mid point of the ninth floor heading south and miraculously had not yet come upon any victims. By managing to close the north wing fire door, Aide Bob Maher and Nurse Eileen Gormley Santiglia had saved countless lives.

But Frank Droney's heartbreaking discovery broke their string of luck.

"Holy Mary Mother of God," the Irishman suddenly said as the crew neared the south end of the elevator lobby. He knelt in front of the hoistway doors of car three, the very elevator where Tim Kelliher and the crew from Engine 10 had pulled off a daring rescue only moments before, one floor above.

There, at his knees were the charred, still smoldering remains of two people who apparently had been waiting for an elevator that never came. They were burnt beyond recognition, not even their gender being distinguishable.

Droney made the sign of the cross. There was nothing to be done. He too wondered what they would find ahead.

"Move on, the devil has done his work here," he said, stabbing a plaster hook into what remained of the plenum above the elevator doors which was still burning. Someone turned a hose on the burning drywall and the bodies without a word.

Marty Conroy was the first to say it, although loathing to having to give in.

"I need a blow, bad," Frank. "Gotta get some air."

Bill Kenney took a look at the bodies and suddenly felt his stomach churn. They all needed air.

"Everybody to the first room on the west side," he said.

"If the window isn't broken, break it. Suck up what you can in three minutes. Then we move out again."

Kenney didn't have to give the order twice. A moment later he heard the crash of a helmet against a window to open it.

Someone was letting his feelings be known, he thought.

# Twenty-One

~~~ ୬ ~~~

*"My God, what happened here..."*

On number nine, the fire monster, sensing the pincer attack from the north by multiple Engine and Ladder crews and the assault of Engines 3 and 4 from the south, made a last, ferocious stand.

There was little left to burn in the south wing, yet the fire and smoke continued unabated until Lieutenant Frankie Burnes finally identified the source. It happened as the two Engine Companies, advancing slowly northward, cleared the intersection of the east and west corridors and Burnes spotted an orange glow ahead in the dense smoke.

"This mother won't die," Burnes screamed. He called out to his crew.

"There's the source! We've got heavy fire shooting out of the trash chute. There's still a frigging blast furnace feeding this thing!"

The mistake was obvious. In Lee's haste to position men and assets all over the building and
~~~

prepare for any number of scenarios, the fact that the source might still be active had somehow been overlooked. In fact, there was fire six floors down in the trash chute that was still burning out of control.

"Abbate, Murphy..." Burnes hollered to the men on the nozzles of the two hoses continuing to pour water on the blaze and cooling patient room doors, "advance 20-feet and hit that trash chute hard. You can't miss it – it's the blow torch shooting out of the wall on the right." He waved forward four more men. "Attardo and Biancamano, back 'em up. Kieselback and McInerney, grab those hoses and give 'em plenty of slack."

Like a well-drilled squad of Marines, the six men put their backs into dragging the heavy, pressurized lines forward in a giant step toward the source of the fire. There was no hesitation. Every man holding the canvas hose could taste the victory that was only paces away.

Behind them, firefighters John Officer, John Slattery, Eddie Walsh, Eddie Kelliher, Billy Walsh, Johnny Baine and Frank Stoto were making careful forays into every patient and treatment room, closet and storage area looking for survivors and victims. It was more than the smoke that made them hold their breath every time they opened a door.

With the blazing source of the fire in sight, Danny Abbate and Billy Murphy let loose a torrent of water directly at the trash chute and kept advancing until they were literally standing directly in front of the 18-inch opening. They aimed the two nozzles, each spraying water at a rate of some 300-gallons per minute, directly at the open hole. The trash chute door had been completely torn off its hinges and blown clear across the corridor into a bathtub in a treatment room. It wouldn't be found for days.

The fire monster, only minutes before generating heat so intense that it instantly vaporized the torrent of water directed at it, began to weaken quickly. The sheer volume of water being poured down its throat would not allow it to swallow fast enough to sustain its raging heat. It was drowning.

From the depths of the trash chute came a piteous, yet blood curdling cry. It was the whining, tormented moan of red hot metal being doused with cold water. To those still trapped in patient rooms, it was nothing more than the sound of a fire being smothered. But to men who fought the fire monster every day, who faced its grotesque appetite for death and destruction in real life and in their dreams, it was the resonance of evil screaming in pain. It was a sound that brought a smile to the faces of firefighters everywhere, a victory symphony only they could hear.

Unwilling to give the beast even the slightest respite from their attack and any chance of recovering, the hosemen ignored the bits and pieces of flaming debris still dropping upon them from overhead, and continued their assault until only light, moist grey smoke was emerging from the opening. It was the last gasping breaths of evil.

The fire monster was finally dead. It was finished with Hartford Hospital, having done all it could to create a nightmare that an entire city would remember for decades to come, a lurid dream that would haunt 16 families forever, a trauma that even hardened, veteran firefighters would carry with them all the days of their lives.

Even as the last flames of the inferno died, from the north wing emerged Ladder 1, Engine 1 and half of Engine 5's crew who had needed to stop and break a window on the west side to suck in a quick three gulps of air. That's all it took to give them back their legs. They joined up with Engine 12 and the remaining crew from Ladder 5. Then the army of firefighters continued their advance into the south wing. Almost immediately, they came upon the skeletal remains of a person, presumably a nurse, draped over the counter of a reception desk.

"God bless her soul, the poor thing," said John Slattery, making the sign of the cross.

"From the looks of it, the bastard was on her before she could even think about running. My God, what happened here..." Slattery asked out loud as he looked around the charcoal ruins. There was no answer. His stomach, already full of bile and smoke, churned. He held back the urge to wretch, only the presence of his crewmates keeping it down. The bedraggled collection of men from a half dozen of the city's fire houses were fighting their own battle to keep from being sick.

But they pushed on, Frank Droney and his crew from Ladder 1 using their plaster hooks to rip down the last burning and smoldering remnants of what had been a pristine hospital corridor. In the hands of an experienced man, the plaster hook was a lethal tool used to tear out a plaster or drywall ceiling or wall. A Company of men would work long into the night to make sure every cinder was torn out and extinguished using the tool and irons like the Halligan bar. The tools resembled something out of a medieval arsenal.

Finally, through the smoke ahead of them, still heavy despite the cross breeze which had kicked up and was rapidly clearing the corridors through smashed windows, the brave men from the north wing saw the outlines of a crew ahead and could feel the mist of water spray in the air. They looked ghostly, figures on a most ghastly stage.

It was Droney who noticed it first.

While the team that had successfully fought back the fire in the north wing took some silent satisfaction that they had beaten the monster and were victorious in saving and evacuating nearly all of its occupants, the boys from the south end of the building looked not only tired, but beaten and defeated.

They were bent over, sucking air from the Scott Air Packs that had finally arrived only moments earlier, the sad, vanquished reflection in the whites of their eyes exaggerated by the contrast of the black filth covering their faces.

Ladder 1's Captain Dwight Schaeffer sought out Frankie Burnes.

"How bad, Frankie?" Schaeffer asked the crestfallen senior officer of Engine 3 who had battled through the worst of the south wing inferno side by side with his guys and the crew of Engine 4.

The Lieutenant dropped his head, shaking it. He could barely speak.

"Worst I've ever seen, Cap."

He was silent.

"A little girl, her mother and father, old timers, nurses…God only knows who else…I don't even know how many…lost count."

Schaeffer put his hand on the shoulder of the exhausted leader of Engine 3.

"You did what you could, Frankie," the Captain said. "Christ, imagine how many more would have died if you hadn't fought through this hell...but how did it move so fast?" Schaeffer muttered, looking around him in awe at the damage he was seeing. "We passed more in the center section. They never had a chance."

"Fire Door was wide open, Captain. Either never got closed or it was blown open," Burnes answered. "It appears someone tried to swing it shut. There's a pile of what looks like it might have been a person behind the door."

Schaeffer shook his head.

"We gotta get some priests up here," Joe McSweegan said softly. "Quickly."

"Roger that, Joe," Schaeffer responded. "Artie," he called out to Art Kieselback, "get downstairs and find a phone, will ya? Let dispatch know the scene is clear... and that they should send the padres right away." Kieselback disappeared toward the south wing stairwell.

"What 's the status of entrapments?"

"We've still got plenty of people left in rooms with the door closed. We're waiting for some of the smoke to clear, "Burnes said. "Some of them can walk, some will have to be carried down in their beds. It's going to be a long night."

"Yah, no telling how many floors they're going to have to evacuate," Schaeffer added. "But let's worry about number nine first and start getting some of the remaining survivors off the floor. Tell everybody up here not to touch any remains until we get instructions from Car 1 and the Coroner's office."

Deputy Chief Poveromo appeared out of the south stairwell. He was badly winded from climbing the stairs, overseeing the evacuation of all patients from the upper three floors working with Deputy Chief Ed Mullins. A man handed him an oxygen mask. Poveromo refused it, fuming inside that his guys had had to fight the entire way practically on their hands and knees looking for oxygen. If they didn't have a mask, he'd be god damned if they would see him sucking on one. He was already thinking about the hell he was going to raise with the City Council about the state of affairs of the department's equipment. But right now, he had other matters to attend to.

"I just gave the Chief an update," Poveromo reported. "He's going to meet with the hospital administrators now to see how we proceed. Don't know how many people we're going to have to move, but I suspect quite a few hundred."

Poveromo looked around the two dozen or so firefighters on number nine. He knew they had hours of work ahead of them, relief coming only as the guys from the night shift reported in. They looked like they were ready to drop now.

"What I do know is that after the coroner's office has been here and examined the evidence and taken photographs of the deceased for the investigation, we're going to move the remains down to number eight. We will set up a temporary morgue there until the bodies can be identified."

The Deputy Chief paused and looked down at the blackened, water-covered floor, trying to avoid their eyes. He needed to give them a minute, having just given his men probably the worst orders they had received all day.

Removing the remains of the fire victims was not only gruesome work for the firefighters, but each body they touched was another reminder of how they had failed to arrive in time, how they could not reach those who had perished.

They'd done their best. No one would ever know just how fierce a fight they had waged to save so many. But each and every victim was a reminder that having accomplished a miracle just wasn't good enough to fulfill the self imposed rules of their creed. What was it that John Larkin always said? His words, oft repeated in fire houses around the City and in his own living room, would make them all second guess what had happened that day:

"You gotta be at your best when things are at there worst."

They had been at their best in the worst of situations. But to a man, they would take little solace in knowing that this monster had simply had a running start in a place they could not quickly reach, or that no one could have done better against the odds that were overwhelmingly against them even before the first alarm had come in.

A sense of helplessness, a numbing of their innate belief that they were up to any of the fire monster's tricks, that they only lost the battle on those rare occasions when they made a mistake, descended over the dozens of Hartford firefighters who had played a role in stopping the rampage. Unconsciously, they allowed themselves a moment for the depth of the tragedy in which they had been pawns, to sink in.

For the first time, they looked around and saw the total destruction they had somehow survived, but also the horrific number of those who had not. Into each of their egos wormed a doubt that the enemy they fought each day was bigger and more powerful then they.

Some felt a shiver of fear.

Others, resignation – not unlike what a soldier, after prolonged exposure to the potential of sudden death, carries with him into battle.

And still others, despondency. If the beast they hunted could stalk and feed upon the helpless with such ease, in a place psychologically embraced as a cathedral of care and refuge for the sick and infirm, then there was no place exempt from its taste for flesh and bone.

There was not a man among them who was untouched by the magnitude of the heartbreak on the ninth floor or who left Hartford Hospital that day the same person who had arrived hours earlier, full of confidence, even a bit of swagger.

In the end, it was good that they did not understand the root cause of the calamity.

For to know that all the pain, loss and destruction was the result of an act of vengeance, might have driven them over the edge of reason.

# Twenty-Two

~~~ ❧ ~~~

*Could this really be happening?*

On the streets surrounding the hospital, the Hartford Police were frantically working to pull off a miracle of their own even as smoke continued to pour from the burning building: create some semblance of order out of the miles of vehicles gridlocked on Seymour, Jefferson and Washington Streets and Retreat Avenue. The job was proving almost impossible.

Already, more than 90 ambulances and hearses were stacked up on Seymour Street, ordered there by the Governor. Combined with the huge number of fire apparatus and supporting vehicles, utility company trucks and local and State Police cars already on the scene, the line of Cadillac-based ambulances and funeral cars made the main entranceway into the Hospital nearly impassable.

On the surrounding streets, which all served as main thoroughfares for the south end of the city, traffic was stopped nearly dead. Some of it was normal, mid-
~~~

afternoon transport in and out of the business district downtown. But most of the cars were filled with curiosity seekers and gawkers, or sadly, panicked relatives and friends of patients in the Hospital.

Desperate for information about loved ones, the hospital switchboard was ablaze with lights signaling incoming calls. Operators were overwhelmed by thousands of calls from people frantic with fear. Even if they got through, operators could provide little or no information. Frustrated, many callers drove to the hospital despite continual radio and television broadcast messages telling them to stay put at home and wait to be contacted. Hartford Hospital telephone operators and administrative secretaries were also trying to reach the relatives of some patients who were being discharged to arrange to have them picked up or to have transportation provided. The situation was nearly impossible.

Every available police officer was either in the building helping to evacuate patients, on the street trying to untangle the traffic nightmare or controlling the great crowd of onlookers who gathered as close to the scene as they could, just to watch.

For some of the watchers, being there had to do with making the "surreal" real. Could this actually be happening? For others, it was the excitement of it all, as if the circus had come to town.

The circus? Many in the crowd remembered how that had turned out in June, 1944 just as America was bracing for the painful victory on the beaches of Normandy. Others had to see it to believe that Hartford could be hit with yet another, strange, tragic and historical fire. The great, unsolved conflagrations that destroyed St. Patrick's and St. Joseph's Cathedrals had occurred less than five years earlier, stunning the city. What was it about Hartford and devastating fires, they wondered.

But little by little, control and organization began to take the upper hand. Just as the men whose job it was to fight the fire monster that would have consumed the hospital and every person in it if left to its ingrained, evil will to destroy – the police, the administrators, doctors and nurses, security guards, switchboard operators, secretaries, maintenance workers and kitchen help – everyone else who had a job to do, did it.

Outsiders, too, played a pivotal role in supporting the efforts to regain the hospital's footing. Red Cross volunteers, with the assistance of a Hartford Police escort to fight their way through the traffic gridlock hurried blankets and stretchers to the scene. The Red Cross Director, John Russell, and William Scanlon, vice chairman of the relief organization's Disaster Services, arrived to help direct the flow of supplies through the heavily congested fire scene. Even the Red Cross Canteen came to provide coffee and food for those waging the battle. Doctors arrived from all over the city, some to check on the well being of their patients, others to just lend a hand where needed. Hospital personnel who had completed earlier shifts came back to work without being called. There were even instances of former employees suddenly appearing to offer their help.

No one was above pitching in. Including the clergy.

Even before the coroner's office had arrived, a half dozen priests, a rabbi and a minister, all of whom had heard the news on the radio and rushed to the hospital, were escorted by Chief Thomas Lee up the long south stairwell to the ninth Floor. The religious men came to beseech God's forgiveness for the victims and grant to them eternal peace and pain from suffering.

Lee came to see with his own eyes if the horrors that had been described to him by his shocked men were real or imagined.

A brief look was all he needed to confirm that the last few hours of his watch hadn't been a dream, but a real life nightmare. He would spend many a long hour rethinking the decisions made and the efforts expended that fateful afternoon. Could they have done anything differently, anything that would have made a difference? Ultimately, that judgment would come from experts all over the country who examined the Hartford Fire Department's response to the catastrophe. Ultimately, it was universal in its praise.

After catching their breath, the firefighters began the second phase of their operations. The first was to kill the fire. The second was to complete the evacuation of all survivors still taking refuge in patient rooms. The third was to remove the remains of the victims. The fourth was clean up and salvage and ensure that no flicker of flame or a cinder of hot ash remained anywhere in the fire zone. That meant using the plaster hooks to tear down any remains of the ceiling and to rip out sections of wall that were suspect to be hiding potential flare ups. The work was brutally difficult in a filthy, still heat-filled environment, but the job wasn't done until they were sure the fire monster truly was dead. It wasn't until nearly midnight that the job was finished. By the time they were done, nearly the entire ninth floor had been completely gutted.

Although every city hospital had been put on alert and prepared for an onslaught of new patient admissions to make room for those displaced from Hartford Hospital, in the end, no patient was transferred.

Simultaneous to the steady stream of patients being evacuated via the stairwells from the 12th all the way down to the seventh floor by every available firefighter, policeman, nurse, orderly or aide, hospital administrators were taking steps to absorb those routed from their beds into other sections of the building.

Part of the process involved assessing what undamaged space was available in the building and the condition of every patient. High on the list were those who were ready or nearly ready to be discharged from any ward of the hospital. The administrators found considerable room available, particularly in the lower levels of the south wing, near the Maternity and surgical areas of the building.

Patients determined to be ready for release or nearly ready to return home were carried to the first floor lobby and given the choice of being discharged by private cars, ambulance or taxi. Of the nearly 800 patients still remaining in the Hospital, nearly two thirds were discharged. Those too ill to be released were relocated to floors unaffected by the fire. The exhausting trek of the firefighters, police and hospital personnel up the long, hot, water-drenched staircases would last until past 9 p.m. that night. At times, a river of water an inch deep cascaded down the steps of the stairwells as the evacuation progressed.

For the hundreds of observers crowding around the front of the hospital near the horseshow driveway, the magnitude of the disaster was becoming painfully clear as the parade of those to be discharged or moved to other locations passed across the glass staircase. It was a chilling scene, as they watched the massive evacuation in stunned silence.

Among the crowd, nearly invisible amongst the miles of fire hose snaking across the horseshoe green and the chaos and cacophony of moving men and equipment, Tim Kelliher Jr. and his new friend, the German Shepherd, Sarge, continued to watch and wait.

Barely an hour had gone by since Tim Jr. had arrived on the scene, but it seemed like a lifetime since he had last seen his father and he was on the verge of tears. The excitement of the fire was long gone for the boy. Now, as he saw the condition of firefighters emerging from the building, their faces blackened, gasping for breath and wretching from the smoke, he feared for the safety of the man who was his idol.

For Sarge, a great canine beast who theoretically had no sense of time, he only knew that his master had been taken from him. The human who gave him shelter, fed and cared for him and showed him affection had disappeared. The dog was confused by what he saw and the chaos around him. He waited with no less anxiety than the boy who unconsciously stroked the fur on his back.

Each of them had an emotional investment in the great drama being played out in front of their wide eyes. The two barely blinked looking for signs of the people who meant so much to them. The fact that one of them was a boy and the other a dog made no difference. They had something else in common, something much more important, a value they had each learned from the person for whom they waited.

In the Marine Corps, they called it "Semper Fi."

In the Fire and Police Departments, it was known as "Brotherhood."

Tim Jr. and Sarge only knew it as a feeling that made each of them want to run into the burning building and find the men for whom they waited.

It was the same emotion that made men risk their lives for each other, fight side by side for right, made fathers love their sons, sons love their fathers and dogs protect their masters.

It was an emotion summed up in a single word.

Loyalty.

# Twenty-Three

~~~ ❧ ~~~

*The whole thing was a dream…*

Impossible.

James Anglun stood among a large crowd gathered on Washington Street a block away on a slight hill overlooking the Hospital. He was far enough away that the chance of his being seen by coworkers was slim. They were all inside, he thought, working together, fighting the fire, already trying to recover.

Was it a fire he started? He knew the answer, but could not find the courage to admit it.

Impossible.

The word silently crossed his lips over and over. This could not be happening. This is not what he intended. This was not the kind of man he was. This was a mistake.

Would they believe him?

Would they understand that he only meant to cause a bit of mischief to embarrass his boss? To repay him for his disrespectful treatment of someone just trying to do his job?
~~~

He knew the answer to those questions, too.

No, they would consider him a criminal, an arsonist.

He shook his head and fought the urge to bury his face in his hands.

For God's sakes…they would forever brand him as a murderer.

Incredulously, he stared at the long line of hearses and ambulances. How many had been burned? There was talk in the crowd that many had died. Someone with a transistor radio shouted out that the body count was up to seven now. Seven? Seven people dead? Because of him? Because of his desire for vengeance?

Impossible. That's what it was. Impossible. The whole thing was a dream. If if he wanted to, he could walk back to the hospital right now, go to his office and get back to work. He was imagining all of it. He was in some sort of hypnotic state.

He was hallucinating. That's what it was. He was dreaming the whole thing, only imagining what would happen if he threw the cigarette butt into the trash chute.

He clenched his eyes shut for a long while, hoping if he held them closed long enough that the scene in front of him would fade away. The ambulances and hearses would not be lined up on Seymour Street. The horseshoe driveway would not be filled with fire trucks. The smoke would disappear. The smell of burnt flesh would not be palpable in the air.

Finally James Anglun summoned up the last drops of courage left in his soul, sucked in a deep breath, and forced his eyes to open.

And then he cried.

# Twenty-Four

~~~ ஒ ~~~

*"Please, I've seen enough..."*

By 4:30 p.m., slightly less than two hours after the first box alarm had come to the Dispatchers, the fire was dead, the smoke had largely dissipated and the whole operation had turned to recovery.

T. Stewart Hamilton, who had spent the better part of the last critical hour overseeing evacuation and reorganization efforts that would go on well into the night, finally made his way to the ninth floor to see the carnage for himself.

Accompanied by Chief Lee and Deputy Chief Poveromo, he entered the floor from the south stairwell fully expecting to see the worst. Still, he was unprepared for the alien world into which he stepped.

For an instant, he thought he had stumbled into a movie set. His superbly organized mind, that of a doctor and administrator for which all was required to be orderly and accountable, simply could not grasp the contradiction that awaited him on the ninth floor. This
~~~

can't be real, he thought as the startling images burned into his brain.

Hamilton stopped dead in his tracks, frozen in place by the sheer totality of the destruction. Later he remembered his first glimpse of the burned out corridor as so overwhelming that he was staggered.

For a moment, he was reminded of a terrifying event he had experienced as a child with his parents visiting the Rhode Island shore.

Standing alone at the ocean's edge, he had suddenly felt the water being drawn away from his feet. So strong was the tidal pull that it knocked him off his feet and he began to be dragged into the surf. The water grew into a wave several feet high that continued to build until it towered over him. His father had plucked the young Hamilton from the water just as the wave was about to crash down up on him, saving him from being drowned.

Now, as the images of what he was seeing began to register, he felt that same helpless horror —the death and destruction grew into a tidal wave that rose to monumental proportions in his mind, far more powerful than he was able to process. For an instant, he longed for his father to come and rescue him again. But it was not to be. He would have to save himself.

In those first brief minutes standing in the burned out corridor of the ninth floor, the cool, almost aloof composure for which T. Stewart Hamilton was known evaporated, and he was stunned o the point where he fell against Lee, who caught him as his knees buckled.

"Are you all right, Dr. Hamilton?" Lee asked him, suddenly aware of the crushing weight of responsibility that had been thrust upon the shoulders of the hospital administrator. Lee lived with the accountability of making decisions that put men under his command in peril every day. It was a part of his life, an element of all his thinking. The Fire Chief could only imagine how overcome the doctor turned white-collar executive felt at this moment. He held Hamilton's arm to steady him.

With Lee by his side, Hamilton walked slowly up through the corridor, dazed, stopping occasionally to peer into the patient rooms with open doors to see the damage. Lee told him that where a door was closed, the bodies of victims were waiting to be examined by the coroner. Hamilton visibly flinched when Lee said the word "victims."

At the junction where the south fire door stood open against the wall, hardly recognizable as a door it being so bent and charred, he saw the remains of Dr. Norman Hedenstad being examined and photographed. Someone else was scraping the charcoal like substance that covered the door into a container for analysis.

"Do we know who that is?" Hamilton asked.

Lee beckoned to one of the nurses who had volunteered to assist with the identification of the bodies and spoke to her quietly. She shook her head sadly.

"We can't be sure at this point, Dr. Hamilton," Lee told the Hospital president. "But the nurse believes it is a 'Dr. Hendenstad.' Perhaps you knew him?"

Hamilton looked as if he had been struck in the face with a hammer. The final reality had fallen upon him.

The three men got as far as the elevator lobby where two more bodies lay in front of car three.

Hamilton turned ashen, now visibly shaken by what he had seen.

"Please, Tom, I've seen enough," Hamilton said. "I must get back downstairs and see to the evacuation." Lee nodded, but thought to himself that the Hospital president had been spared the worst of it by the doors that remained closed. The entirety of the horror of what had happened on number nine had only been seen by his men, the firefighters who had risked their lives in a hopelessly impossible rescue attempt.

In that moment, Lee thought he had seen the end of T. Stewart Hamilton as a leader, and indeed, the chief administrator was demonstrating signs of extreme duress. But in the days ahead, he would fool many people with his strength and resolve in facing and dealing with a nearly incomprehensible disaster.

Captain Dwight Schaeffer escorted Lee back to the administrator's suite of offices as Lee personally organized the removal of the bodies to the temporary morgue on the eighth floor, where preliminary autopsies were to be performed.

The Chief then turned command of the fire scene and supervision of the entire department complement over to Deputy Chief Poveromo in order to assist State Police Commissioner Leo J. Mulcahy, acting as the official state Fire Marshall, and State Police Major Carroll E. Shaw, who conducted the official investigation of the fire. Later, Governor John Dempsey, who had personally ordered the assistance of the State Police and National Guard and the support of other city hospitals, joined the group for a first hand briefing by Lee, Mulcahy and Shaw.

Downstairs, the evacuation of patients was ongoing as the discharge of patients progressed. As a semblance of order once again descended upon the Hospital, some fire crews were being relieved and sent back to their stations in order to bring some normalcy back to the fire coverage necessary to protect the city. Engine 1, which had been the first to arrive on the scene within minutes of the 2:39 p.m. alarm, was the first apparatus to leave the scene, pulling out at 5:38 p.m. that evening.

Captain Bill Kenney was quiet as he took his seat in the front of the cab of Engine 1 and turned his eyes as they drove by the armada of ambulances and hearses still lining Seymour Street. He didn't want to look at anything else that would remind him of the death and destruction that he had seen on this day.

With the immediate "breaking news" story losing its urgency, reporters from the two Hartford papers, the Associated Press, WTIC radio and television and dozens of other reporters turned to the stories of heroism that were beginning to emerge.

Stories of nurses leaping into patient rooms with flames just inches behind them and slamming doors shut – saving all in the room.

Of doctors, who like Norman Hedenstad, ran to the fire floor to protect their patients.

Of a medical resident, 28-year old Dr. Anthony Fons who literally put his back against the burning door of a patient room to keep it from bursting open and incinerating the three people inside.

Of reporters like *The Hartford Time*'s James Stewart and Morton Boardman who put their notebooks in their jacket pockets and stopped taking photographs to grab a hose line, help with the evacuation of a patient, or push wheelchair-bound patients to safer grounds.

Of doctors and nurses refusing to leave their stations, even as the fire closed in.

Of firefighter Dick Tajirian leaping off a 100-foot tall ladder to get inside the fire floor – perhaps the most important single action taken by a fireman that day.

The stories were countless. But in the days and weeks ahead, most would be forgotten in light of news coming from the investigation that pointed to so many avoidable causes for the fire. Improper use of the trash chute. The installation of flammable materials in the hospital corridors. The delay in calling in the fire. The "What ifs?" that might have prevented the fire or limited the death and destruction.

Engine 12, under the supervision of Captain Timothy Kelliher Sr. was the next apparatus relieved from the scene.

Exhausted, Kelliher and his crew, driver Clinton Rowland, Sal Tedone, Bobby Parent and Tommy O'Neil, emerged from the front lobby as a team and walked under the portico where they had begun their fight.

On the horseshoe green, Tim Kelliher Jr. saw a stirring at the front lobby doors and watched as his father and crew emerged and began to take up engine 12. He shouted to his father, trying to get his attention but the noise outside was too great. The young Kelliher was satisfied just to see his father, so relieved that he was safe, but he couldn't help jumping up and down on the green, waving his arms in exuberance. As if understanding, Sarge began to bark to add to the celebration. That did it.

Captain Kelliher, remembering that he had seen a strange dog in the middle of the blaze earlier that afternoon looked up in surprise and saw his son leaping for joy. The Captain took off his helmet and waved to the boy. His face was coal black and his grey hair was matted against his forehead from sweat. He was beyond exhausted, but dug down deep and smiled for his boy, hiding the despair he really felt over the disastrous events of the afternoon.

Like the majority of men who had fought the blaze that day, he didn't for a minute think of himself as a hero. He had only done his job. But Tim Jr. waived back at him, his chest bursting with pride. It was a moment neither would ever forget.

It dawned on the boy that his mother was probably beside herself worried about both he and his dad, so he decided to head for home. It was a long walk. He turned toward Seymour Street and began the journey, then remembered his longhaired friend. When he looked back, Sarge was still there, still waiting, his eyes trained on the front door from which people seemed to come out of. Tim walked back to the dog and sat with him again, stroking the thick fur on his neck.

"It's ok boy," he said to the dog. " I don't know who your master is, but he'll come for you. I promise."

As the afternoon sun began to set, the boy and the dog remained huddled together on the horseshoe green and resumed their long, agonizing wait.

# Twenty-Five

~~~ ~~~

*A sea of tears...*

A man of considerable discipline, State Police Major Carroll E. Shaw began interviewing eyewitnesses to the events on the ninth floor at precisely 5 p.m., hours before the evacuation and relocation of patients were completed. A total of 25 patients and staff were to be questioned under oath, some of them still filthy from the smoke and wearing soot covered hospital gowns and slippers. But Shaw refused to wait. He wanted to hear the accounts of these all-important witnesses – in some cases people who had been chased by the flames and barely escaped with their lives.

Shaw saw nothing wrong with his decision. From his perspective, this fire was no different than any other investigation that involved a homicide or fatality. His training demanded answers quickly while the evidence was fresh, and unfortunately he was not of a mind to consider that some of the witnesses were in varying emotional states. For those required to be
~~~

interrogated so soon after the appalling events they had witnessed, the experience bordered on cruelty. In the ultimate irony, two of the witnesses were survivors of the Hartford circus tent fire in 1944.

However, in their statements, patients and Hospital staff were unanimous in their recollections. Universally, they commented on the incredible speed with which the fire had spread from the south corridor through the central section and elevator lobby area of the ninth floor. The witnesses would testify until midnight, at which time the investigation was adjourned until nine o'clock the next morning.

But even as Shaw began taking testimony, Hartford Police Captain Thomas J. Hankard, head of the Detective Division, inspected the remains of the victims with the coroners and finally came up with a confirmed tally of those killed.

In total, 16 people, a doctor, one nurse, two members of the Hospital staff, five visitors and seven patients were identified as victims. Each had perished in the corridor or in a room where the door had been left open or blown open in the south and central sections of the ninth floor.

As Hankard and the coroners finished their gruesome work, stretcher-bearers gathered up the remains of each victim, some little more than piles of charred bone and ash, and carried them down to the temporary morgue on the eighth floor.

The clergy continued to pray over the dead as their remains were collected and did not leave until the last casualty had been removed. One floor below, Commissioner Mulcahy, Chief Lee and Governor Dempsey talked in hushed tones over how to handle the press conference that was scheduled at 6 p.m. Virtually all of Hartford was waiting for some definitive news of the tragedy, having depended only on wildly speculative reports most of the afternoon.

The worst was yet to come for the shocked community. The appalling number of casualties had not yet been released to the public. Dempsey, especially, knew that the country's eyes would turn on the small city once the grim facts were known. Everyone involved, from his office down, would be the subject of intense scrutiny in the weeks ahead.

The Governor, a man known for his compassion, wasn't concerned about the terrible black eye the State and City had suffered or the grilling that was sure to follow. What kept going through his mind as he watched the parade of stretchers pass by him carrying yet another body, was not only the grief the families of the victims would have to endure, but also the sheer hell of media attention that would follow them for months.

From the 13th Floor down to the eighth was one world; from seven to the lobby was another. The latter was a whirlwind of activity as the evacuation and relocation of patients continued, surgeries on critically ill patients were performed as planned if not slightly behind schedule, and even new babies were delivered in the Maternity Ward.

Despite the calamity that had befallen Hartford Hospital, life within the Seymour Street microcosm of the city went on. Mixed with the stench of smoke, which had dissipated but still hung in the air throughout the Hospital, was the aroma of dinner meals being served by available staff. The hospital kitchen carried on with its routine, the only difference being the confusion of trying to determine how many patients to cook for.

While Stewart was adamant about making room for patients who continued to depend on the hospital for treatment, he was just as determined to release as many as possible that were ready or nearly ready for discharge. As a manager, he knew that he had to reduce the strain on his organization for a short period, just to give it time to catch it's breath and rebound from the shock. He had a plan to provide care for those patients who needed follow up that he would discuss later that night with his Department Heads. Stewart was determined that no matter how severe the criticism that he and his hospital would receive in the coming months following the investigation, no patient would find fault in the way in which they had been cared for.

He made the determination late that afternoon that the Emergency Room would not accept new patients, with the exception of life or death situations, for at least the next 24 hours. He also wanted every patient in the ER who could be treated by private physicians or whom were occupying beds on an "observation" basis, to be released as soon as possible, meaning by that evening.

One of those patients being held for observation was Charles Whitemore. Slightly after five o'clock, he groggily emerged from the deep sleep of the sedative that the agitated veteran had been given earlier in the afternoon.

Restrained to a gurney because of his highly anxious behavior and incessant, loud emotional pleas for his beloved "Sarge," within a few minutes of regaining consciousness he was yelling again.

A nurse finally took pity on the poor man who had suffered what thankfully amounted to only minor injuries in a hit and run that had left him lying in the street earlier in the day.

An observer might have guessed her to be a bit older than she was, the stress of her job in the ER giving the young nurse more stress wrinkles than she deserved at the age of 27. She worked long hours that often demanded exhausting physical effort and intense, sometimes traumatic duty.

But as an ER nurse, her soft brown eyes went a long way in comforting people who were quite often more frightened than injured or ill. She had a natural way of calming her patients. The nurse held one of his Whitemore's hands, tied to a metal railing on the hospital gurney with strips of soft cloth. With the other, she lightly stroked the side of his face trying to soothe him.

"Where's Sarge?" he begged her, tears streaming down his face. He rolled his head back and forth in complete panic. "What will I do without him? Oh, God…"

"Charles," the nurse said to him, "tell me who 'Sarge" is and perhaps we can find him…"

Whitemore looked at her like she was crazy, a wild look in his eyes.

"He's my whole life… don't you understand? Did the car hit him? Is he dead? Is that why you're hiding him from me?" he lashed back, unable to control his emotions.

"Wait, Charles," the nurse responded. "One thing at a time, ok? I'll help you. But you must calm down. My name is Cookie and I'm your friend." She paused to let him contemplate her words. "Believe me?"

He hesitated for a moment, then shook his head.

"Good," she said. "First, who is Sarge?"

Whitemore buried his face in the pillow beneath his head, his hands still tied to the bed and sobbed inconsolably.

"Charles, tell me, I will help you…" she said again. She sat on the edge of the bed and held both his hands now, trying to ground him with her touch. Cookie O'Malley had seen enough disturbed patients in her career to know this poor man had experienced some awful trauma in his life, probably war related. The "Semper Fi" tattoo on his wrist was a dead giveaway. It was awful to watch what some of these poor veterans went through.

She massaged his hands with her thumbs trying to get his attention and finally broke through.

"Sarge… he's my friend," Whitemore sobbed. "My only friend… we live together," he managed to whisper through his tears.

"Where was Sarge when you were hit by the car, Charles? Do you remember?" she asked.

"He was walking with me. We walk to the Park Street Green every day. I had his leash in my hand…"

"His leash?" the nurse said in surprise. "Sarge is a dog, Charles?"

"Of course! But not just any dog…"

A tear came to her eye as she realized what was happening to the man and the realization that she might not be able to help him.

"I know, Charles… Sarge is your friend," she said.

Whitemore began to cry again.

"Don't Charles, it will be all right," she said trying to comfort him. "I'll tell you what. Let me go out to the nurses station and I'll check to see if there are any notes on your chart about Sarge. Will you be all right while I'm gone? It will just be a moment."

He looked at her, his eyes showing a glimmer of hope.

"I'll be right back," she said. "In the meantime, you try to calm down and maybe we can get those restraints off your wrists when I come back, ok?" She flashed him a big, confident smile.

"Yah," the veteran responded, his voice so low it was almost a whisper.

Despite all the craziness she had persevered on this insane afternoon, Cookie O'Malley took the time to go to the desk and review Charles Whitemore's notes because she knew it just might be the most important thing she did all day. She recognized the despondency in Whitemore's voice as more than just feeling sorry for himself. Without even know his background or history, she could tell that he suffered from depression and probably other psychosis. And for that reason she knew how important Sarge was to this man. A lowly, four-legged canine might be his only link to sanity and the difference between his independence or spending the rest of his life in an institution.

If the dog was alive, she was going to find him. But how, she wondered, does a nurse working in a hospital that happens to be experiencing a three-alarm fire go about such a thing?

At that very moment, the answer walked by. It was a Hartford police officer she recognized. He was escorting a man in handcuffs who had been brought in from the Morgan Street jail early that morning complaining of stomach pains. The prisoner had spent the day confined to a guarded examining room, nervously watching dozens of firefighters pass through, their faces blackened by smoke. Some stopped to spend a few minutes breathing from oxygen masks.

The jailbird knew there was a fire in the building, but he didn't know where, how close or how bad it was. He never thought he'd look forward to getting back to his cell, but this place was making him real nervous. He kept calling out for attention, but was ignored. Now after things had calmed down some, a nurse came in to inform him that the results of the tests they had him take earlier in the day had been delayed by the fire, but that he was all right. It was nothing but a bad case of indigestion.

"Good," he said curtly, throwing the blanket that was covering him on the gurney to the floor and yelling to the cop who was standing outside his room.

"Let's get the hell out of here, man... this place gives me the creeps!" he said.

Cookie knew the young policeman from his frequent visits to the ER with accident victims or guys like the one he was escorting today.

"Jimmy," she hollered out to him as the cop passed. "It's Jimmy isn't it?"

The officer stopped and turned to face the nurse. He was a good looking guy, a little over six feet tall, just about Cookie's age and definitely ex-military. She could tell by the "high and tight" haircut that framed his sharply chiseled features in a way that quietly said, "Don't mess with me."

"Why yes, ma'am, it is," he answered, slightly flattered that she knew his name. She was a really good looking woman who'd caught his eye on more than one occasion. "Jimmy Murphy. Can I help you?"

"I sure hope so," Cookie beamed and told the police officer the story of Charles Whitemore and Sarge. Murphy was sympathetic. A year in Korea had changed his outlook on life, especially when it came to people in need. That was the real reason he became a cop.

"Ya know, I think I may know the officer who took that call this morning when your patient got hit," he said. "Let me get my friend here back to Morgan Street and I'll get a hold of him. I'll call you from the station. See if you can get a description of the dog. I can check the report to see if... what was his name – Sarge?" Cookie nodded. "To see if there's any indication of how Sarge was disposed..." He stopped.

"I mean, what happened to the dog. If there's no mention, I can check the dog pound and if he's not there I'll take a cruise through the neighborhood. Maybe he's just confused and running loose."

She smiled at his kindness.

"I'll need your telephone number here at the hospital," he said, smiling back at her. Then he paused. "And maybe your home phone?" he asked hopefully with a touch of shyness that made his request a compliment.

She grinned at him flirtatiously.

"Actually, I'd be glad to give you both, Jimmy. You're so kind. Thank you for your help."

"Glad to do it, ma'am." The cop turned to continue his walk with the prisoner.

A mischievous look appeared on her face.

"Jimmy..." she called out to him.

He stopped and turned.

"Yes, ma'am," he said.

She winced.

"Jimmy, if you call me 'ma'am' one more time you can forget about that second number. I'll bet we graduated from high school the same year. My name is Cookie," she said with a warm smile.

He laughed. "Cookie it is. "I'm sorry. My mother raised me right. Blame her."

"Seems like she did everything else pretty well," she answered, blinking her eyes seductively. He blushed.

"Yes ma'am," he winked, teasing her and continued on his way.

"You do have a way with the ladies, hey man?" the prisoner commented as they walked out to the waiting patrol car.

"Shut up," Murphy said to the handcuffed man. "Or I'll take you to the Wethersfield Prison instead of Morgan Street."

"What???" the jailbird panicked.

The cop laughed out loud. "Why are you in lockup anyway, man?" he asked.

"Did a little too much celebrating over the weekend. Got loaded. Guess I got a little out of hand."

"What were you celebrating?"

"Being sober for a month," the prisoner said with a straight face, then laughed hysterically at his own joke.

Even Jimmy Murphy had to laugh.

"Keep an eye out for that dog or I'll tell the judge you were uncooperative, you criminal." For perhaps the first time that afternoon, two men standing outside of Hartford Hospital laughed aloud.

The sound went unnoticed in the sea of tears that surrounded them.

# Twenty-Six

~~~ ❧ ~~~

*A tomb of terror, sadness and death…*

One by one, Deputy Chief Poveromo relieved each fire company to return to its station and prepare for the next alarm. For those fortunate firefighters who had been first responders or part of the Second and Third alarms on the day shift, most were relieved by their night shift counterparts and were free to go home after laying standby hose lines on the ninth through 12th floors.

There were other companies, such as Engine 6 and Ladder 1 who were held over at the Hospital through the night to continue probing into the walls and ceilings of number nine with their plaster hooks, digging deep to find any tiny spawn of the fire monster. The firefighters were all too familiar with the fact that a single spark could reignite the whole mess and spread quickly to other floors. They left nothing to chance. There'd been enough sadness that day to last them all a lifetime.
~~~

The profoundly tired men who remained worked through the night in the acrid, smoky air, sweating profusely in their heavy gear despite the chill of the night that penetrated the floor through all the smashed windows. It wasn't until seven o'clock the following morning that they were dismissed from duty.

The scene was eerie that night, like something out of a horror movie, as they pierced walls and ceilings with their lances under the ghastly light of a string of bare light bulbs that had been hurriedly hung the length of the ninth floor corridor. The harsh light from the bulbs only exaggerated the gruesome, burnt out cave the Hospital ward had become and shadows jumped with every move the firefighters made. Less than 24 hours before, this had been a thriving, hygienic place of peace and healing. Now it was a tomb of terror, sadness and death.

Along with the firefighters, Detective Hankard had ordered Hartford policemen to stand guard through the long night outside each room and by every location where a death had occurred. The blue suited officers appeared to be a sort of honor guard for the victims of the fire. But Hankard had other reasons for the guards. This was a crime scene, until proven otherwise, and he intended to protect what was left of it as much as possible.

Hankard was not happy with the press conference held earlier that evening, when the State Police Commissioner had quickly identified the cause of the fire as "most probably a cigarette butt carelessly tossed into a trash chute and the delayed reaction of hospital maintenance workers to report the ensuing fire."

The Hartford Police Department's Chief Detective was not interested in contesting the delay in pulling the fire alarm. Some had speculated that it was as long as six minutes. Ultimately, his instincts told him, the evidence would prove the gap was much longer.

No. What intrigued Hankard much more was the nagging thought that this was not an act of "carelessness" or even accidental for that matter. He just wasn't convinced. The speedy conclusion bothered him not only because it was based almost entirely on the testimony of 25 battered and physically and emotionally exhausted witnesses, but also because he knew from experience that additional evidence would ultimately surface. That evidence would either confirm or confuse the initial findings and probably lead to questions the investigators hadn't even thought to ask yet.

Further bothering Hankard was the statement made by the County Coroner's office that all 16 of the victims had died of "smoke inhalation, with some showing minor burns." His stomach churned at the misleading information.

He had seen the bodies, counted them. Most had not died of smoke inhalation. Hankard didn't even want to think about how horribly they had died. The detective had seen much death in his long career and the many ways in which it occurred, either by accident or homicide. One only had to see the remains of a burn victim to know there was no more horrible way to die.

Why were the State Police so quick to release such a statement? Did they actually believe that describing the cause of death to be "smoke inhalation" would ease the pain of the victim's families or the burden on the city's reputation – and culpability?

It was all moving much too quickly for the career detective, and he was puzzled by the reasoning. But somehow, his instincts told him this was going to be another Circus fire, the cause of which had never been definitively established. Theories abounded, but no one ever proved if the fire was set or the tent burst into flames as the result of some accidental event. He was desperate for a different outcome this time. Not only to satisfy his own instincts, but to bring some sort of closure to the families of the victims. Better to know the truth than to spend a life wondering what it was, he thought.

The late evening edition of the *Hartford Times* and the morning's *Hartford Courant* both nailed the cause of the fire as "accidental due to a cigarette butt being tossed down the trash chute" and quoted the coroner's office on "smoke inhalation" as the cause of death for all 16 victims.

The news was out. To change it was analogous to forcing a magical Genie back into his bottle, Hankard knew. First, to prove the conclusions wrong, he'd have to provide solid evidence that the fire was not accidental – but arson. Second, he would have to find proof that would discredit the Coroner's report.

The former was possible only if he could find an individual with a motive, whether he was a sick son of a bitch who liked to see things burn, or someone seeking vengeance. It would involve intensive police work and a million interrogations. Hankard was more than up to that task, it wouldn't be his first experience at finding a needle in a haystack. But he knew the latter was all a matter of literally fighting City Hall.

That was not a battle he figured to win.

# Twenty-Seven

~~~ ঌ ~~~

*Semper Fi…*

The Emergency Room was empty with the exception of one patient by seven o'clock that night. Charles Whitemore still lay on a gurney, although the disturbed man's restraints had been removed. Cookie O'Malley stayed with him as they both waited for the phone to ring. Whitemore was silently saying prayers he had learned as a boy hoping for a telephone call that he was more and more convinced would never come. Cookie had put her faith in a policeman who thus far had done everything he promised he would. She wasn't so quick to give up hope.

At that moment, Patrolman Jimmy Murphy was prowling the south end looking for a glimpse of a large German Shepherd who answered to the name of "Sarge." It had become his mission. All over the neighboring streets, fellow officers were doing the same thing as they conducted their nighttime patrols, and with each turn up a street, each hoped to catch sight of
~~~

the large dog in their headlights. The search had been going on for hours, but as of yet had produced no results.

The officer who had responded to the accident clearly remembered the giant dog, having feared for his life when he approached his master lying helpless in the street. He recalled watching the German Shepherd race after the ambulance that took Whitemore to Hartford Hospital, but that's all he knew other than the dog was not injured in the accident. That news alone was of great comfort to the grieving veteran, but not nearly what he hoped for.

Murphy wouldn't give up. One, because he genuinely cared for the fellow Marine Corps veteran of Korea. Two, because there was a certain phone number of a particular nurse at stake.

It hit him just as he drove by the accident sight for the umpteenth time and made the left hand turn onto Franklin Avenue that would carry him to Jefferson Street and then to the hospital on Seymour Street.

Seymour Street. That was it. That was where the entrance to the Emergency Room was.

Against every Department policy he could think of, Murphy hit his lights and sirens and nailed the accelerator, taking his patrol car on a path back to the hospital. He radioed a fellow officer in the vicinity to meet him.

The scene at the hospital was eerie. It was cold and dark outside at 7:15 p.m. and several fire apparatus were still on the scene, their strobes and spotlights casting long, urgent shadows against the otherwise darkened entrance to the building. The lights were on as usual in much of the building, but the upper floors were visibly dimmer with only emergency or makeshift lighting available. Overall, one had the sense that the building had been severely wounded.

The long line of ambulances and hearses had disappeared and had been replaced by repair vehicles, utility company trucks and State and Hartford Police cars as Murphy pulled up to the horseshoe entrance to the hospital. He pulled up behind Engine 1, still parked at the portico and asked a couple of security guards outside if they'd seen a big dog. One of them pointed towards the Green.

There in the shadows, Murphy finally spotted what he was looking for, with one additional surprise.

The silhouettes were unmistakable, and unmoving. Both the figures were sitting on the green, patiently watching the front doors. One was obviously a boy, from his size perhaps a young teenager, Murphy thought. The other was standing straight and tall, with two large, pointed ears standing erect. No question about it, it was a boy and a dog.

Murphy parked his car in the horseshoe just as a fellow officer pulled in behind him.

"Hey, Danny," Murphy greeted the cop and shook his hand. "Thanks for the assist, buddy."

"It's on me, Marine," Dan Harrison responded, taking off his hat and wiping his brow. "Been a long day, hey bud?"

"That it has," Murphy responded. "Sure would like it to end on a good note."

"Amen to that."

The two patrolmen slowly walked towards the two solitary figures, Murphy brandishing a flashlight.

"Be careful, Dan. This is a big dog and he could be a handful."

"Nah, there ain't a pooch alive I can't handle," Harrison laughed.

As they closed within six feet, the dog jumped to all fours and let loose a fearsome growl at the two approaching officers. Harrison jumped back.

"May have spoken too soon there, partner," he said.

Murphy laughed. "Let's take this easy."

"Hey son," he called out to the boy, aiming the flashlight at his face. "What's your name?"

"Tim. Tim Kelliher, Jr. My father is Captain of Engine 12. He was in there this afternoon," he said.

"Who's your friend?" Murphy asked calmly. "Is this your dog?" he asked.

"No. I found him out here alone. He's been here for hours. I think he's waiting for someone who's inside but I don't know who it is. I didn't want to leave him alone."

"Do you know his name?"

"No. I just call him 'boy' and scratch his back. But he never takes his eyes off the front door."

Murphy took another step closer to the dog. Then he took the leap.

"Hey Sarge, you all right buddy?" he asked in a gentle, reassuring voice. The dog immediately began wagging his long, bushy tail and took a step towards the officer.

"Sarge? Is that your name, boy?" The dog ran the few steps to Murphy and clawed at his leg with a giant front paw.

"He knows," Murphy said. "He can tell I know where his master is just because I know his name. He's so smart." Murphy ran his hands through the dog's mane, as he knew Whitemore would and looked up at Danny.

"Hey Dan, how about taking Timmy here and paying a visit to the ER. Ask for nurse Cookie O'Malley and her patient and tell them we've got a surprise outside here."

"Yeah!" Tim yelled and began running toward the front door even before Dan Harrison could respond.

"Ya know, I think we're going to have at least one happy ending today, Jimmy. Good work, buddy."

"Semper Fi, Dan."

"Roger that." Harrison jogged to the front door, put his arm around Tim and the two entered the front door, headed for the ER.

"Just wait a minute more, Sarge, I think we may have found your master. Ok?"

Sarge whined and anxiously stared at the front door.

Several minutes later, Murphy saw a group of people approach the door, one in a wheelchair being pushed by Cookie. It was Whitemore, followed by Harrison and the young Kelliher.

From 50-yards away and through the glare of the spotlights bouncing off the plate glass windows of the lobby, Sarge saw his master. He knew. The dog tore loose from officer Jimmy Murphy's calming hold and raced towards the Hospital, barking loudly, his thick furry tail flying with the wind. He would have swum a river to get to the man in the wheelchair.

Cookie saw him coming and smartly jumped in front of Whitemore and opened the door to the lobby. The dog might have smashed through it had she not.

Charles Whitemore stood up just in time to catch the leaping German Shepherd in his arms and to feel the slobbering licks on his face from the giant dog, the best and most loyal friend he'd ever had. You would have thought the two had been separated for years instead of hours.

Whitemore fell back down in the wheelchair from the weight of the onslaught of the loving dog that was beside himself with relief. The veteran himself couldn't stop the tears from flowing down his face and kept repeating, "Thank you, God, thank you…"

"Now there's something you don't see every day," Murphy said to himself out on the green, watching, finally feeling the sensation that he had been searching for since becoming a policeman. He had helped someone in need, and it felt damn good.

From afar, Murphy suddenly heard his patrol car radio calling. He sprinted to the car and grabbed the receiver. It was dispatch telling him to report to a domestic violence call a couple of blocks away.

"10-4, rolling on that call," Murphy responded. Duty beckoned.

He jumped back into his car and began to back up out of the horseshoe. Just as he turned onto Seymour Street, he saw Tim Kelliher running towards him, waving. Murphy pulled the car to the side of the road and waited for the boy.

Tim reached him seconds later, and handed the Officer a rumpled piece of paper.

"Here," he said breathlessly. "The nurse asked me to give this to you."

Murphy reached down and tousled the boy's hair. "Thanks, buddy. And good job taking care of Sarge." Tim beamed. "Tell Officer Harrison I asked him to give you a lift home. I'll buy the coffee tomorrow."

Murphy unfolded the wrinkled paper, read it and a grin emerged on his face. The message was simple.

"Looking forward to your call, Marine. Jackson, 524-1789. I'm off on Sunday. Cookie. P.S: Both my boys here say thank you. Me too, hero."

The young patrolman laughed out loud, slammed the patrol car into drive and hurried to his next emergency. In his entire 25-year career as a cop, it was the only domestic violence call he would ever respond to wearing a smile.

# Twenty-Eight

~~~ ❧ ~~~

*"Move on, put it behind you..."*

No one who had witnessed the horror or the shock of the day was untouched.

Detective Tom Hankard went home early the next morning, sometime after three a.m. following a final briefing from Mulcahey and Shaw on their findings, which hadn't changed. Chief Lee was there too, but struck Hankard as strangley quiet. He wondered if the Chief wasn't plagued by the same nagging thoughts he had.

The City's Chief Detective chose to walk home to his small house in the south end, to take advantage of the solitude and quiet the stroll afforded his ability to think things through.

In no frame of mind to answer the thousand questions he knew they would have for him, Tom Hankard was almost grateful that his wife and kids were asleep when he arrived. He hadn't eaten in more than 18 hours, but had no appetite. Instead, he poured
~~~

himself two fingers of scotch, neat, and sat in his easy chair, staring at a blank television screen.

The scotch helped erase the sickening images he had been carrying with him for many hours now, since the "counting." It also numbed the anguish he felt following his decision not to challenge the status quo. It bothered him terribly to give up on a case where so many innocents had suffered and died, but he knew, in the end, that satisfying his own doubts and craving for justice would only serve to keep a story alive that would haunt the families of those killed. And worse, chances were, like the Circus fire, he would never find an answer. Fighting the Mayor and the Commissioner of the State Police? Hankard wasn't afraid of anyone or anything. But waging that battle, even if there was a chance he could win, wasn't worth a bucket of warm spit.

At the hospital, the lights in the Administrative suites burned brightly all night long.

T. Stewart Hamilton worked like a man possessed, managing the final patient evacuations, discharges and relocations and putting together a plan of action for the following morning. He was running on pure adrenalin, but the more he worked the stronger he became. The pain of working through his physical exhaustion somehow allowed the shock his mind had endured to dissipate. Even while his body cried out for sleep, his thoughts sharpened. By daybreak, he had a plan of attack in place.

Most of the Hospital's Department Heads also worked all night, each preparing briefings for their staffs and a plan of recovery they would implement. The most important thing was to get the hospital back on its feet, operating with the same efficiencies that it had before the fire. But even more important was the need to instill confidence and pride back in the men and women who made Hartford Hospital a success.

Not all of his peers noticed, but some wondered about the absence of James Anglun. After all, wasn't this a situation where his expertise in maintaining and repairing the physical plant was most needed? Those few who noticed his darkened office didn't waste a lot of time fretting over his whereabouts. You were either part of the team or you weren't.

Hartford Police continued to try to manage the traffic situation on the main roads around the Hospital, with the number of gawkers beginning to dwindle only after 10 p.m. It had been a long day for the blue uniforms and their patience was tested by the unnecessary complication of thrill seekers blocking roads that were critical to the emergency responders. By midnight, the roads were clear, but extra police were assigned to the main roads, manning barricades on Jefferson and Seymour Streets that would not come down for another 24 hours.

Firefighters from companies all over the south and central areas of the city gradually returned to their stations to be relieved by the night shift men, most of whom had also spent the last few hours at the hospital having reported early after the third alarm had been declared by Chief Lee.

The fire had been a tough blow to the Department and there wasn't a man who had been there who wasn't affected in some way. This hadn't been the kind of fire that brought them together in back slapping celebrations in any number of bars and taverns across the city for a few beers and a toast to their brotherhood. No, they had lost too much today. They'd done everything possible – even the impossible – yet 16 people had died. They all knew it was a miracle there were no firefighters among the dead.

Tonight was a time for them to go home, to hug their wives and children and to sit in silence with that beer to reflect on all that had happened. Most firefighters lived by a simple creed after a bad fire, especially those where there had been a loss of life.

"Move on, put it behind you," was what they said to each other on the outside.

Sometimes it wasn't so easy on the inside.

Those who had been on the ninth floor, who had felt the fire monster roar over their heads, those who had stood on the top rungs of 100-foot high ladders shouting instructions to trapped patients and survivors to help themselves, those who had done the counting and seen the death, perhaps this time might never quite get over it.

Sleep came hard that night to men who were steeled for and had seen the worst things imaginable in their lives.

Captain Tim Kelliher dragged his tired bones home long after midnight, wordlessly greeted his wife with a smile, then hid in the bathroom under the guise of taking a hot shower.

The thought struck him as he stood beneath the steaming water that as he neared the end of his career, it was getting harder and harder to wash the stink of smoke from his skin. But it wasn't only smoke, was it? Mixed into the odor was also the stench of burning flesh and death, sorrow, grief… and frustration.

16 people.

Dead because they couldn't be reached.

Men under his command who didn't have the proper equipment, weren't able to breath or even communicate.

Ladders that didn't reach trapped victims.

Was the new odor a loss of faith – the hopelessness he felt at this moment?

The man known and respected throughout the Department for being tough as nails and willing to take on any bureaucrat when doing the right thing was at stake wondered if the drops of water rolling off his face were only from the shower.

He grieved for the 16 and felt sorrow for the unbearable sense of loss he knew their families were suffering this night. But he felt overwhelming sadness for all those men who had put their lives on the line on this December afternoon and were agonizing over the same question he was.

Was there something else they could have done?

He sat with his wife for some time afterwards, sipping on the cold beer she had poured him. They were silent. That's the way she knew it had to be as her husband relived the day and every decision he had made. On the way to bed, he stopped by his son's room, and quietly opened the door a crack. He'd seen Timmy at the fire, had sensed the fear his boy had felt for him even from a distance, but had also caught his look of pride. He was a good boy and he loved him immensely. Kelliher wondered if his son would still be proud of his old man tomorrow when he read the newspaper and understood the full magnitude of what he had been watching from the horseshoe green.

He hoped so.

But it was a hard question for a man to face.

Was there something else *he* could have done?

# Twenty-Nine

~~~ ঌ ~~~

*"Fire of undetermined origin..."*

James Anglun waited outside the nondescript Seawall's Drugstore at the corner of Clifford and Broad Streets, several miles from the hospital, pacing and chain smoking. He had walked all night through the south end, alone in his thoughts, ducking into the shadows each time a car would pass. In his psychotic, paranoid state, the man who had caused incalculable grief in an act of vengeance was convinced the police were looking for him. He was sure they had found some evidence, something he had left behind that would indelibly link him to the crime, and that he was the object of a city-wide manhunt.

In his wildly raging imagination, he was further convinced that if the cops didn't shoot him on sight they would handcuff him and lock him in a cell forever with hardened criminals who would torture him for his shocking crime. He knew that no explanation, no consideration for the slight he had endured that had
~~~

caused him to take the drastic action of which he was accused would be considered. No one would ever know the truth, the humiliation he had endured.

Anglun needed to know what *they* knew. The answers would surely be plastered all over the front page of the *Hartford Courant*, the morning newspaper that he now waited anxiously to be delivered to Seawall's.

He looked at his watch. It was nearly five a.m. Just another few minutes before the early edition of the newspaper would be delivered and he would know.

Just then, a patrol car passed by, slowing, it seemed, to look over the haggard looking executive with the disheveled hair who needed a shave. For a moment, Anglun thought they had him. He considered running, but waited. The police car abruptly picked up speed, turned on its lights and siren and sped up Broad Street towards Maple Avenue. He was safe, for the moment.

Several minutes later, a small pickup truck pulled up in front of the drugstore and a boy in the back tossed a bundle of newspapers out on to the sidewalk in front of the door. Anglun behaved as if he was waiting for a bus and agonizingly paused for the truck to drive away before attacking the bundle.

Finally alone, he pulled a paper from the loosely bound stack and carried it gingerly through an alleyway leading to the back of the building where he could peruse it without danger of being seen.

Slowly, cautiously, as if the pages of pulp-based newsprint hid a venomous snake waiting to sink its fangs into the hand of the curious, Anglun opened the paper to reveal the startlingly bold, oversized black

Times New Roman serif typeface that screamed the morning's headline:

**"16 Killed in Fire at Hartford Hospital,
Patients, Doctor, Nurse Among Victims"**

He stared, wide-eyed at the headline, finding the words unreal, like the cover of a pulp fiction novel. Was this really possible or just a nightmare that would not end?

Finally, collecting his wits, the panicked administrator found what he was looking for in the very first words of the first paragraph's report of the fire. He read them once, then again, then once again…

"Fire of undetermined origin roared through the ninth floor of the 13-story Hartford Hospital Friday afternoon, killing 16 persons."

He was elated. The words "Fire of undetermined origin…" twirled over and over in his mind. The report went on to indicate that investigators believed that the fire had originated in a trash chute, and most likely had been caused by a recklessly discarded cigarette. But more importantly, in his insanely narcissistic state of mind, what he read said that the authorities had not mentioned that it was *his* cigarette. He read it over and over, seeking mention of his name.

Nowhere did it say, "James Anglun did it."

He was home free.

Quickly, he formed a plan. He would hurry home, shower, shave and change into a fresh suit and race back to the Hospital. He would explain to his wife and children that the emergency dictated that he work all night and was so urgent that he had not had a moment to call them. He was so vitally important to the hospital that they needed his expertise. They would understand. Certainly they would. They might even think him a hero.

At the Hospital, to those who asked, he would respond by explaining his absence was dictated by a family emergency. Then he would dig into his job. For of course, T. Stewart Hamilton and the rest of the ingrates who ran their precious departments would be counting on him to rebuild the ninth floor and get the hospital back in running order.

Who knows, he laughed to himself as he began the walk home, he might even toss in a new painting or two when he proposed the plans and the budget for repairing and remodeling the destroyed ninth floor.

A dark, evil grin came to his face.

How was that for irony, he thought with devilish delight.

# Thirty

~~~ ~~~

*"Twas just another day at the factory…"*

Through the long night, those who had faced the fire monster's fury wandered to their homes for a brief respite before returning to duty.

Chief Thomas Lee sat with his wife sipping coffee, revisiting the now almost obscene words he had left her with the previous morning.

"Let's hope it's a quiet one today, sweetheart."

Lee, the man in charge, was privately inconsolable. There was not a second of the hours he had spent since being informed of the fire that he had not revisited and second-guessed himself. He was wracked with guilt, but did not know where to place it in the order of his thinking. It ate at him.

What else could he have done?

In another few hours, exhausted and emotionally distraught, he would have to hide his inner torment and face the press, the Mayor, the Governor, the State Police experts and worst of all, his own men. The very men
~~~

who had fought without hesitation or regard to their own safety to do the impossible.

And he would have to do it without emotion and without giving away the torture that he felt inside. After all, he was the man in charge. It came with the job.

At dawn, T. Stewart Hamilton drove to his home in the west end under the guise of changing into a fresh shirt before beginning one of the most important days of his life. Actually, he made the long drive home just to be able to wrap his arms around his wife and to feel her hold him. He did not know if he could face what had to be done without someone to help him stand up to fate.

Amy Hamilton met her beloved husband in the driveway. She knew that what he had experienced was not just a tragedy for victims and their families, but also for this man who considered Hartford Hospital his very own child.

He lived for its success. He agonized over its future. He dwelled on its errors. Amy wondered if he could carry the burden of all 16 victims, as she knew he would, and survive. He was amazingly strong minded and strong willed. To lose just one of those victims might have staggered him. She worried now that the great loss of life would be a burden of responsibility that would bury him.

In the privacy of their driveway, hidden by a finely trimmed hedge of tall arbor vitaes, she silently met him with open arms into which he fell for support.

They spoke no words. There were none to speak.

An hour later, Hamilton drove back to the Hospital, his legs strong and his back straight once again. There was work to be done, and it was his to lead.

In a different part of the city, one not so elegant or finely pruned but closely knit and equally proud, those who had fought the fire monster face to face also returned to their homes and families. Some openly wept at the sight of wives and children, others were simply quiet. Some took their creed to heart and "moved on." At least outwardly.

Frank Droney sat in his favorite chair in the front room of his apartment and watched the sun rise, grateful to see another morning. He closed his eyes trying to erase the images, quietly saying prayers for those who had been lost but also for those who had been saved. He thanked the Lord for keeping the "Probies" safe and for not losing a man. And he vowed to stare down the monster again when the next opportunity came. He knew he wouldn't have long to wait.

Bob King, on the other hand, walked in the door to his small south end house wearing a grin that would light up the block. Inside, his guts were as torn up as any other man who had a command role in killing the beast. But his inner strength and care for his family made him hide what he felt. They worried enough for his safety.

With a quick hug for Ag, his wife, his son Bob and the light of his eye, nine-year-old Cathy, Lieutenant King retired for a quick shower, followed by breakfast with the family. There'd be no talk of the fire at the table on this day. He would save that for the firehouse. Like the day he'd stepped off of the *USS Oklahoma City* fifteen years before, his job and duty done, he was home and grateful to be there.

John Larkin, who had left for his shift the preceding morning whistling the old Irish ballad, *"I'll*

*Tell Me Ma,"* walked in the door the next morning after a night spent helping with the evacuation of patients and searching for hot spots, whistling the same song. Like his friend Bob King, his memories of war helped him through the bad jobs firefighters sometimes faced, and to keep it all in perspective. He did his duty then turned his mind to Mary, Peter and Jeff, his private altar of worship.

"Good morning to ya," he said as they met him at the door, surrounding him in a group hug. "Now let's not be having this," he said laughingly. "Twas just another day at the factory. Who's ready for some pancakes?" he asked, winking at his two boys. Larkin didn't know it, but his picture was on page one of the *New York Times* that morning, showing him helping to carry a patient in a hospital bed down a flight of stairs. The ribbing he took at the firehouse for his sudden glancing blow with fame did a lot to rebuild morale at Engine 6.

Ritchie Tajirian, the 25-year-old firefighter who had literally leapt off the top of a hundred foot ladder pointed straight into the sky to get inside the building, did exactly what he did after every shift. He went straight home, took a shower and climbed into bed.

"Hell," he said, thinking for just a moment about the death defying leap that only a handful of survivors actually saw and the last thing he said before he made it.

"I guess this is what I get paid for."

Less than 60 seconds later, the attic rafters were rattling from the sound of his snoring.

# Thirty-One

~~~ ๛ ~~~

*No words could describe the devastation*

As the first shift began to report the next morning, Saturday, December 9, department meetings were already being held throughout the hospital. Each department head had developed a plan of recovery, but one overriding element was to be put into effect commencing at nine a.m. that morning.

T. Stewart Hamilton had made the difficult decision to open the ninth floor for inspection by each department of the hospital. He wanted every employee from the top down to personally witness the devastation that was once a pristine, bustling patient unit and to see where 16 people had died in a hospital that had been considered the safest in the country. He knew that no matter which words he chose, he could never impress upon those who did not see the destruction first hand just what kind of horror had occurred on the ninth floor.
~~~

Hamilton was not unaware that for some employees, the inspection might be overwhelming, even frightening. In particular, the taped outlines of where victims bodies had been found, evidence for the coroner's office and the State Police investigation made the scene particularly real, and gruesome. Many of those who toured the floor had known the hospital staff that perished, including Dr. Hedenstad. To see where their friends had burned to death was beyond chilling. The bare bulbs hanging from the ceiling only emphasized the charcoal covered doors and the gutted walls and ceilings. The effect was as morbid and vivid as a visit to the morgue.

But one by one, the employees of each department toured the south, center and north wings from one end to the other. Hamilton himself led the parade, making sure it was a slow procession that forced his people to take in every ghastly detail. He let the brutal images settle into their minds. At the end of each department tour, he spoke, briefly, with carefully chosen words that served to remind every hospital employee of their role in preventing a reoccurrence of the mind-boggling disaster.

"Look around you, please," he began, speaking slowly but firmly. "I want you to remember what you've seen here today. The devastation. The destruction. The horror."

The silence in the blackened corridors was deafening as he spoke.

"We don't know for sure why this happened," he continued. "I'm certain it will be some time before we know with confidence. But I think it is safe to say that it will prove to be the result of a mistake in judgment." He paused.

"I only pray that it was an accident. "

Hamilton looked around the corridor at the faces staring at him. Always there were some that appeared startled at the suggestion that the fire was *not* an accident. It was obvious that it had never occurred to them. The concept had taken him a long while to accept, but he knew the possibility existed.

"Nonetheless, we must all remember one thing," he continued. He waved his arm around the black corridor.

"This can never happen again." Hamilton paused.

He raised his voice for emphasis.

"I *vow* to you this will never happen again.

"Never.

"Ever."

Hamilton dropped his head and stared at the blackened, melted remains of what once was a polished, brown linoleum floor.

"But let there be no mistake, no confusion or misunderstanding of what I am saying," he continued.

"What has happened here occurred on my watch," he said solemnly. "As the President and Chief Executive Officer of Hartford Hospital, the blame, the responsibility for what has happened here must lay squarely on my shoulders. There will be no finger pointing as it regards the disaster, no excuses for what has happened.

"But in order for me to stand behind *my* vow that this will never happen here again, I must have your unwavering support to ensure it. That is the vow of responsibility *you* must pledge to me and to this Hospital."

Amidst the tears and hand wringing that Hamilton saw in every group, were the nods of agreement.

Every employee saw the results of what they believed to be carelessness with their own eyes, smelled it and tasted it. They would never forget this blackened, charred landscape or the smell of death that hung in the air. And despite Hamilton's effort to carry the burden of responsibility upon his own back, the employees of Hartford Hospital knew that only they could provide the unending vigilance that would ensure his pledge. Nothing more needed to be said. The truth was as certain as the acrid smell of smoke that made their eyes water and their throats burn even all these hours since the fire had finally been extinguished.

By early afternoon, every day shift employee had toured the ninth floor. Later that afternoon, at shift change, the process was repeated.

During the day, Hamilton dispatched hospital and private physicians to visit every patient who had been discharged the previous day to ensure readmission was not necessary. Amazingly, not a single patient who had been discharged earlier than anticipated required additional care.

T. Stewart Hamilton had summoned up the courage to get through the first day following the fire. Slowly, with the help of dedicated administrators and doctors, nurses and staff, order was beginning to return to the hospital. There would be many more bad days ahead, many hours of sadness, remorse and soul searching to follow.

But Hartford Hospital had survived, had taken a deep breath and was moving forward.

# Thirty-Two

~~~ ঌ ~~~

*Finally, they were coming for him…*

Among those hundreds of employees who toured the ninth floor the following morning was James Anglun. In fact, he was present throughout most of the morning viewings, behaving as if he was studying the damage and formulating a plan of reconstruction.

He spoke to no one other than to utter perfunctory greetings. Several times he thought that he felt Hamilton's eyes upon him, but was unsure if the attention was real or imagined. Truthfully, James Anglun was such an innocuous presence to the hospital president that Hamilton later could not recall even seeming him at any time that morning.

But Anglun, with his paranoid suspicions mushrooming by the minute, was sure that his boss was on to him. And if he was, it was only a matter of time before he would feel the cold steel of handcuffs on his wrists.
~~~

Anglun's hastily contrived plan to impress his wife and two children with his dedication to the crisis had seemingly worked, and there was a great outpouring of concern by his family when he announced that he was heading right back to the office. At the hospital, not a single person had commented on his absence, a fact that was at once an enormous relief and a profound letdown. Like his disastrous performance and Hamilton's inability to even recall his name the previous day in the conference room had proven, Anglun knew that he was an afterthought among the key hospital administrators. He lusted to be a member of the inner circle of Hamilton's trusted aides, yet he was practically invisible to the man.

He had already exercised his rage over the humiliating slights with catastrophic results. Now, his anger expended, he felt only deep sadness at his failure to matter. Anglun was so narcissistic, his personality disorder so profound, that he had yet to feel grief for the deaths he had caused or the pain he had inflicted on countless families.

Returning to his office, his clothes and hair and skin reeked of the stench of smoke that permeated the ninth floor, but took some comfort from the foul odor. In his rapidly twisting mind, the nauseating smell was almost a badge of honor. It made him one of them, a part of Hamilton's team.

For the next several hours, he buried himself in paperwork and spent considerable time with the phone to his ear, conducting what appeared to be urgent conversations with contractors. There was no one on the other end of the line. In the midst of this charade, T. Stewart Hamilton was at his door. Anglun, startled, dropped the phone from his ear and looked up at the

Hospital CEO with the look of a deer caught in the headlights of a car. He froze.

"Oh," Hamilton said, finding Anglun's behavior odd, "sorry to disturb you, James. I just stopped by to..."

Before he could finish his statement, Anglun jumped up from his chair and backed up against the credenza behind his desk. He threw his hands in the air, as if giving himself up, a look of horror on his face.

"Why, James..." Hamilton said, shocked by his subordinate's reaction. "What...?"

Anglun was overcome with dread and clutched his chest as if he could not breath. Without warning, he brushed past Hamilton and ran from the office into the lobby and out the main door of the Hospital. A security guard last saw him running down the sidewalk that bordered the horseshoe driveway, which only hours before had been full of fire trucks and covered with miles of canvas covered firehose.

Hamilton was completely perplexed.

"Good Lord, what an odd man," he said to himself. "I only wanted to set up a meeting to talk about planning the reconstruction."

He stopped to speak to Marjorie Hayes, Anglun's secretary. She also looked stunned.

"What was that all about, Dr. Hamilton?" she said.

"Beats the hell out of me, Marjorie. When he returns, please tell him I need to see him at once so we can get to work on the ninth floor."

"I will, Doctor Hamilton," she said, shaking her head. "He's been acting so strange lately."

The exhausted CEO shrugged his shoulders. "Perhaps the stress of the last 24 hours or even some problems at home. I don't know. But I have too many other things to worry about right now." He walked away, scratching the back of his head.

Anglun was still running when he got to Washington Street, where he had parked his car earlier that morning. He fumbled with the keys, scratching the paint around the door lock before finally unlocking it. Sweating profusely, he jumped inside the car and slumped low beneath the steering wheel.

His mind raced.

Hamilton knew.

They all knew.

He could not process the ramifications other than one. His life was over. The thought occurred to him that he had never done anything to hurt another human being in any way. But here he sat now, an arsonist. For God's sake, a murderer.

He wrung his hands together in panic. Oddly, they felt wet and sticky. He looked down, puzzled, and trembled. Horrified, he saw that his hands were covered in blood. He wiped his fingers across his starched white shirt, thinking he was imagining the gore. The front of his shirt was streaked with crimson trails. Anglun screamed aloud and smashed his forehead against the steering wheel, trying to will away the nightmare. But it would not end.

Panicking, he jumped out of the car, unlocked the trunk and pulled out a red metal can. He took it with him as he resumed his seat behind the wheel, holding it to his chest, hoping to hide his shirt, which he now imagined was drenched in blood.

Somehow he managed to insert the key into the ignition and started the car. Without looking, he jerked the wheel to the left and pulled out into the busy

Washington Street traffic. An older woman coming up behind him slammed on her brakes trying to avoid his Oldsmobile sedan, but it was too late. She rammed his rear fender before coming to a stop.

Anglun ignored the impact and floored the accelerator, aiming for Jefferson Street about a block away. It was still barricaded by Hartford Police who were guarding the main drive by the hospital to keep the gawkers at bay. Only emergency and contractor vehicles were allowed through.

The crazed executive ignored the yellow wooden barricades, swung the steering wheel of the grey Olds hard to the right and smashed through the barriers, sending police scurrying in all directions beneath a rain of splintered wood.

He floored the car again and a block down made another hard right on to Seymour Street. Without slowing, he turned left and slammed into the apron of the horseshoe driveway. Fifty feet from the front door under the portico that firefighters had mounted to manage the exhausting hose pull up to the ninth floor just 24-hours before, Anglun screeched to a stop. He stayed in the car with the motor running and looked up at the building where he once thought he would enjoy a remarkable career.

Hospital security guards and Hartford policemen blocking the front entrance looked curiously at the car and the odd behavior of its driver. From behind him, Anglun heard the sound of a siren.

Finally, they were coming for him.

He didn't hesitate to do what he knew was necessary.

Grabbing the metal can, he unscrewed the cap and proceeded to pour its liquid contents over his head and upper torso until he was drenched. He noticed that not even gasoline would wash the blood off his hands and shirt.

Reaching inside his jacket pocket, he pulled out a pack of Camel's with shaking hands. Hurry, his racing mind told him.

He shook out the pack and managed to find a cigarette that was still dry and stuck it between his lips. Then he pushed in the dashboard lighter.

A moment later, red hot, it popped out from the dash. He reached for it and lit his cigarette, then took a long drag from the butt and blew out the smoke. He brought the lit end to his face and studied it just as he had yesterday. Then James Anglun spent a final moment thinking of his wife and children, hoping they would forgive him.

In perhaps one of the few moments of his life when he wasn't completely self-absorbed, he prayed that *everyone* would forgive him.

Without another thought, as casually as he had flicked the cigarette into the trash chute at Hartford Hospital the previous fateful afternoon, he dropped the fiery tipped cigarette butt into his lap, awakening the fire monster that instantly set the man ablaze.

As officers saw the tongues of flame leap up inside the car, they charged forward to try and save the driver. Before they could reach him, James Anglun felt the fire monster come to life and grow over him. His last conscious thought was one of amazement at how beautiful the beast was yet how painful his kiss felt.

The fire monster sucked the air from his lungs and quickly burned through the epidermis of Anglun's skin before rescuers could even approach the car. Within seconds, he was fully engulfed. Always hungry for more, the beast began to eat the interior of the car even before it had completely consumed the victim in its grasp. There was nothing for the responders to do but watch in horror as smoke and flames poured from every crevice of the car.

In sickening irony, James Anglun finally had the audience he craved.

* * *

At the Hartford Fire Department Headquarters at 275 Pearl Street, Dispatchers Dan Kelley and Dick Walsh were back at their stations, managing alarms and the flow of information to the 21 fire companies spread throughout the city.

It had been another busy day, but nothing like the previous afternoon. So when the alarm bell in the office signaled a Box Alarm had been pulled somewhere in Hartford, Dan Kelley almost nonchalantly got up from his seat and read the Morse code ticker tape signal to see where in the city it had come from.

His face turned ghostly white.

"What is it Dan?" Dick Walsh hollered over to his partner, alarmed by the shocked look on his face.

"What the…" Kelley said, reading the tape again and again to make sure his eyes weren't deceiving him.

"What is it?" Walsh repeated, jumping up to see for himself why his partner had turned so pale.

Kelley handed the tape to him.

"Where…?" Walsh demanded.

He looked at the tape, startled by his colleague's reaction. Then his eyes went wide and his face turned ashen as he stared at the strip of paper in his hand.

"That can't be… it's impossible," the Dispatcher stuttered.

"It says Box 5141."

"Yes," Kelley said, shaking his head in disbelief.

"But that's…"

"I know." He struggled to say the words. Was it possible for the fire monster to have risen from the grave?

"It's Hartford Hospital."

##

# Epilogue

~~~ ൠ ~~~

*The story behind the story*

*Out of Reach, The Day Hartford Hospital Burned* is a novel that combines historical facts concerning the tragic December 8, 1961 fire with both real and imagined characters and events. It is an historical fiction account that portrays an imagined cause of the fire while examining how events might have transpired that fateful day.

The foundation for the novel is based on the real life fire that took the lives of 16 people and devastated Hartford Hospital. To the great credit of the hospital, the disaster is an open book within the community on Seymour Street, which maintains a permanent, museum quality exhibition commemorating the event and paying respect to those who died.

Hartford Hospital has held true to T. Stewart Hamilton's vow, "Never again" by refusing to allow the catastrophe to be forgotten. Rather, the event is commemorated to remind all hospital employees that
~~~

diligence to safety is as much a part of their jobs as is the well being and healing of those whose lives are entrusted to their care.

Through extensive research and interviews with firefighters who "lived" the Hartford Hospital fire and the recollections of their family members, *Out of Reach* attempts to fictionally reconstruct much of the strategy employed by Chief Thomas Lee and his department to fight the blaze and minimize the loss of life.

In both the fictional and real accounts of the fire, Lee and the Hartford Fire Department performed with extraordinary commitment and exceptional skill in stopping the conflagration and preventing it from spreading to other areas of the hospital. The grief and sorrow experienced by the families and loved ones of those who perished are beyond calculation. But it is not an exaggeration to say that the loss of those 16 lives was a painful and lasting blow to the men who fought a fire they literally could not reach. Hardened veterans cried. Some never stopped asking the question: "Was there more we could have done?"

The answer to that question is much more certain than the final findings of the investigation as to the cause of the fire.

As Chief Lee would repeat often over the ensuing years, he believed that most, if not all of the victims were dead long before the Fire Department was called in to perform a miracle. The delay in reporting the blaze coupled with the location of the fire virtually ensured those trapped behind open doors or exposed hallways would perish before help could arrive. Experts from around the country applauded the department's efforts, against all odds, to kill a fire that could have caused a tragedy of far greater proportions if it had not been prevented from spreading.

The final findings were not nearly so kind to the designers of the building, which until the fire had been considered one of the safest hospitals in the United States.

The trash chute design was, in and of itself, an accident waiting to happen. There had been numerous instances of fires in the chute before December 8, but still hospital personnel continued to utilize it. Four days after the fire, Lee permanently banned the trash chute from further use. Hospitals across the nation soon followed.

Additionally, lab testing of the ceiling, wall and floor materials revealed the use of highly flammable substances. Hospital architects had gone to great lengths to design a structure that made the spread of fire from one floor to another a near impossibility, but unfortunately had not put nearly as much thought into the combustibility of materials used in decorating the rooms and corridors. Once the blaze began, the flammable materials combined to create a virtual fire storm in the 275-foot long ninth floor, with temperatures at one point exceeding 1,400° F and the production of highly toxic smoke and pressurized gasses.

As to the cause of the fire, the origin of the blaze was traced to the trash chute. The prevalent smoking culture of the times made an improperly discarded cigarette butt a prime target as the culprit. But no definitive case could ever be established. The cigarette theory holds true, given that smoking was allowed in nearly all areas of the Hospital and the trash chute had on numerous occasions been used as an ashtray.

The bigger question, one that has never been answered to the satisfaction of conspiracy buffs, is that if a lit cigarette was indeed the cause, was it discarded by accident or intentionally? And if it was intentional, was the cause of the fire arson? Did someone mean for people to die? Were they murdered? Therein lies the premise of *Out of Reach*: What if?

As to heroes, there were many that day. In *Out of Reach*, some are fictitious characters. But they are far outnumbered by the real life heroes of that awful day.

Young Richie Tajirian actually *did* jump off the top of a 100-foot ladder to reach a thin metal windowsill that would allow him to gain access to the fire floor. By getting into that window and taking charge of survivors trapped in the south wing, he saved dozens of lives singlehandedly and gave the responders eyes on the fire. The instances of heroic behavior on the part of firefighters and hospital staff are innumerable. But for individual acts of bravery, hundreds more might have perished.

Every man mentioned in this story was an actual Hartford firefighter who participated in killing the "beast." They tackled an impossible situation without hesitation and with extremely limited communications and breathing equipment. If ever there was a true to life gang who demonstrated John Larkin's creed, "You gotta be at your best when things are at there worst," the 70 plus firefighters who worked the Hartford Hospital fire exemplified it.

In the 150-year history of the Hartford Fire Department, 56 firefighters have been lost in action. Two of them were veterans of the Hartford Hospital fire who later died in the line of duty: Marshall Slavkin in 1968 and William Kenney in 1981. Thomas Fischer, who worked the Box 417 alarm at Zion and Ward Streets earlier that same day, was killed in the line of duty in 1974. May this story help to preserve the memory of their bravery and ultimate sacrifice.

The names of those lost in the Hartford Hospital fire are permanently memorialized in its permanent display. They speak to every member of the staff each day as they pass by its strategic location near the front lobby. But perhaps more importantly, the voices of these 16 have spoken loudly for change in building codes and fire safety improvements in every hospital in America. The changes to design and construction have been extensive. Nowhere are they more evident than at Hartford Hospital.

In *Out of Reach*, T. Stewart Hamilton, who in real life so ably led Hartford Hospital back to its level of prominence in the medical community and restored its pride, asked his fellow employees to help him keep a vow, to which all agreed.

But imaginably, despite their voices being forever silenced, it was the 16 victims who ultimately provided the greatest impetus to answering his plea heard across the nation:

"I vow to you this will never happen again.

"Never.

"Ever."

##

## Acknowledgements

From start to finish, *Out Of Reach* owes many thanks to many people.

First and foremost, to my wife, Bobbie, my perpetual love, partner, counsel and the inspiration of my life and work whose undying faith helps me to persevere when the words will only come one at a time. To my loving family, Jack, Jay and Andrea, for always seeing in me more than I deserve, and to Charlie, my grandson and the most profound gift of my life, who one day will find books written by his "Papa", a thought that fills me with joy. And to my beloved Grandfather, William J. McGrath, a man who epitomized love and humility, who instilled in me a passion for history and filled my imagination, thank you for being there for me.

Special thanks also to my friend Lisa Orchen, whose remarkable insights and sensitivities make her the consummate editor and author's friend; to Joyce Rossignol, my very first editor who taught me to love the art of writing; to my very special friend, Cathy King whose encouragement and support is boundless, and to her father and my eternal friend, Bob King, a role model who is, and always will be a gentleman and my hero. To my age old friends Genevieve Allen Hall, Steve Bazzano, Carol Russo, Gail Donahue, Carla Unwin, Michael Jordan-Reilly, Debbie Bartlett, Cheryl Zajack Barlow, Sharon Tomany Marone, Lisa Rivero Jankowski and Earl Flowers, my everlasting thanks for pushing me uphill.

But perhaps *Out of Reach* owes most to my newfound friend and teacher, Hartford Fire Department

Captain (Ret.) Timothy J. Kelliher, Jr. Just as his grandfather and father before him and now his son Timothy Patrick, Captain Kelliher devoted his life to the Hartford Fire Department. For 25-years he loved his job and gave his best every day to the Department, earning extraordinary respect from the men he worked with and commanded.

Tim Jr. was a witness to the Hartford Hospital Fire in 1961 and watched his father assume a command role in averting a far worse disaster. His memories, insights, amazing knowledge of the science of fighting fires and innumerable anecdotes are the backbone of this novel. *Out Of Reach* could not and would not be without the help of Captain Timothy J. Kelliher and the countless hours he shared in helping me to shape this story. Somehow, he guided this writer in sorting out the intricacies of a very dark and complicated moment in Hartford's history. To Tim, my eternal gratitude and a salute to the "Fighting Kellihers."

Thanks also to veteran firefighters Frank Droney and again to Bob King who gave their all on that awful day in 1961 and so graciously shared their memories. A special note of gratitude to Hartford Hospital Fire Marshall Michael Garrahy, whose grandfather Patrick was a deputy chief who worked the fire in 1961, for his generous help in personally guiding me through the facility and the facts. And finally to my boyhood pals, Bill Bartlett and Peter Larkin, whose own fathers served with distinction for many years with the Hartford Fire Department and particularly on December 8, 1961, thank you for sharing with me your own, sometimes painful recollections of that fateful day.

*F. Mark Granato, October 2014*

# About The Author

**F. Mark Granato's** long career as a writer, journalist, novelist and communications executive in a US based, multi-national Fortune 50 corporation has provided him with extensive international experience on nearly every continent. Today he is finally fulfilling a lifetime desire to write and especially to explore the "What if?" questions of history. In addition to *Out Of Reach,* he has published the acclaimed novel, *Finding David,* a love story chronicling the anguish of Vietnam era PTSD victims and their families that was nominated for a 2013 Pulitzer Prize, *The Barn Find,* chronicling the saga of a Connecticut family brought to its knees by tragedy that fights to find redemption, *Of Winds and Rage,* a suspense novel based on the 1938 Great New England Hurricane, *Beneath His Wings: The Plot to Murder Lindbergh,* and *Titanic: The Final Voyage.* He writes from Wethersfield, Connecticut under the watchful eye of his faithful German Shepherd, "Groban." Readers are encouraged to visit with Mark on his Facebook page at "Author F. Mark Granato" or at fmgranato@aol.com.

Made in the USA
San Bernardino, CA
29 January 2016